# LYCOS

## GUARDIAN SHADOW WORLD BOOK THREE

## KRIS MICHAELS

WWW.KRISMICHAELSAUTHOR.COM

# PROLOGUE

**T**wo *years ago:*

Guardian Shadow, Lycos, sat in the corner booth of his favorite D.C. bar. He enjoyed the atmosphere. The crowd, as usual, was diverse. Men with men, men with women, women with women, the dancers didn't give a fuck, and neither did he. Right now, the only thing he cared about was making her way through the grinding bodies on the small dance floor. Her tight ocean blue dress clung to every enticing curve of her holy-fuck-stop-all-traffic, accident-causing, body. Her thick black hair would have fallen to her shoulders if she hadn't twisted it up and skewered it with long ornamental pins. Ornamental his ass.

Lycos leaned back in his seat and let her see his intimate regard. He had a reputation, one he didn't discourage, but one he hadn't earned either. They'd been exclusive for years, except when the job required them to perform, and, as far as they knew, nobody else was aware of their sporadic domestic bliss. Their relationship started as one of convenience and had become one of stability for both of them. Were they in love? No. They'd had that talk often. He wasn't sure either one of them was capable of that particular emotion. What they had… worked. When it no longer did, they'd walk away. He'd be sad to see the end of it, but the only constant in life was change.

He stood as she approached and, even in her four-inch heels, she barely reached his chin. She was his little doll, although she wasn't fragile. In fact, Moriah was the deadliest woman on the face of the earth. He claimed her mouth as her arms circled his neck. If any of the bastards that were eye fucking her when she walked past them wanted her, they'd have to come through him first. Not that she needed him to protect her, but she allowed it, and that was some heady as fuck shit. She untangled herself from him with one last rub of her hips against his erection.

"Tease." He hissed as she slid into the booth.

"I don't think it's a tease if I'm a sure thing." She picked up his tumbler of Grey Goose and took a drink. She set the glass down and turned to him, leaning into his side, laying her head on his chest. "What's wrong?"

"Why do you think something's wrong?"

"Grey Goose. Your go to when you're stressed."

"They have you on video."

Moriah shrugged as if his concerns were nothing. He rolled his eyes at her cavalier attitude. She glanced up and caught him in the act. She huffed, moved away from him and flopped onto the backrest of the booth. "Look, they saw nothing. I watched. I saw what Asp set up, and I examined it when he was inside the house waiting for that bastard. I stole the clothes I wore from a stall in Cartagena, and I put stacks in the heels of my boots. Too tall, no face. Dead man tell no tales, right?"

"Desert Eagle?"

"What? I like *that* gun. Not like they can trace it or the ammo to me or connect me to Colombia. I was in Egypt on assignment, remember?"

"You shouldn't have killed him. I wanted you there to back up Asp, not to take the Columbian fucker out. You should have left when Asp did." Lycos was livid when he'd learned she'd popped a cap through that bastard's brain. This wasn't the first time she'd taken justice into her own hands. He sometimes wondered if the people doing her evaluations saw anything other than her beautiful face. The woman had deep, dark scars. He'd been with her for years, and he knew only the smallest details about her past.

"Don't tell me what to do, lover. I don't like it."

"I don't want to see you taken down. Stop with the vigilante justice, Miho, or sooner or later, it will come back and trap you."

Moriah blinked at the use of her given name. She took his Grey Goose and downed it in one swallow. "Stop worrying about me, Ryan. I'm not yours. I never will be. Perhaps it is time we say goodbye." She slid around the table and got out. Lycos stayed seated. She pulled down her skintight skirt and turned to face him. "I will always be there for you, my dear, sweet, friend. Stay safe. Whatever it takes."

"As long as it takes, my beautiful doll."

"I'm not a doll."

"I know," he said to her back as he watched the swing of eyes, both male and female, follow her out the door.

He motioned to the waitress and ordered another Grey Goose. He knew he'd been pushing what she tolerated when he criticized her actions, but he'd never expected her to break off their arrangement. He watched the throng on the dance floor pulse and grind against each other while he tried to decide what he felt. He took his drink from the waitress and dropped a fifty on her tray. She smiled enticingly, but he ignored her. He took a long pull on his GG. Sad. He was sad the time with her was over. Wasn't that a shame. He should probably feel more, but... that wasn't him. Or her.

Oh, for fuck's sake, who the hell was he trying to

fool? That *was* him, and he'd hoped like hell it would have been him with Moriah. That wicked deadly assassin was one of the only constants in his life, and now that shred of normalcy had just sauntered out the door, taking his dreams of a wife, two point five children, and a fucking golden retriever—although in his case it was a wolf hybrid—with her. Sad didn't *begin* to describe what he felt.

He shot the rest of his GG down and lifted his glass toward the over-attentive waitress. She acknowledged his request.

He'd come here tonight to talk some sense into his Moriah, not sever the only romantic relationship he had. The waitress did a drive by with his GG. He caught her hand, shot the Goose, and gave her the glass back. He also dropped three fifties on her tray. "Keep them coming."

"Anything for you, sugar." She grabbed the bills and winked at him.

His eyes drifted over the dance floor. He'd heard the definition of insanity was doing the same thing over and over and expecting a different outcome. Was he insane? A sneer spread across his face. No. At least not according to Guardian's shrinks, and he fucking saw them often enough.

The waitress dropped off two doubles of GG. "Don't tell management you're alone. If they ask, your date is somewhere out there. I'm not supposed to serve you more than one drink at a time, but you look as if you might need two."

Lycos lifted the glass in a silent salute to his bar goddess and took a sip of the magical elixir, the liquid of champions, or in this particular instance, runner-up. *Second place is first loser, asshole.* Tonight, after he'd persuaded Moriah to give up the vigilante bullshit that would plant her on the wrong side of their employer, he was going to invite her to see the safe house he'd built—for them. He'd even made changes to his original design anticipating Moriah would someday live there with him. He'd held the self-delusional belief Moriah would think him worth her effort. Lycos' gaze followed the path she'd used to destroy that dream. He snorted in self-derision. He should have known better. He'd been on his own for the majority of his life. Alone was familiar. Alone was safe. Alone didn't get his dreams stomped to shit.

# CHAPTER 1

**P**RESENT DAY:

Stratus, the organization headed by three women known only as the Fates, had suffered a debilitating blow, and the repercussions rippled throughout the global organization. The Fate known only as "One" stared at the image of a woman on the computer screen in front of her filled with a novel emotion—a sense of impotence. Unknown entities held Two, and the enforcement arm of Stratus was being excruciatingly slow in finding where she'd been taken.

"What are we going to do?" Through the microphone of her computer, Three's voice echoed her own thoughts.

"What we've already done. The move to our fall back locations is complete. Two does not know our safeholds." The fall back positions were Three's idea when they'd first taken over the Triune. Each woman had selected a location with no ties to anything related to the Fates or the businesses they controlled. No one was told of the locations in order to keep them safe in case someone should infiltrate their ranks, or as in the case of Two, be captured and presumably tortured for information.

"That wasn't my concern. Protocol has been followed. To a point." Three cleared her throat and leaned in toward her monitor. "It is time to erase."

One's shoulders slumped. Erasure was inevitable. The action was as necessary as air to breathe and water to drink. The effects of an erase would be seen in the slow wave of death that would ripple across the face of the earth and eliminate any and all personnel connected to missions active when Two was taken. The insulated core of Stratus would remain. The left hand did not know what the right did. In fact, on the same hand, the index finger was unaware the ring finger existed. A vacuum kept their core personnel from being able to understand the implications of their work or identify the complex organization behind it.

"I concur. We start with Two. Do we know where she is being held?"

Three sighed. "Several places we've been monitoring have had recent transports."

"Take them all out." The loss of their sister was hard, but as Fates, capture meant death. Their only hope was that Two could resist any drugs or torture until they could terminate her.

"It has already been planned. The order need only be given."

"Then give it. The extent of erasure?"

"I have a document." The sound of Three tapping her keyboard preceded the file popping up on One's screen.

One double-clicked on the icon. The list wasn't as extensive as she'd assumed. Five works in progress, hundreds of people, and millions of dollars, lost. A waste of resources and some good operatives. Twenty-two sisters would perish. A shame. The collateral wipe eliminated over six hundred others. Six hundred people connected to so few missions. It was amazing how the familial ties and casual acquaintances of the people they manipulated undulated through the population. What was that old saying... something about six degrees of separation? She looked at the list and scrolled down the columns. The names, addresses, occupations, and ages of the people streamed across her monitor. No, not six degrees... six hundred... men, women, children.

She should feel something for the loss of life other than the irritation of shifting the organization's focus and moving Stratus' teams into erasure mode. One flicked her eyes back to the small square where Three waited.

"I concur. Erasure is needed and warranted on all lists you've sent me."

"I will set the wheels into motion. Now, in regard to replacing Two." Three tapped her keyboard again, and another document appeared on One's screen. "These are the candidates I have interest in. Do you have your list?"

One double-clicked her mouse and sent her list to Three. "We can discuss the candidates tomorrow after we have reviewed each other's nominations."

How easy it was to move forward. She should feel something for the loss of Two. Her mind flitted across the feelings that were registering. No regret. Only irritation and anger at the loss of footing Two's capture had caused them. One shrugged her shoulders. It was just as well. Emotions only clouded the mind's objectivity.

"On to the next matter at hand. We have a potential opportunity in Venezuela."

One minimized the list of six hundred names no longer germane to the conversation. "Two was not involved?"

Three shook her head. "No. This came to light yesterday. She was taken the day before."

"Ah, well then, let us proceed." One leaned forward. They would need to replace the monetary stream they'd lost with Two's capture. A nation in turmoil was always prime for exploitation.

# CHAPTER 2

Lycos crouched and waited in silence at the base of the dock connected to the bulkhead of the massive seaside estate. The cement around him faded into the billowing fog that hugged the ground. A deep rolling cloud covered the lush grass that blanketed the vast, carefully maintained lawns. Heavy haze smudged the line between the water and land. The surf lapped at the cement barrier, and it registered in his thoughts, but the sound was just another input to be analyzed and dismissed. His target's approaching footfalls alerted his senses long before the man's mist-obscured form came into view. The soft, repetitious tread of a seasoned runner grew louder.

He reached out and grasped the piece of grey cord stretched across the running path. Vincent Clément, the man jogging down the trail, was a bastard and a monster, and probably the most feared and well-connected gangster on the planet. The Sardinian had tenaciously climbed to the top on the bloody pile of his competitor's bodies. When his father, the leader of the oldest mafia crime family, legitimized him, Clément was able to add his old man's reach and influence to his. The backing of his father catapulted the man into an elite category. Victor used that fear and power to order and pay for the assassinations of four very powerful heads of state, men who'd opposed Clément's vision for Italy. The first assassination dropped the leader of Italy's financial institutions. The second contract, against the leader of the Italian General Confederation of Labor, had been botched. The assassin had been caught and forced to talk.

Guardian had briefed Lycos with every scrap of information the Council had provided. That was fourteen hours ago. So far, the world knew nothing of either event. Clément didn't know his contractor had been captured. He still thought himself invincible, and that vanity led to his downfall.

The soft footfalls grew louder. Lycos closed his eyes and drew a deep breath before he turned his head and focused on the footpath. Every nerve in his body sang with anticipation. The mandate was to make this assassination look like an accident.

His forte.

He lowered as the footfalls hit the crest of the small knoll thirty paces from his position. His body shifted under the dock when he ducked to see through the boardwalk that ran adjacent to the running path. Steady fingers gripped the cord and waited... Five, four, three, two, one and *pull!* He tightened the material, sending the man in a sprawled-out flail onto the running path.

Launching from his position, he leaped to the boardwalk and dropped onto Victor before the man had an opportunity to recover. He grabbed one of the large rocks he'd pre-positioned by the running path. With practiced ease, Lycos dropped the stone beside Victor's head, grabbed the man by the hair and slammed his temple into the rock. The body beneath him went limp. A quick check of the gangster's pulse confirmed the perfectly placed strike had killed the bastard. He pulled the metal rod to which he'd attached the woven cotton line from the ground. To camouflage his presence, he replaced the plug of dirt and grass over the hole the rod made in the lawn.

The cotton tripwire left no scratches or visible bruising on Victor's legs. Scrapes on the man's hands and knees lent credence to the accident Lycos orchestrated. The target fell while running and hit his head. *Another unfortunate accident.* Methodically, he erased all evidence of his presence. He retrieved his SCUBA gear, donned the mask and tank, and walked out into the Mediterranean. A skiff anchored in a cove two miles up the coast would take him to a small fishing port, and from there he'd make his way home. Before the water consumed him, he glanced back toward the dock. The bastard's crimes against humanity were not expunged by his death, but Lycos' actions stopped further pain.

*Number twenty-seven.* He knew each target by name. He'd kept score.

The water enveloped his body. A baptism. He'd resurface alone as another person in another life, until Guardian called again.

They always called.

Evil could only be defeated by a greater evil. None were as vile as he.

Bethanie Clark tightened her death grip on the hybrid SUV's steering wheel. It was so damn dark and she, well, exhaustion saturated her bones. Her trip had started at three-thirty yesterday morning. Leaving New York City under the cloak of darkness, she'd driven straight through the day, and now, almost twenty hours later, the darkness of the Smoky Mountains surrounded her. She was back in darkness in more ways than one.

She'd left civilization just past the little town of Balsam, North Carolina—population forty-nine. The previously blacktop surface had become hard pressed gravel that climbed in narrow, switchback turns that made it impossible to see more than a few feet ahead. Worse, those hairpin turns had no guardrails to prevent her small vehicle from plummeting to the bottom of the deep ravines. She flicked the switch on the column of the steering wheel illuminating the high beams of the headlights. The powerful fissures of brightness enhanced the way the granite outcroppings loomed next to the car. The dark shadows obscured the surface of the road as she drove by, and she questioned whether or not the bright lights were a good idea, but without them, she saw hardly anything. So, high beams it was. Her grip tightened again when she glanced out the passenger side window. Inches separated the car from a wall of jagged granite. A glance out her driver's side window revealed a sheer drop-off one lane away that fell into complete blackness. Bethanie flexed her fingers slightly before she resumed her metal-bending grip on the steering wheel. She made sure she was as far to the right as she could safely move before she slowly pulled around the massive outcropping of rock and trees that loomed ahead. A small sigh of relief pushed out of her lungs. The road was visible in her headlights, and it was straight, well... straightish.

She glanced at her son, asleep and unaware of the panic that threatened to consume her. Her phone's GPS had led her to the top of this mountain. The GPS fritzed in and out as she drove around the face of the mountain. It had been doing that since she'd started the climb. She slowed to thirty miles an hour as the vehicle crept farther along the dark roadway. The directions to this 'safe place' had been entered into her phone back in New York. She prayed she hadn't made a mistake. She'd prayed a lot during the last twenty hours. Actually, she'd been praying continuously over the past three years. It seemed an answer had appeared, and she'd grasped it, desperate to escape what was coming.

The crunching of the gravel under her tires ground to a stop. The GPS muttered 'arrived at destination.' The volume had been turned down to a whisper so the mechanical voice didn't wake Ethan. In the array of her headlights stood a squat log cabin tucked into the side of the granite face. Two windows, a solid-looking door, and front porch peeked out amid a stand of pine trees. Images of every cowboy movie she'd ever seen while growing up flashed through her mind. Whole logs were literally fitted together, one on top of the other, to form the walls. The posts of the porch had once been trees. The columns were stripped of bark, but a few stout branches remained and jutted out several feet from a trunk. A lantern hung off one. On another dangled a sizable metal box—just as she'd been told.

Leaving the car running, she opened the door and stepped out into the night. The crunch of rocks under her feet announced her arrival at the porch. She stepped up on the wooden stairs and stretched toward the box that hung high above her head. Using the app she'd been instructed to download, she held up her phone and keyed in the six-digit number she'd memorized and waited... and waited.

A spasm of fear tightened her gut. That fear

fought hard against the exhaustion that overwhelmed her, but neither of those emotions dimmed her desperation. A metallic click made her jump and drop her phone. Over her heart, her hand tightly clenched her t-shirt. *Oh, shit.* Her eyes flashed around the porch and then back to the car quietly running not ten feet away. She pulled in a breath of air, pushed it out, and pulled in a deeper breath, before she bent over and picked up her phone.

Using the flashlight app to illuminate the metal box, she stepped up to the top step and lifted onto her toes to reach it. With her fingertips, she twisted the bottom portion of the container open. A set of keys dropped from the box. *Of course, she jumped again.*

Bethanie tried to laugh at her own skittishness, but she *was* scared. Her life and that of her son depended upon her *not messing this up*. She bent down to pick up the key ring with at least ten different keys on it. She tread carefully and quietly on the wooden porch, shining her flashlight at the substantial metal door in front of her. Odd for a log cabin to have a metal door. Wasn't it?

Her tired mind dismissed her thoughts as she fumbled to find the right key. It took three different keys before she located the one for the deadbolt. She stepped in and reached to the right, praying for a light switch. Her fingers patted around in the dark until they found a switch. She flicked it up and blinked at the blinding light. She'd missed seeing the spotlight on the front porch. Squinting up at the five billion-megawatt halogen light, she opened the door a bit farther and flipped the next switch in line. The interior of the cabin illuminated.

Bethanie pushed the door open farther and drew an easier breath. *Oh, well, all right then... not really expecting that.* She glanced back at the car before she moved inside the cabin. The front room boasted an overstuffed couch and chair, plus a recliner, in front of a flat screen television. There were numerous machines under the screen, probably for DVDs and such. She glanced out the window and moved through a small but modern kitchen, a bathroom, and two bedrooms. She checked each window latch, closet, and room, before she made sure the deadbolt on the back door was locked. Satisfied the little house was empty and secured, she headed back to the vehicle she'd switched to in Allentown, New York where, as instructed, she'd left the new Ford Harvey had allowed her to use in the parking lot of a movie theater.

"Ethan, honey... time to wake up."

"What?" Her son sat up. His blond hair stood straight up on one side, and his face was creased with sleep. "Are we there?" He yawned and blinked owlishly out the windshield.

"We are. It's really nice inside. Help me carry our stuff in, and we can explore for a little bit before we go to sleep."

Ethan had been a trooper; he'd tried to stay awake

and keep her company as she drove. The young man was always trying to protect her. He was eleven going on forty. She turned off the car. He grabbed his backpack with all his valuables, and she wheeled-slash-dragged in two of the suitcases that held their clothes.

"Cool." Ethan stopped in the middle of the doorway.

Bethanie pulled one suitcase up the porch stairs before retracing her steps to fetch the other. "It's nice inside. Why don't you go see which bedroom you want?"

She'd returned to the porch with the second load of suitcases when Ethan came outside.

"I put your suitcases in your room, Mom."

She bounced the first suitcase up the stairs. "Thank you. Which room is that?"

"The big one." He headed toward the car.

"Okay, thank you. There's just the groceries left. Wait for me, and we can carry the cooler together."

"I can bring in the plastic bags." His voice cracked a little as he called back. He was turning twelve in a month.

Bethanie pulled the cases behind her and headed into the house. She wheeled the tote that held their bathroom supplies into the bathroom and made quick work of putting the supplies away in the nearly empty cabinets. She did note, however, there was new toothpaste, toothbrushes, shampoo, and soap under the counter. She carefully moved the unopened products aside and put their items where Ethan could reach them.

"Mom, I got all the bags in." Ethan leaned against the door frame as he watched her collapse the tote.

"Thank you. Let's go get the cold food and unpack it."

"Can we eat? I'm hungry."

"You're always hungry."

"I know, all my awesomeness takes fuel. "

"You are awesome," She smiled. "Fuel it is."

"I'm almost taller than you already." He stood toe-to-toe with her and smiled.

"I'm still your momma, young man." Ethan laughed at her when she spun him and swatted his butt. He was a good kid, and she was happy about that. He was right, at eleven he looked her in the eyes, and she was five feet two inches tall. His father was a big man, well over six feet and heavy with muscle. Ethan took after his father, and he would no doubt tower over her soon.

They went out of the little cabin together, and she pulled the cooler out of the trunk. It didn't hold much. Staples, milk, eggs, mayo, butter. She didn't buy or pack the food, but whoever had was brilliant.

They worked together to carry the cooler into the house. Ethan grunted right alongside her as they worked together to get the ice chest into the small kitchen.

"Peanut butter sandwich?" she asked as she

started shifting the cold foods into the refrigerator after turning the temperature down just a bit.

"Yum. That will work."

"There are paper plates and plastic knives, forks, and spoons in one of those bags."

"I saw them." Ethan worked to pull out the bag of utensils and find the peanut butter while she put away the rest of the cold items and started on the dry goods.

"Do you need help?" She glanced over at the table where Ethan had set up his workstation.

"No, I found everything. Do you want one?" He lifted the knife out of the jar, a huge blob of peanut butter hung precariously from the plastic.

She motioned toward the knife. "No, thank you. Careful, it's drooping."

"Oh, crap."

"Language."

"It was crap, Mom. It isn't a bad word, not like shit or..."

She lifted her eyebrows and blinked at him. "It is still not nice to say."

"All the kids say it."

"Are we like all the kids?"

"No, ma'am." He sighed the response as he carefully spread the mound of peanut butter on a piece of white bread.

She turned her back on him so he wouldn't see her smile. They had this discussion at least once a day. When she was little, she could remember her parents chastising her and her sister for the same thing. Heavens, she was tired. She never thought about her family unless she was exhausted. She turned and leaned against the counter watching her son. He was so handsome. She once again prayed his father's physical attributes were the only thing Ethan inherited from the evil son of a bitch.

She smiled at him when he stuffed a huge bite of bread into his mouth and pulled a plastic cup from the sleeve she'd put on the counter. "Milk?" Bethanie walked over to the fridge.

"Soda?" The muffled request was barely understandable through the mouth full of peanut butter.

"Milk?"

"Milk." That sigh again.

This time she did chuckle.

"How long are we staying here?" He licked the side of his hand where a glob of peanut butter had fallen as he was eating his sandwich.

"I don't know. Until I can figure out a few things." Because how else do you explain to an eleven-year-old boy that his recently deceased father's criminal associates were hunting for you? The papers had described Harvey Simmons' death as an accident, but she didn't believe it. She wasn't even sure he was actually dead. How did she explain to Ethan that the bastard who controlled their life when he was alive was now ruining it in death? *You didn't.* You told him it was adult things. After pouring the milk and setting it beside him, she sighed and rubbed her tired, gritty eyes.

Ethan took another big bite of sandwich.

She pulled out a chair at the small table and sat down to watch him finish his food.

"What am I going to do about school?"

"Well, we are going to take a vacation for a while, and then maybe I'll be your teacher for a little bit." She had no idea how to homeschool him, but she could figure it out. But not until she got the all clear. Until then... well, they'd make those decisions day-by-day.

"You?"

"Yes, me. I'm pretty smart, you know."

He narrowed his eyes at her and took another bite of his sandwich. When he did that it scared her. That calculating and assessing look was all his father. She'd lived through over a decade of the man's unfeeling scrutiny.

Ethan finally cocked his head and nodded. "You're very smart. James' mom said so." He glanced at her from the corner of his eyes, a little smirk on his face. "Even if all that plant stuff you like is weird."

"She did, huh?" James' mother was a sweet woman, but she didn't understand Bethanie's love of herbs, botanicals and growing things. Bethanie had watched James on occasion so Patty and Darrin, James' parents, could go out on date nights. Harvey had never allowed Ethan to spend the night at other children's houses, and James' father worked for Harvey. He was cut from the same cloth as his boss, and Bethanie was required to follow the mandates set down by Ethan's father.

"Can James come to visit us here?" He grabbed the plastic cup and took a long drink of milk. The mustache it left received a cursory swipe of his tongue, which missed just about everything.

"Probably not. We don't know how long we're staying, and it is a long way away from New York." And if James knew where they were, his father could find out. God only knew if Darrin would use that information for his own gain, but he could, and she wasn't going to give him that opportunity. She handed Ethan a napkin and pointed to his milk mustache.

He sighed at her before he raked the napkin across his face. "What time is it?"

She tapped her phone and sighed. "Three in the morning." She'd been awake for twenty-three and a half hours. Before that, she'd gotten only a couple hours of sleep. Events had transpired quickly. Her yawn, no doubt triggered by the mental math she'd just done, spread across the table like magic, and Ethan's jaw cranked open, too.

"Okay. Teeth and then bed."

"Can we explore tomorrow?"

"Yes, but only if we go together. You can't go anywhere by yourself until we both know the surrounding area. Okay?"

"Yeah, okay." The words were slurred with another yawn.

She put the peanut butter and bread away, rinsed the plastic ware, and threw away the paper plate while he brushed his teeth and used the bathroom.

She waited for him to get into bed and left the bathroom light on after checking on him one last time. Leaving the light on was as much for her benefit as his. If she thought she could get away with it, she'd curl up in his bed with him. Protect him. But he was too big for that, at least according to him. Damn, she didn't want him to grow up so fast, but life had a way of forcing the issue. She untied her shoes and toed them off.

The mattress under her was soft, and the blankets were warm as she pulled them up over her clothes to her chin. In the utter silence of the little cabin, she could hear her son's small snores. He slept the sleep of the innocent. If only she could keep him that way.

If it was up to her, she'd fight to the death to keep Ethan away from his father. According to the newspapers, that problem was over. Harvey J. Simmons was reportedly dead. The papers said he'd been killed in an explosion. Bethanie would believe it when she spit on his damn corpse. She'd waited, expecting him to show up, to call, to let her know in all his insidious ways that he still controlled her. But weeks had passed, and he hadn't contacted her. She'd almost let herself believe he was dead; that they were safe.

But her life, which had been surrounded by

deadly threats for almost as long as she could remember, couldn't be that simple. Her son's father had enemies.

At least according to those women, he did. The women from Guardian Security had paid her a surprise visit. She replayed the shock at finding them in her apartment after she'd dropped Ethan off at school. The terror, then disbelief, then a horrid realization and disgust at Harvey's outreach of vileness. If she believed them, and she had no reason not to based on the documentation they'd shown her, Harvey had powerful adversaries in the criminal world who now claimed what Harvey had built. Ethan was a threat to those claims. She had no idea what they thought an eleven-year-old boy could do to them, but the women who approached her were insistent she and her son were in grave danger. She curled her arms under her head and stared up at the ceiling.

The two women who'd reached out to her, who'd built this plan to get them out of New York and away from this unseen menacing harm, were convincing. If the uncensored information they'd provided proved anything, it showed her they were connected and had documents that no one should be able to access. They had *proof* of that bastard's crimes. The first woman, Jewell King, provided document after document listing the atrocities Ethan's father had committed and showed her the trail of money and the devastation his actions had caused.

Bethanie didn't doubt the veracity of the information she'd seen. For three months she'd been a victim of Harvey's undivided attention while he used her body to gain an heir. At sixteen, she'd have rather cut her wrists than lie with that bastard, but she'd had no choice. None. Harvey and the people before him had taken everything from her. She was alone in the world. Until Ethan. In an act of unbelievable generosity, Harvey had provided her an apartment and an allowance and instructed her to raise her son. Harvey would claim him after he'd matured. His visits had gone from once a year, to every six months, and over the last year, Harvey visited monthly. She lived with the daily fear that the next visit would be the last time she saw Ethan.

She sighed and rolled to face the door, still listening to her son sleeping in the other room. She was so tired. Tired of being afraid. Tired of waiting for Harvey to show up and demand Ethan, his heir. She didn't remember a time when she hadn't had to look over her shoulder, to be afraid. When was the last time she felt safe? Before Harvey. Many, many years before Harvey.

# CHAPTER 3

L ycos watched the dog in front of him. He was some sort of weird mix of red wolf and possibly Mastiff, though the attempt at re-introducing red wolves to the Smoky Mountains was considered a failure. Dog's ears twitched as he listened to whoever was in the cabin. Lycos moved to see beyond a clump of overgrowth which kept him out of direct view of the safe house. If anyone looked out the windows, they wouldn't see him. He'd stared out each one of those windows and had memorized the terrain, learned the obscured fields of view, and knew how to minimize each of the cabin's liabilities.

This morning his ass was planted on the ground *outside* his old safe house because he'd received an alarm indicating someone activated the lockbox. Naturally, he assumed it was one of the other Shadows who knew about this location. Only four people besides him had that code. Thanatos, Moriah,

Smoke, and Tempest. Thanatos was in Africa, Smoke was on some damn assignment with Homeland, of all things, and Tempest? Well, no one had seen Tempest in over two years. The assumption was that the man was dead.

That left Moriah, and one thing he was absolutely certain of, Moriah wouldn't show up here. The woman hadn't talked to him since that night at the club when she'd walked out on him. He didn't figure the stubborn as fuck assassin would change her mind and reach out unless her life depended upon it, and even then, he wouldn't give that gamble even odds. So, the question remained. Who *was* in the cabin? He glanced at the SUV again. It was a rental. That much was blatantly obvious. The decals on the car window were a dead giveaway.

Dog lowered to his belly and relaxed, his eyes intent on the front porch. Lycos listened to the birds as they flitted from branch to branch. It was cold, but not frigid, although late winter in the Smokies was a temperamental bitch. This year the snow had held off. Light dustings and a few accumulated inches in December had most everyone thinking the winter would be temperate. Not so, one ten-day forecast predicted an imminent blizzard. Bring it on. It was one of the many reasons he lived out here. He loved the untamed nature.

He took in the roofline of the cabin. He needed to winterize it before long. The solar panels on the back slope of the safe house would keep the small cabin powered as long as whoever was in the house got up on the roof and brushed the snow off the panels. If that became too difficult due to injury or extreme weather, the house had a generator, and a 500-gallon buried diesel fuel tank. He'd trucked the fuel up the mountain himself, and even though he didn't use the safe house any longer, he made sure it was available for his... co-workers. He chuckled at that thought. Like they had a union or some shit.

He'd spent a handful of winters in that cabin. It was acceptable shelter, and he'd been comfortable, but he'd finally completed his new location. He lived on the other side of the ridge, and if one didn't know exactly where the entrance was, they wouldn't be able to find his mountain home. Small creases at the corner of his eyes deepened as he smiled. He liked his home. He'd excavated and built it himself. He was the only one that had ever stepped foot on those floors. Well, him and the dog. But Dog didn't take to being inside, so he came and went at his pleasure. Mostly went.

The animal stiffened, and Lycos' eyes flicked to the door. It opened, and Dog growled, low and deep in his chest. A hand on his hindquarters quieted the animal. Lycos watched the door open, anticipating Tempest to walk out on the porch. *Aww... fuck no. Son of a motherfucking bitch.* Nope. This was not happening. *No, no, no. Not a fucking kid.* Who in their right mind would bring a kid up here? He'd fucking kill whoever gave out that code. Kill them dead and then stab them again just for the delight of stabbing them. Motherfuckers!

The kid shuffled to the end of the porch and sat down on the step. He had a plastic cup and a paper plate. He carefully set the cup down and balanced the plate on his knees. Dog's head did the tilt-a-whirl thing. *Yeah, I have no fucking clue what is happening either, boy.*

The boy, maybe ten or twelve years old, turned slightly and started on his left-hand side, scanning the area he could see, eating his sandwich as he looked around. He watched some birds darting in and out of the trees. The boy shielded his eyes and glanced upward. Lycos looked heavenward, following the miniature human's observation. A golden hawk circled lazily on the air currents. The kid finally tired of watching the hawk and continued his examination of the world beyond the porch. He didn't leave the step, and he kept still as he watched.

Lycos frowned. Did Tempest have a son? Was that the reason he'd disappeared? If he did have a kid, why would he bring it here? What the fuck had to have happened to make that move?

Dog twitched beside him. The kid had pulled some crust off his sandwich and was tossing it on the ground. Several small sparrows hopped on the ground in front of the cabin. Perfect, just like a *Disney* movie. All the kid needed now was talking mice and a fairy grandmother.

Dog lifted and edged forward. Lycos touched the

animal's flank, but it didn't acknowledge the command. Of course, it didn't. Contrary fucking animal. The canine sat down almost obliterating his view. The asshole. He wrapped his huge hairy tail around his feet and cocked his head. The small human had the dog completely en-fucking-chanted —or confused.

Probably confused. Hell, *he* was confused, and he had opposable thumbs for fuck's sake. One thing was for damn sure. He wouldn't break cover until he knew who was in that cabin. He'd used curiosity to lure far too many of his targets to their untimely demise to be fooled with the tactic.

He shifted slightly after scanning the area. Dog tensed again, and Lycos' eyes slid to the door. The woman who came out was... well, she had on a pair of jeans that fit the globes of her pert ass like a glove and a sweater that hugged the generous swell of her breasts. Two of his favorite parts of a female. She shrugged on a large jacket over her form-fitting turtleneck before she sat down with the boy. They talked, and smiled, and laughed at the snowbirds which were hopping around on the gravel in front of the cabin. She said something, and the boy hopped up and ran into the cabin with his plate and cup.

The woman stood and crossed her arms, almost hugging herself. The breeze blew the crazy curls of her short blonde hair around. She pushed it out of her eyes and turned toward the trailhead near the cabin. Lycos watched her closely as, like the boy, she gazed through the trees, but he didn't sense the wonderment he'd observed in the child. No, the woman displayed worry. The boy ran out of the cabin with a jacket. He hopped down the stairs and shoved his arms through the garment as he headed toward the trail. She called to him to wait and turned to lock up the cabin.

Lycos lifted a metaphoric eyebrow at the action. She was in the middle of nowhere. The normal human tendency was to assume isolation; this woman, however, didn't. Her worry was more than a cautionary tale, at least to him. Yet another reason to use extreme caution.

He observed them as they headed to the trail that would lead them to the ridgeline. If they followed it all the way, they would be gone for an hour. Lycos waited until Dog's ears started with the swiveling radar movement before he shifted position. If the woman and child were still close, the dog would have had a steady bead on them.

He cautiously circled the clearing, staying well within the trees to avoid being seen. He would go into the cabin via the back door. The woods would cover his approach until the last minute. After ensuring he was alone, he made his way to the door, slid his key into the lock and let himself into the cabin. Dog sat at the open door. The animal would warn him if someone approached.

He passed through the kitchen, noting the supplies laid in. Not enough if they were staying for any length of time. He eyed the furniture in the living room and then headed to the bedrooms. Both beds were made. The child's room was obvious. He had a backpack full of electronic devices. A DVD player, handheld games, a Bluetooth speaker and headphones.

In the woman's room, he found a purse. He dug out the wallet and rifled through the contents. A driver's license from New York. Bethanie Clark. The date of birth made her twenty-seven, almost twenty-eight. He put the wallet back and grabbed her phone. The screen lock took thirty seconds to break. He pulled up her call log, and his eyes narrowed. There was nothing for the last four days. Lycos brought up her voicemails and checked all her messages, texts, emails and voicemails to include deleted messages. There was literally nothing on the phone. He flipped it and opened the case. A tingle of apprehension ran down his spine. The phone had a chip attached to the case. Tracker or listening device, he wasn't sure and couldn't be unless he removed it. Not in this lifetime. He'd make sure he knew what he was dealing with before he exposed himself in that fashion. He replaced the back of the phone and put it back in the case. He swiped through the apps and stopped when he saw the app that had allowed her to open the key box. He'd developed the app. Whoever had sent her here knew him. He double tapped on the icon and blinked at the six-figure code still displayed across the screen.

Well, fuck. Things just got interesting. He'd assigned that code to Moriah. Why in the hell would she send a woman and a kid into the middle of nowhere, to him? He shut the device down and dropped the phone back in her purse and ghosted out of the house. He had a phone call to make, and in order to do so, he needed a Sat phone and a secure connection.

"Look!" Ethan ran ahead and scooped up a massive pine cone. It was at least eight inches long, and it hadn't opened yet. He held it up to her showing her the base.

"That's impressive." Bethanie took the cone and examined it.

"Right? Did you know the pine cone is a good example of a Fibonacci sequence?" Ethan ran his finger from the base of the cone and followed the spiral around the base.

Whew, there was no way she was going to home-school her son. She had no idea what the Fibonacci sequence was. Ethan had always been ahead of his peers, so much so the headmistress at Ethan's private school had arranged advanced classes for him.

"I didn't know that. Can you explain that to me?" She continued walking, and he fell into step with her.

"It's so easy. It's all about patterns. Like this pine cone. On the spirals, both ways you can see the order.

See this is one, two, three, five, eight, thirteen, twenty-one."

"Wait, how do you get those numbers?" Bethanie stopped and watched as her son traced the spiral.

"You add the last two numbers to get the next one. Mr. Cavetti said patterns like this happen in most of nature because everything comes from an origin point. The point on the pine cone is here. So, you start here with one."

"Have I told you today how brilliant you are?"

She ran her hand through his hair, and he pulled away with a drawn out, "Mom."

"Well, you are." She drew a deep breath and enjoyed the scent of pine.

"Why did we really leave home? Why are you scared?" Ethan tossed the pine cone away and shoved his hands into his pocket.

"Well..." Hell, it was time to speak the truth, wasn't it? "Let's go sit down over there."

Ethan sat down on the trunk of an old tree that had fallen and grabbed another pine cone. His fingers traced the spirals as he waited for her to speak.

"I need to tell you some things, about your father."

Ethan glanced up at her. He set the pine cone down and wrapped his arms around his stomach.

"Not long ago, your father was in an accident."

"He's dead, isn't he?"

Bethanie's head snapped toward her son. He shrugged. "James' dad told James. He told me."

"When?"

"About two weeks ago."

"Why didn't you say something?"

"Why didn't you?" Her son stared at her, his eyes narrowed, waiting for her to answer.

"Because I didn't know if it was true, if he was actually gone. We didn't have the best relationship." Understatement of the century.

Ethan blinked and looked down at the pine cone. He started rocking back and forth before he asked, "Did he hurt you, like James' dad hurts his mom?"

Her stomach clenched and then dropped. She shook her head. "No, honey, he used to threaten me, but he never once hit me." His head snapped up, and he stared at her. She watched him closely. Emotions floated over his face before he looked down again.

"If he's dead then he can't ever take me away from you."

She barely heard his words. "No, he can't." She put her arm around her son and pulled him into her. "He can't ever take you away from me."

His sagged. No matter how big he grew, she didn't want to imagine a day where she couldn't hold him and soothe his fears or try to absorb his pain. Harvey would have taken him, and she'd tried to prepare Ethan for the eventuality. To prepare herself. It would have killed her. In her heart she knew it would have broken her beyond repair to know Harvey had Ethan.

His shoulders shook as he cried silently. She dropped kisses on his hair. She didn't have any emotions for that bastard, but for the pain her son was feeling, tears flowed down her cheek.

He sat up and wiped at his tears. He sniffed, "Mom?"

"Hmmm?"

"I'm happy I don't have to go live with him. I hated him."

"You... but you never said anything..."

Ethan shrugged. "He scared me, and I didn't want to go live with him. I wanted to stay with you, and I told him that. He said he'd hurt you if I didn't do what he said. He told me I could never tell you and that we'd both be sorry if I did. He said my... weakness wouldn't taint him. What does that mean?"

"Oh, Ethan. He scared me, too. He was a very different man, but he can't hurt you or me. He's gone." Bethanie wiped at her own cheeks. The horrible things she'd tried to keep from her son, the things she believed she'd shielded him from, were things he'd been dealing with alone. "He's gone, and we are going to be fine."

Ethan sniffed and wiped his nose on the sleeve of his jacket. "If he's dead, he can't take me away from you, and he can't hurt us, so why are we here? What is the real reason we left?"

How did she answer that without painting his father as the monster he was? He could never know the abomination Harvey Simmons had been. *Never*. Bethanie drew a deep breath and walked a verbal tightrope. Truth on one side and lies on the other.

When he was older, perhaps she'd be able to tell him, but not now. He wouldn't understand or be able to deal with the truth. "Your father made some enemies."

"Not a surprise." Ethan's snark forced a chuff of laughter from her.

"Yeah, well, we came here because nobody really knew if we were in danger from them." The explanation was as factual as she could make it. She wiped at her tears again and picked up the pine cone he'd placed on the ground in front of him.

"Why would they want to hurt us?" Ethan pushed at a rock with the toe of his shoe.

"I don't know, but there are some people who are trying to fix that. They're the ones who sent us here. That's why we left our car and have the rental. So, no one can track us. We're safe here." God, she prayed they were safe. If someone came after them here, there was no hope for help. They were so alone.

"You're sure?"

"Positive." She made herself smile at him and prayed that searching look he gave her didn't make it past the very thin veneer she'd pasted over her insecurities.

He leaned into her and nodded. "Okay. Hey, Mom?"

"Yeah?"

"Don't tell James I cried, okay?"

"Never. It will be our secret. I promise."

# CHAPTER 4

Lycos slid through the trees and worked his way back to the side of the granite outcropping. He watched Dog scramble to the top of the boulder that obscured the trail to his front door. The animal lifted his nose into the wind. His ears twitched, and he gazed down the mountain before he sat down and huffed.

Lycos chuckled as he passed the animal. Poor Dog. He was upset there wasn't anything to chase. Sooner or later a small animal, or hell a large one, would lure Dog away. Lycos walked down the trail and slid through the crack in the facade of the mountain. The naturally carved chute led him into his home. He moved a fabricated rock, deactivated his security alarm, and opened the door. The shape of his door followed the natural contours of the rock and varied in width to replicate a solid boulder when it was shut. The lights activated at his movement. He took off his boots and placed them on a rack beside the door.

The radiant warmed floors were heated by a thermal spring. Naturally occurring thermal springs littered the Smoky Mountains, and he'd harnessed one to warm his home. As he moved through the massive cavern that held his living room and kitchen, the lighting switched on, illuminating his path as he headed to his office. He followed the natural incline to a higher set of caves. His bedroom, the office, and a room he used for storage were located here. He used naturally occurring cracks in the granite for skylights. The openings led to a bowl on top of the mountain where he'd placed his solar panels along with the septic tank, and the pumps that drew fresh water and the heated spring water up the mountain.

Lycos dropped into the chair in front of his desk. The monitor activated at a touch of his mouse. He leaned over and flipped a switch. He heard the distant whirring as his satellite dish unfolded. The camouflaged netting over the dish would obscure any view of his presence.

He waited until his phone had obtained a connection and hit the digits of the hand-held device.

"Operator Two Seven Four."

Lycos smiled and shook his head. How many years had the same woman always answered his calls? Too many, probably. She had to be an artificial intelligence program.

"Sunset clearance, third operative," Lycos said the

words that would get him the answers he needed. Or should he say, the questions he hoped like fuck Bengal would have the answers to.

"Standby third operative."

"What's wrong?" Bengal's harsh rasp came across the line.

"Has Moriah been compromised?" That was the only reason he could think of for someone other than her to use his safe house with her code.

"Standby." Bengal's clipped words didn't bode well, but Lycos refused to allow any emotion into his consideration. He stared at the small picture on his desk—the only picture he had in the entire house. The snapshot had been taken from a distance. Faces weren't visible, even if it was digitally enhanced. The photo was of him, Fury, Bengal, Moriah, Anubis, Thanatos, Tempest, Asp and Smoke, the original Shadows. There were more now. Lycos didn't associate with them. Refused to. Fury was dead. Bengal and Anubis were killing paperwork now. Tempest? Probably dead. Moriah had severed him from her life, and Thanatos, well, that man was like a brother to him. He'd hurt the day Thanatos no longer walked the earth. That is if he lived long enough to see that happen. Again, a gamble that shouldn't be given even odds.

"Archangel."

Shit. *The* boss. "Third Operative."

"Moriah is not compromised. Why did you ask?"

"Her code was used to access one of my safe houses."

"Standby."

Lycos held the phone away from his ear and lifted an eyebrow. Another click sounded, and a female voice came on the line. "I'm on."

"Third operative is online. Explain what is happening at his safe house. I'm out." Archangel's barked order preceded an audible click on the line.

"Bossy, isn't he?" the woman's voice mused.

"I think he has the right. May I ask what's happening?" This person on the phone wasn't Moriah. Moriah had a deep sexual huskiness to her voice. This woman was... perky.

"Right. Okay, we needed to relocate the woman and her son. There is a mission going on that you are not cleared for but, suffice to say, we needed some-place no one would look."

"I'm not cleared for? Are you sure?"

"Okay, technically, you're cleared, but you don't have a need to know. Specific enough for you?"

"I deal in facts."

"As do I. The fact is you don't have a need to know."

"Indeed. But I *am* involved because Moriah offered up my safe house. Good to know."

"It was an informed decision. Look, this woman and her son have been dealt a fucking raw deal. They need to know they are secure and safe. We listed and rejected twenty different locations. Yours was selected because it is on no one's radar."

"For a reason," Lycos ground out.

"I need you to watch out for them. We don't have reason to suspect they were trailed."

"There is a tracking device in her phone."

"Mine. I wanted to make sure she made it. The phone is new. The rental's GPS has been obliterated, and it has been purchased by a shell company from the rental agency. Nothing that can be traced back to Guardian or the woman."

"A lot of trouble to go through for someone who has just been dealt a raw deal."

"She has an eleven year old son. That kid, he's family."

"Whose family?"

There was a long pause. "Our family. Watch out for him."

"I'm on deck. I won't be here much longer." He was hot for an assignment. He'd sent the signal a week ago and checked his dead drop three times a day, as required.

"I'll handle that with Archangel and Anubis."

"Bengal?"

"I can handle Bengal." She laughed, a slow, sexy laugh.

Lycos leaned back in his chair. This woman was the one Bengal had married, Jewell King. So, the kid was important enough for them to pull him from the rotation *and* violate the sanctity of one of his safe houses.

"What is the level of threat to the woman and her child?"

"That is unknown at this time. We'll need..." The woman blew out a long breath of air before she continued, "... a month, no, at least two months, before we will know for sure. It could be nothing, but we need to make sure that boy and his mother are safe."

"Who is the child's father?"

"That is not important. What is important is who his brothers are."

"And?"

"And *they* are family."

He chuckled, "I could find out."

She returned the laugh, "I've heard you're good with computers."

"That's what I've been told." He had several highly refined talents: computers, building things with his hands, killing people. You name it, he could master it. He enjoyed a challenge. Usually. What was unfolding now? Not so much. He didn't do kids. Hell, he barely did people. Kids were... different, messy... obnoxious.

"Don't try. We don't want anything to trigger a reaction from those who could be watching. The people we are shielding them from are as good as we are."

"As good... or better?"

"God, I hope they aren't better, that shit keeps me up at night."

"I'll ask again, what is the threat level to these assets?"

She sighed. "We don't know. This could all be overkill, but information is unclear and what we do have is... well, it is swirling. We don't have a serious grip on anything right now. Bengal or Anubis will reach out to you if we determine it is a nonissue."

"I copy, and if it is an issue?"

"Well, then I guess your talents will come into play."

"Is that authorization?" He followed Guardian's mandates—all of them—all of the time. "I will have that sent to you. Not my department."

He could hear the woman typing in the background. Multitasking. He could like this chick.

"There, the circumstances and request have been forwarded to Archangel. The rest is on him."

"Roger." Lycos leaned forward to disconnect the call.

"Hey, for what it's worth, I'm sorry. I know what it's like to have someone thrust into your life without your knowledge or approval."

"And yet you did it."

"I did. I had to," the woman admitted.

"Because they are family."

"Because they were in danger and, yes, they are family. And wow, did I just have a revelation. I need to go apologize to my brothers." She laughed a little.

Lycos smiled despite himself. He did like Bengal's wife. Maybe he'd like her a little more if she hadn't dropped a woman and her child in his lap.

"Tell Moriah she owes me an explanation when she has the time."

"Yeah? Well, she's busy for the foreseeable future."

"This request doesn't come with an expiration date."

"Noted."

"Third operative is clear." Lycos disconnected the call and hit the switch to fold and lower his satellite antenna. A smaller directional antenna rotated toward the safe house.

He leaned back in his chair and mentally flicked through the phone call. A swipe of his fingers jiggled the mouse and activated the computer screen. He minimized the architectural plans he'd been working on and toggled through the camera system, opening the video surrounding the log cabin. He'd mounted and then camouflaged ten wildlife cameras around the safe house. He activated them, one-by-one.

The assets were sitting on the front porch again. He nodded to himself and worked through the cameras. With the wildlife cameras, he could monitor their comings and goings without making contact.

He watched as the woman threw back her head and laughed. Her short mop of curls swirled around her face. Lycos sighed and swiveled in his chair. They didn't have enough supplies to last a week, let alone a couple months. That was going to be a problem.

He gazed up through the natural crevice skylight he'd constructed in his office. The low hanging clouds rolled past indicating coming snow, or possibly rain, depending on Mother Nature's fickle ass. Lycos groaned and glanced back at the cameras displayed on his monitors. When he went through everything this morning, there hadn't been a stitch of clothing appropriate for the kind of winter they'd encounter in the mountains in either of the closets.

Fuck him. He needed to head down the mountain. Food and clothing, for two months. Real winter clothing, not the jackets he'd seen. Sixty days. Fifty-nine if he counted today. Lycos nodded to himself and grabbed the keys to his truck. He had to walk one hell of a distance to get to his vehicle, but such was the price for living in a mountain. One he'd gladly pay.

He glanced at the camera again. The assets would be fine for a day. He looked at his watch. Two days. By the time he got off the mountain, it would be late, and then he'd still have to drive into a city that had what he needed. He'd be back tomorrow night, late. God, he hoped the woman had enough common sense to stay out of the weather.

He headed down the incline to the lower portion of his home. She'd made it out of New York. She'd made it to the top of the mountain. He was banking on her being cautious and hoping the fear he sensed this morning held for a few more days. He didn't have an option. Winter at these elevations wasn't the temperate climate they were currently experiencing. When winter came, it would dump a fuck-ton of snow. Assets not having proper clothes was an issue, and if shit went south and they had to make a run? They'd freeze before they escaped. Not. An. Option.

# CHAPTER 5

"**M**om, look!" Ethan whispered as he pointed to the sky.

A shooting star blazed across the heavens.

"I saw it!" she whispered back. They lay on the porch under two blankets and stared out at the vast array of stars. In the city, seeing one or two stars was an event, here... oh, beautiful heavens... the *multitude*!

"Did you make a wish?" Ethan turned his head to look at her, his eyes wide and happy.

"I didn't. Was I supposed to?"

"Uh huh. I did. I wished for a real dad."

Bethanie blinked back her shock. "Oh, baby."

"Sorry?"

"No. Don't be sorry for feeling what you feel."

He turned back to the sky and nodded to himself. "When I grow up, I'm going to be a good dad. I'll play with my kids and go to their things at school. I'll hug them a lot."

Bethanie reached out and took her son's hand in hers. She squeezed it and whispered, "You'll be one of the best dads ever."

Ethan squeezed her hand back. "Yeah, I'm going to try."

"Sometimes trying your best is the only thing you can do." She blinked back the tears that obliterated the stars from her eyes. Her son was such an old soul. His maturity should have been a wonderment, but it wasn't. Life for both of them had been hard. She'd tried to shield Ethan from Harvey, tried to make up for his lack of a father figure. She'd had no idea how badly she'd failed—until now.

Ethan yawned and pointed up at the sky. "I read a book at school that said the stars group together to form constellations. In old times, people made up stories about hunters in the sky, but really, the constellations were ways for people to navigate." He pointed his finger. "That is the North Star, so that is the Big Dipper, and if you follow it, you can find the Little Dipper."

"Can I ask you a question?" Bethanie smiled as she looked up at the sky.

"Sure, what's up?"

"When did you get so smart?"

He laughed a little. "I grew up, Mom. It happens."

"Yeah, it does." Sometimes sooner than people wanted, that was for sure.

"Mom?"

"Yeah?"

"When are we going to get permission to get back online. I mean, we left in the middle of the night. James has got to be freaking out. We had plans to do our science project next weekend."

"Oh, I don't know. I wouldn't expect for at least two weeks or so. They want to make sure we are safe. I'm sure your teacher will assign James another partner. It will work out." *Please, God, let it work out.*

Ethan rolled onto his belly and lifted up on his elbows. "I'm going to get really bored."

"Nope. I brought books, board games, and you have all your video games and movies. Plus, we have all this nature. I can't see us getting bored, even if we are not connected to the world." Bethanie turned her head toward her son. "No phones, no internet. That means no Facebook, no online games."

"You just want to go hunting for all that weird cra... uh stuff in the forest."

"Language."

"Mom, crap isn't a bad word."

"I still don't like it."

Ethan sighed heavily and rolled toward her. "I want to go home."

"I know. So do I, and we will. We just need to take a time out for a while."

"But we can go back, right?"

"Yes, we can go back." The lie stuck in her throat. There was no way to know if they'd be able to go back to their life... or how she was going to pay for his private school, their apartment, insurance, food... anything. She glanced up and caught a glimpse of a shooting star. She closed her eyes and made a frantic wish. It was simple and held everything she'd ever wanted in one breathless, silent plea. *Please, God, let us be safe and happy*.

Ethan yawned again. She got up and held out a hand. "Come on, bedtime."

"Can I sleep here?"

"No way. We sleep inside with the doors and windows locked." The sounds of nocturnal animals in the woods made her jumpy. Sleeping out here? No, she'd be awake all night and keeping up with her son took energy. She needed sleep.

"Okay." He reached up, and she helped pull him to his feet. "Are we going exploring again tomorrow? Somewhere different?"

"Sure. But we need to figure out how to mark our way if we go off the big path." They'd stuck to the big path for the last two days. She wasn't surprised that Ethan wanted to see and do more. He'd been patient as she gathered bits and pieces of trees and bushes. It was almost winter, and the ever-green variety of foliage was amazing. She had several books that she used to look up the species of plants in the region.

"We can leave a marker, tie a cloth to tree limbs." Ethan yawned as he shuffled into the house.

Bethanie gathered the blankets and shut the door

behind them. She threw the deadbolt and locked the mechanism on the door handle.

"Excellent idea. Let's talk about it in the morning. Go brush your teeth and get ready for bed." When the bathroom door shut, she made the rounds. Windows in the kitchen, living room, his bedroom and hers, all double checked. She went back into the kitchen for a glass of water and glanced at the back door. She knew it was locked but still reached over and made sure the deadbolt and locking mechanism on the handle were engaged.

A ghost of a shiver raised gooseflesh on her arms. What she wouldn't give to know they were safe... to be able to sleep without waking in fear at the slightest sound. The door to the bathroom opened, breaking her from the grasp of her fear.

"Okay. Pajamas and then bed." She waited until he slid under the covers and put the water on his bedside table.

"G'night, Momma."

She smiled and bent down to kiss his forehead. She was still Momma when he was tired or sick. "Night, Ethan. I love you."

"Love you," he parroted, his eyes already closed and body heavy with sleep.

She went into the bathroom and brushed her teeth before she grabbed a novel she'd been reading and settled into the corner of the couch in the front room. It was too early for her to even try to sleep. This late in the fall, darkness came early, and without the constant barrage of television, with the exercise of their exploration, and the fresh air, Ethan had crawled into bed at eight-thirty.

Losing herself in the world of magic, elves, fae and happily ever after, it took a moment for her to realize something was wrong. Jolting forward on the couch she strained to listen. She could hear Ethan's small snores, but there was something more... a car!

Her legs hit the floor, and she launched across the room. Swatting the light switch, she plunged the room into darkness. Her head snapped to the hall where the bathroom light shone like a beacon. She ran down the hall and flipped it off.

*Phone!* She scrambled into her room and grabbed her phone off her dresser. Her fingers squeezed the side button, willing the device to power up. As the face illuminated, she held it to her chest and tiptoed back down the hallway to the front room.

She pushed to the far side of the window to see down the long road that rounded the mountain. "Oh, no. No, no, no..." whispering words into the darkness didn't stop the shine of headlights that approached. The hand that held her phone shook against her chest.

She glanced at the face of her phone, swiping it open. There was a button that looked like a game. She had only to open the icon to send an emergency distress signal. The women had told her to use it only as a last resort if she or Ethan were in life-threatening danger. She slammed the illuminated face of the phone against her chest again and tried to breathe.

The truck made no attempt to hide its approach. It pulled into the clearing in front of the cabin right next to the vehicle she'd driven here. *Oh, heavens, she should have hidden the car!* The engine shut off. From where she stood, she could see the huge truck clearly.

"Oh, God..." the whimpered plea strangled from her as she watched a massive man drop down from the elevated truck. He shut the driver's side door and headed straight for the porch.

Her back hit the wall. She heard his steps as they mounted the stairs and walked across the porch. A startled gasp caught in her throat when a soft knock sounded on the door.

"Bethanie Clark, I'm with Guardian. I have supplies for you and your son."

It took several seconds for the words to make sense. She glanced at the door but didn't move. It could be a trick. This man could be one of Harvey's enemies.

"Look, I know you're scared. You used a six-digit code to get the keys out of the metal box. One of the women you talked to is about your height, but she has long black hair and an attitude. She's Asian and talks as little as humanly possible. If I wanted to hurt you or your son I wouldn't have driven into the clearing. I would have waited until you were asleep, broken in, and done what I needed to do. I have keys to this cabin. I built it."

A rattle of metal sounded outside the door, and she watched in horror as the deadbolt twisted to the open position and then locked again. The lock embedded in the doorknob twisted open and then locked again.

"I have food and clothing. I'll put it on the steps and leave. You'll need to bring it in. It's going to rain or maybe snow tonight."

She heard footsteps track across the porch and down the steps.

"He brought us food?"

"Holy shit! Ethan!" Her heart exploded. She grabbed her chest and him at the same time.

"Are you scared?" Ethan whispered as she smooshed him against her.

She hissed, "Yes, of course, I'm scared, and you scared me more!"

"Shit, sorry."

She could hear the concern in his voice. She drew deep, ragged breaths and tried to calm down. "It's okay." *No, it wasn't okay.*

She pulled him into the corner with her and kept him close as she watched the man make trip after trip to the porch. When he finished the last of his trips, there were six huge coolers and at least thirty bags of groceries on the porch. Three large boxes on the other side of the porch held God only knew what.

He made one last trek across the clearing and walked up to the door again. He turned and looked directly at them, although she knew in the darkness they couldn't be seen.

"I'm leaving now. You'll need to put the food in the coolers into the refrigerator and freezer. Make sure you turn down the freezer. I guessed on the clothing sizes. Layering if they are too big would be your best bet."

The crunch of gravel under the man's feet and then the slam of the truck door preceded the flash of headlights against the far wall of the cabin. They stood silently as the motor sounds receded.

"Can we get the food?" Ethan finally asked her.

"Let's wait for a while, okay?" She wanted to watch the road and make sure he didn't double back.

Ethan nodded and leaned toward the window. "He brought a lot."

She glanced at the porch. "He did." But it wasn't the supplies that held her attention. No, the man could have come into the cabin *at his will*. It didn't matter that she'd locked everything. He'd clearly demonstrated that there was no way to stop him from entering the house. What could she do to protect them? How could she ensure they were safe? Once again, someone other than herself controlled her and her son's safety. She closed her eyes and tightened her hold on Ethan. *Would this nightmare ever end?*

# CHAPTER 6

Lycos shifted out of his jacket and snapped the drops of moisture off it before he stepped through his front door. He hung the camouflaged Gortex on the peg to the right of the door and toed off his muddy boots, placing them on the mat under the pegs. The rain-snow mixture had started about an hour after he left the safe house cabin. The forecast was for a gentle warming tomorrow, and then a massive cold front was supposed to push through. The next twelve hours were probably the last of the temperate weather.

He was glad he'd made the trip to Charlotte and stocked up for himself and the assets. He slipped into dry boots and retraced his steps to where he'd staged his food. It had taken five hours to drive his truck to his hidden staging area and then trudge all his supplies through the mountain terrain. He could have waited a month or two before he restocked, as he was planning on bringing supplies back when he'd completed his next assignment. Now that his on-deck status for Guardian had been rescinded, he combined the resupply effort. He usually dropped a couple grand on food and clothing for the winter, anyway. Adding supplies for the woman and kid wasn't a hardship. Hell, he'd probably overspent for two months, but kids ate a lot, right? If he'd had access to food when he was growing up, he would have eaten constantly. He was always hungry at that age. That hollow, empty, needy feeling echoed through most of his memories. Pain was the other constant. Childhood sucked. Enough said.

He glanced at the clock as he shoved the last ten-pound bag of flour into a plastic bin that held all his baking supplies. The effort kept his staples dry and away from any unwanted visitors who might find their way into his home.

He rolled his shoulders and glanced at his watch before he made it into his office and rewound the tapes of his surveillance of the cabin. The woman had waited almost an hour before cracking the door open. Huh... She had the boy shut the door until she approached and knocked on it. The kid was probably instructed to lock it too. She carefully examined each bag before she allowed it into the house. He watched her go through the coolers before she dragged them to the door. He should've thought about that and bought more coolers to make the load lighter. The diminutive woman struggled to tug the weight of the filled containers. He chuckled as she held up the clothes. Yeah, the coats were too big. She didn't try on the snow boots, but she did examine everything before she took them into the house.

Lycos reset his surveillance. If the woman kept up her cautious nature, this assignment might not be a royal pain in the ass. Right. He rolled his shoulders and walked over to the floor-to-ceiling bookcase. Out of routine, his hand traveled to the eighth shelf up from the floor, and then over to the seventh book from the left. He pulled the top of the book and heard the latch behind the shelf click. Pulling on the reinforced wood, he dislodged the unit and swung it open. The vault door was an engineering success. He'd built the vault. He'd cut the metal and reinforced the simple looking door, making it damn near impenetrable. The seven-digit combination was a matter of muscle memory now. He waited until the light flashed and placed his hand on the wall-mounted scanner. The door clicked open, and he walked into the weapons vault which also held one of his many savings accounts. Small bricks of gold and stacks of gold coins lined a shelf to the right. The next cabinet held his trade tools. Passports, visas, foreign currency, driver's licenses, national identification numbers, healthcare cards, pictures of families he never had but who made his covers believable. The architect Guardian employed was worth his or her weight in gold.

The items in this room were apparitions although

they were physical manifestations of his work identities. All were things he couldn't live without, things that allowed him to be what he needed to be to do the job Guardian required. Of course, all of his resources weren't located here. He had other safe places around the world which held the means to become whomever he needed to become. Plus, he was the owner of a figurative ass-load of digital money in secure accounts across the globe. However, he didn't trust the world not to fuck itself one day. He'd be set financially should the world's economy implode. If it didn't? *Gravy*. But the craziness and chaos off the mountain was too insane to ignore. He pulled six more gold coins out of his pocket and stacked them along with the others.

The best of the best in modern warfare comprised the arsenal that lined the walls. The cabinets held ammo for each weapon under the appropriate firearm. Clean, concise and uncluttered. It was the way he liked things. He hated complications; unexpected wrinkles were unacceptable. His eyes traveled to the cabin surveillance monitor in his office. *Unacceptable, unneeded and a pain in the ass. Dammit*. He exited his vault, secured it, and replaced the bookshelf.

His gaze searched the screen, assessing the dark safe house one last time before he padded into his room and then into his master bath. The lights turned on as he entered, and he flipped a switch on the wall that started his shower. The mix of hot water from the natural springs and the fresh water from the well he'd drilled was always the perfect temperature. He used only natural and biodegradable soap and shampoo. He bought enough for a year at a time online. The water he used for the shower and washing dishes and clothes was piped out of his home through charcoal and sand filters to a flat area on the other side of the mountain. One of these days he'd plant a garden. He laughed at the thought. *Or not.* His thumb was not green. He could kill a rock.

The shower fell from the cave wall in a sheet. The waterfall had a natural stone seat under it. Lycos had engineered his home to utilize what nature had provided, and he made damn sure his footprint on the environment was next to nothing. He'd been to too many countries that had obliterated their natural resources and their wildlife. He could see the same thing happening in America—gluttonous people consuming more than they needed, leaving desolation in their wake. He rinsed the shampoo out of his hair and groaned. In general, he hated people and preferred solitude.

He closed his eyes under the downpour of water. Moriah's face flitted across his mind's eye. The relationship they shared had been his one attempt at normalcy. Well, as normal as two assassins could get. He chuckled to himself and stepped out of the shower, stopping the water with a flick of his fingers. He grabbed a towel and mopped off. Sometimes he allowed his mind to cast the 'what if' net. What if he hadn't pushed her in that club back in D.C.? What if he'd tried harder to be more available to her? What if he'd gone after her?

He tossed his used towel back on the hook he'd mounted into the stone wall. If he was honest, the breakup was for the best. She was one of three people who knew his real name. Well, his first name. He'd learned hers, too. She'd reinvented herself many times, as had he. Those names, Ryan and Miho, were just jumbled letters that languished in their past. He had many names now. The plethora of passports, the languages he spoke, and the assignments he took all created new, unique versions of the same person. His existence formed a prism that split the spectrum of death into many different people, all with the same face, and the same consciousness... or lack thereof.

Moriah was right to walk away. Eventually, he would have had to do something about the vigilante justice that consumed her. Now he could claim plausible deniability. Still, she was his first real relationship, if one could call what they had a relationship. Fucking on a routine basis qualified for that title in his book. After a fashion, he mourned her loss. He no longer went to the cities and enjoyed the nightlife they provided unless he was on assignment. Meeting up with her had pulled him from his mountain. Now only assignments and the need for supplies drew him away from his solitude.

He turned back the thick mink blanket and slid into his bed. The lights darkened, and he listened to the small sounds of his home. He chuckled at the sound of the dog's claws ticking as it came down the hallway. "You better not be muddy."

Dog chuffed as he entered the bedroom. The great beast sniffed around the room and left as silently as he'd entered. Lycos had engineered a wolf-sized doggie door for the animal. He'd injected a chip into Dog's neck, much like a microchip people in the cities used to track their dog if they disappeared. This chip, however, activated the door, allowing the dog access to his home whenever he pleased. It worked for Dog, who relentlessly patrolled the mountaintop, and it worked for Lycos. He enjoyed the occasional visit. Besides, he and Dog had an understanding. No dead animals in the house. Lycos rolled over and pulled the blanket up to his neck. Someday, Dog might agree to their understanding.

Lycos stacked the last cord of the old pine tree he'd chopped earlier this summer. He'd have fuel this winter to heat his home if the solar panels stopped working. Which reminded him, he needed to go check the generator at the safe house. It should automatically switch on if the solar array malfunctioned, but preventative maintenance was necessary. He'd seen the woman and child leave this morning before he started work via his camera system. They were an interesting study. The woman was beautiful, and the kid? Well, he didn't seem to be a snot-nosed brat, but looks could be deceiving. He was withholding judgment. But he checked on them before he left this morning. Rewound that digital camera to the time-stamp where the duo had headed out, taking a small backpack with them. He watched them until they were no longer visible as they tracked toward the main trail to the ridgeline. They'd left for their walk before he'd headed out to chop wood.

He glanced up at the sky. Snow clouds were socking in the area. Grey and full, the clouds would release the first big storm of the winter. Normally, winter started in fits and spells in the mountains, but it was going to be damn cold tonight, according to the weather reports. He'd go to the cabin tomorrow. He could fire up the generator, do what he needed to do and be gone before the woman died of a heart attack. *Maybe*. She was wound tight.

He made his way into his cave and slipped out of his boots before he headed up to his office. It was probable the duo were back already. It seemed like the woman kept them pretty damn close to the cabin. He glanced up at the skylight. The clouds were making it dark earlier than usual. He flicked the monitors on and waited for the surveillance cameras to load.

*That's not right.* No lights were on in the cabin. His eyes popped up to the skylight above his desk again. There wasn't a lot of natural light in that cabin and watching the woman over the last week, he'd noted her routine. The lights should be on by now. He rubbed his stubbled jaw and rewound the feed quickly. No... they hadn't come back yet. He flicked his wrist noting the time. A half hour of daylight left... maybe.

Dammit. He stalked back out of his house and booted up, grabbing the emergency pack that was stationed by the door. He made it through the chute, around the massive boulder and let out a long, shrill whistle. Dog would make tracking easier, especially if... He stopped and tipped his head upward watching large beautiful flakes of snow drift down from the heavens. Make that *when* the snow started to accumulate.

He headed around the ridge with a steady, quick pace. Dog would eventually catch up to him. The animal roamed a vast territory but had never failed to find him when he called. It could take an hour or more sometimes. Lycos stopped at the very top of the ridge and filled his lungs, whistling again. He waited for several long minutes before he heard a low, mournful howling response. Good, the animal had heard him. He turned and set a grueling pace toward the safe house. He'd start at the cabin and track them as far as he could in the dark and the snow. When he lost the trail, Dog would lead.

## CHAPTER 7

"Mom, we're in trouble, aren't we?" Ethan clung onto her hand as they stood beside the steep incline.

She didn't remember anything like this. She glanced down at her son and smiled. "We're fine. We just need to look for our markers, right?"

"We've been looking. I'm cold and hungry." Ethan shivered next to her. They weren't supposed to be gone long, but they'd found a trail and had followed it for a short distance. She'd seen what she believed to be a black willow in the distance and wanted to harvest a bit of bark. *Stupid. So damn stupid.* What was she going to do with it? It wasn't like she needed it for its medicinal purposes. Once she'd harvested some bark, they'd been distracted by a couple of rabbits feeding near the base. They'd followed them quietly, watching the greyish-brown furry bundles until they scampered away. When she'd looked up, she couldn't see the willow or the trail. She couldn't find the small pieces of old dish towel they'd wrapped around bushes so they could find their way back, and the temperature had plunged.

Bethanie shrugged out of the huge, red plaid jacket that had a thermal lining in it. "Here, put this on." The thing went almost to her knees. It would keep him warmer. The cold air swirled around her.

"That's yours."

"Yeah, but I've got two sweaters on and you only have that lightweight jacket. I'm not really all that cold. Put this on over your jacket and let me take the pack." *Did mothers burn in hell for the lies they told their children?*

"You'll freeze."

"I'll be fine. If I get too cold, I'll let you know."

"Promise?"

"Sure." Not happening. She looked around and shouldered the little pack that held nothing but the garbage from their lunch and that damn black willow bark. *Stupid. She was so stupid.* Harvey's caustic words played over and over in her head. *Pathetic. Stupid. A waste.* She shook her head. Oh, God... what were they going to do? How could she find a way back to the little house? Night was crowding around them, and it was so damn cold.

She glanced around and then tipped her head back, looking for... hell, she had no idea what she was looking for, but what she saw were the clouds that blanketed the treetops.

"Okay, we aren't going to see the moon or any stars tonight, so we can't find the north star. Moss grows on the north side of trees, right?" She'd heard that once. God only knew if it was true.

"I think that is legend, Mom. Besides, if you're lost, you're supposed to stop and let people find you." Ethan's chattering teeth made distinguishing his words difficult. Or was it her teeth that were making the racket? Yeah, definitely hers.

"That only works if people are looking for you. Nobody knows we came out here, so we have to find our own way back." She kept her words as calm and as a matter of fact as she could. "That trail to the cabin ran to the north. The big trail. Remember?"

She watched her son as he nodded and then sighed. They both stared at the trees. "There. That looks like moss." He pointed up at an old tree. There was a greenish white fungus growing on the side.

"Okay. Then we go that way." Keeping moving was good. Keeping her blood and body active in the cold would help her stay warm. They'd keep walking. To the north. To the ridgeline. Toward the cabin. To safety. She lost all concept of time, just simply kept putting one foot in front of the other.

Cold numbed everything. Her legs and arms no longer worked well enough to help them through the branches and bushes. She'd tucked the hand not holding Ethan's into her jeans pocket trying to keep it warm. The attempt seemed like a good idea at the time, but her hand burned as the denim slid against her cold skin.

She stumbled and fell to her knees. "Whoops." She repeated the word she'd said twenty times in the last hour.

"Mom, we need to stop. You have to take this coat back," Ethan's voice wavered as he spoke.

"'S okay." She braced against the snow-covered ground to push herself up. "See?" She carefully wiped the snow off her stiff, numb hands. "Ready?"

"No, you need to take this coat."

"Nope. You keep it. Let's go." She put her hand on his shoulder and started forward.

He stopped suddenly, pulling her attention from her feet. "What?" She blinked down at him. Her eyelashes were clumping with ice and obscuring her vision a bit.

He lifted his arm. "A dog."

She rolled her head in the direction he pointed. She shoved Ethan roughly behind her. That *wasn't* a dog. That was a wolf. Staring at them. As she watched, the animal lifted his head and let out a forlorn howl. She pushed Ethan again as she stepped backward. A weapon. She needed to protect Ethan. A stick or a rock, anything to protect her son. *There.*

She stepped sideways, putting her hand behind to herd Ethan with her. She grabbed at a branch and so did he. She lifted the thick limb, but her hands were so numb it sagged. She propped it under her arm, tucking it to her body. God help her, she'd tear the fur off that bastard with her teeth if it came closer.

A snap from her right drew her attention for a second. By the time she turned around, the wolf was gone. "Where did he go?" She turned to look for the animal.

"I'm sure he didn't appreciate the aggression." A deep voice boomed from the shadows of the trees.

Bethanie spun so fast she lost her balance and landed on her knees. She grabbed Ethan, pulling him to her. "Who... who are you?"

"We met when I dropped off supplies the other night." He pushed into the clearing and dropped his pack. She clung to Ethan, her mind refusing to work and give her a solution to this new problem. The man opened the bundle and pulled out a small packet. A tinfoil sheet appeared. "Here. Go sit on that branch and wrap this around both of you. His body heat will help you warm up while I start a fire. Put it over your head."

Her arms wouldn't respond. She couldn't move. Even if the wolf came back, she couldn't move. Depleted and exhausted, she could only watch. The words forming in her brain didn't make it to her mouth. *She needed... something. Ethan?*

"Ah, hell. Kid, we are going to have to help your mom. She's half frozen."

*Cold. Yes, so cold.*

"She said she wasn't cold, but she was shivering

before, and she's not now." Ethan helped the man wrap the blanket around her.

"Yeah, moms are pretty strong, or so I hear."

Bethanie tried to move, to warn Ethan not to trust... Her eyes closed for a moment, to gather strength. She had to protect her baby. She had to...

"Okay, kid. We got to work fast, or your mom is going to be in some serious shit. I need you to go into that pack. There are four square silver pouches right at the top. Bring them to me."

Lycos gently wrapped the blanket around the woman. He waited for the boy to hand him the packs and then tore open the thermal blankets. The material crinkled as it hit the cold air. With caution, he cocooned her into three of the thin emergency blankets. He pulled his ski cap off his head and gently tugged it over the riot of blonde curls before he wrapped a blanket around her head and shoulders, covering her face. The fourth blanket he handed to the boy. "Pull that over you."

"I'm not that cold."

"Good for you, dude, but we have to move, and I need you warm and on my six. Understand?"

The kid looked up at him. Big blue eyes and a red nose stared back at him. "No, sir. I don't know what that means."

"That means I'm going to carry your mom, and

you're going to walk right behind me. You need to keep up, and we need to move, or your momma is going to die."

"Die?" The kid's voice trembled.

"Hypothermia is a motherfucker, kid. You keep up, you hear?"

"Yes, sir. I'll try."

The boy sniffed and had tears in his eyes. Great. He needed... yes. He pointed his finger at the kid. "No sir, you'll do. You don't get shit for trying in this life, and trying sure as fuck isn't going to cut it tonight." Lycos gave a sharp whistle.

Dog appeared through the trees and sat down.

The boy took a step closer to him. "Is he your dog?"

"He doesn't belong to anyone, but he's helping us tonight."

Lycos stood, holding the woman in his arms. She weighed next to nothing, but carrying her through the brush and trees was going to be a bitch. "Okay, kid, you and Dog are right behind me. Hold on to his fur at his neck. He'll get you around or through anything on the trail. If you can't see me, don't worry, just keep your hand on that damn dog. Don't let go. I have to get your mom warm. You understand?"

"Yes, sir."

Lycos stepped off, heading to his cavern, it was closer.

"Sir, what about your pack?"

"Leave it, kid. Grab that dog's fur and get your ass

in gear." He waited long enough to watch the kid grab a handful of neck scruff. He whistled sharply and spit out, "Home, Dog."

Lycos trusted Dog to get the kid home. He had to because he needed to haul ass. The woman was an idiot for giving her clothing to the kid. What in the hell had possessed her? That kid wouldn't have had a chance in hell if she'd succumbed to the cold. Was she really that fucking brainless? Why the fuck didn't they start a fire? Find shelter? Share body warmth? He pushed himself, damn near running while doing his best not to jostle the woman too much.

It took him almost a half hour to make it to his home. He held her against him and pushed in the code. He flew through the great room and up the incline, heading straight for his bed. He took off her boots and wrapped her emergency blanket-covered body like a fucking burrito in his king-sized mink blanket.

He rushed through the house again, stopping in the utility room. Shit flew out of the cupboard until he found the thermal packs he sometimes used for hunting. Hand warmers the marketers called them. He ripped open packet after packet, scattering the wrappings as he stormed back to his bedroom. He shook them rapidly before he placed two on her neck, two snaked down her shirt and were deposited in her bra over her heart and two he shoved down her pants to her groin. Most people would try to warm her extremities, but that could cause a heart attack. The ice on her eyelashes was melting, although she wasn't pinking up yet. It was the best he could do for her now.

He ran from his room and slid to a stop at the top of the incline. Dog sat beside the boy, who was still holding onto the dog's fur. Fuck... okay, he needed to make sure the kid was solid.

A quiet voice asked, "Is my mom going to be okay?"

"She's getting warm, kid, that's all I know right now. Let's take off our boots and coats." Lycos strode past the kid and kicked off his boots and jacked off his own coat. He looked back at the boy, who hadn't moved. "Yo, dude, today?"

The boy blinked, turned and walked over to him. Lycos took the blanket and then helped the kid out of both jackets. "I'm going to go check on your mom again. Do you want to come with me?"

"Yeah, I mean, yes, sir." The kid shot him a quick look as he stepped aside quickly. *What the fuck? What was the kid afraid of?* Like he was going to bitch slap him or something? Not likely.

He led the kid upstairs, picked up the corner of the mink blanket, and flicked them back. Her cheeks had some color in them now, and she was shivering. Thank God. They'd have to deal with any frostbite issues later. Getting her core temp up was the requirement now.

"She's warming up."

"But she's shivering now." The boy stroked the mink by his mom's shoulder.

"Yeah, remember when she wasn't?"

"Yes, sir."

"Well, that wasn't good. Not good at all. Shivering is like an internal mechanism to keep your blood pumping. You stop shivering, and you're not long for the world. Cold is a stealthy motherfucker, kid. You stop shivering, and your body stops realizing you're cold. You get really sleepy, and then you die."

The kid swung his wide-eyed gaze to the portion of his mom's face that was exposed. "But she's not going to die, right?"

"Not if I can help it. She's warming up now."

The boy nodded. "I can't lose her, too."

Lycos leaned against the wall. "Your old man gone?"

The kid nodded. Great, the boy didn't have anyone else. Just his mom. He'd lived that scenario, but in his case, his mother didn't have the protective instinct this kid's mom had. He cleared his throat. "Hell, kid, she isn't dead. No need to worry about shit that probably won't happen." What the fuck could he divert the kid's attention with? Food.

"Come on. Let's get some grub. Your mom is going to defrost for a while."

The kid blinked up at him and nodded. He could feel wariness dripping off the kid.

They ambled down the incline as Dog padded

through the great cavern toward the kitchen. "What's his name?" The boy looked up at him as he spoke.

"Dog."

"That's not a name. That's what he is."

"Nah kid, his species is canis lupus lycaon. Dog is his name."

The boy turned his head and narrowed his eyes at him. The little bastard was intelligent, and he was trying to see if Lycos was filling him full of shit. Good for him, he obviously had more sense than his mother. "Fair warning, he isn't a pet. He comes and goes as he wants."

"But this is his home."

"How do you figure?" Lycos looked over his shoulder at the child.

"You told him to bring me home, and he did." The boy shrugged as if his logic was obvious.

"So I did. But he doesn't live here. He lives out there. He just visits from time to time, and he isn't a dog. He's mostly a wolf, so don't go trying to play fetch with the asshole."

Lycos opened his freezer and grabbed a plastic container full of chicken stew. He'd missed dinner, and he was fucking hangry. Hungry and angry all rolled into one exposed nerve. Whatever. Hot water over the outside of the container loosened the frozen stew, and it fell into a large glass bowl. The bowl went in the microwave, a few buttons were hit and presto, instant warm up.

"Go over there and grab a loaf of that crusty

bread." He nodded to the breadbox. The kid headed over and brought it to the table. "Butter is in the fridge." He watched as the boy got the butter out.

"Silverware?" The kid asked as he placed the butter on the table.

"Drawer beside the sink."

Lycos put two bowls on the table and headed back into the storeroom. He threw the shit he'd tossed out of the cupboard back into its place and grabbed six more packs of hand warmers. "I'm going to go check on your mom. You stay here and mind the microwave. Do not take that bowl out. It will be hot. Understand?"

The boy winced. "Yeah, I get it. I'm not stupid," and plopped down on a kitchen table chair. Lycos glanced at him one last time before he dashed upstairs.

He pulled the hand warmers out of the woman's pants and bra and replaced them with fresh warm packets. As he tucked her back in, her eyes blinked open.

"Ethan..."

Fuck, her blue eyes were mesmerizing. Lycos shoved that thought down deep somewhere under a rock. "He's safe. He's downstairs getting ready to eat with me."

"Cold."

"Yeah, you were fucking stupid for giving the kid your jacket. Just saying."

"Had to save him."

"You about got yourself killed."

"Wouldn't matter as long as he's safe."

"Right. We'll discuss how many ways that thinking is fucked up when you get warm. Go to sleep if you can. I'll be back later with something warm to drink. Then we need to check for frostbite."

He didn't want to do that. Didn't want to see what was probably there. If she was suffering from it, they'd have to make a run down the mountain, and the woman's cover would be blown, all because two city slickers decided to take a walk in the woods.

He headed back to the kitchen and found the kid with his head down on the table. Small little snores came from his slack body. Lycos bet the little shit was exhausted. He took out the stew, stirred it, and returned it to the microwave for a few more minutes. He sliced open the loaf of bread and threw it in the toaster oven to warm. Dog padded into the kitchen and sat down beside the kid. His tongue hung out as he panted.

"Too hot for you?" Lycos asked the animal.

The dog cocked his head before he lay down on the floor beside the child. Lycos pointed at Dog. "Do not get attached. We are not keeping them."

The animal groaned and flopped over on its side. Lycos poured water into a kettle and set it on the range. The woman would need some warm fluids soon. He filled his bowl and a bowl for the child.

He tapped the kid on the head. "Yo, dude. Food, then sleep."

The boy lifted his head and slid back into the chair. "Is my mom okay?"

"I think so." Lycos pulled the bread out and slathered a piece in butter before he dropped it in the kid's bowl. The remainder of the loaf went beside his plate along with the rest of the butter.

The kid dunked the bread in the stew and chewed it slowly and carefully. Lycos watched him as he ate. The kids he'd been around were loud and obnoxious, full of sass and stupid questions. This one hadn't pegged any of those hot buttons yet. Thankfully.

"May I have something to drink, please?"

Lycos got up and poured the kid a drink of water from the tap. "Here."

"Thank you."

The boy pulled the glass to him and drank almost the entire cup before he started after the stew again. Lycos noticed the carrots didn't get touched. "Eat your veggies. You need the nutrients."

No argument from young man, but the shiver the kid gave as he chewed the carrots wasn't from the cold. When he finished, he slid from his chair and took the bowl and his spoon to the sink. He returned to the table and finished his water before taking his glass over to where he'd deposited his bowl. The kid walked to the dog and sat on the floor next to it. His hand lingered on the hardwood. "Why is your floor warm?"

"Radiant heating. I have coils under the flooring. I pump hot spring water under the floors to keep it warm in here. Tends to be cold all year around. Caves generally do."

The youth did a 360-degree survey of the grand cavern. "Why do you live in a cave? What's your name?" And finally in a guarded tone, "Did you work with my father?"

*And there were the questions.* He was going to nip that shit in the bud. "Does it matter?"

The kid shook his head. "No, sir." He stroked Dog's grey tipped brown coat of winter fur. "But if you hurt my mother, I'll find some way to make you sorry." Fierce blue eyes rose and challenged Lycos.

Lycos dragged the last of his bread around the bottom of his bowl and sopped up the remaining stew. *Shit.* Had to admire the kid for his backbone if nothing else. "I'm definitely not a friend of your father, okay, kid? More than that you don't need to know." He glared at the young man until the kid dropped his gaze back to the dog he'd never stopped stroking. Lycos poured some of the hot water into a thermos cup with a screw on top. The warm water would hydrate her and help to raise her core temp.

"What's that for?"

"Your mom. When she wakes up, she's going to be thirsty. It's hot and will help her hydrate." He put the top on the cup. "Let's go check on her, then we'll find a place for you to sleep."

The kid jumped a bit when the kettle hit the concrete countertop. Whatever. The boy probably had a right to be on edge. New shit and strange environments.

The kid got up and followed him. Claws scrambled on the hardwood. Guess Dog had decided to depart. Only, it sounded like the damn thing was following them. Yeah, the night was getting weirder and weirder. Lycos glanced over his shoulder as he turned the corner. Sure enough, the wolf was walking right next to the kid, and the kid's hand was holding onto the animal's scruff. Great. Dog had adopted the kid.

When they entered his bedroom, Lycos pointed to a huge recliner in the corner. "Sit over there."

He heard the kid and Dog go over to the chair. Dropping down to his knees in front of the woman, his hand went inside the mink burrito, and he felt her skin. Still cold but warming up. She had burrowed into the mink and that was probably what she needed, sleep and warmth. He still unwrapped her enough to check her ears, nose, fingers, and toes. He didn't see any signs of frostbite, which was a fucking miracle. He wrapped the woman up again. "Leaving you on defrost mode for a while." Lycos flicked the corner of a thermal blanket down, covering her face but leaving room for ventilation.

He rocked back to his heels and stood. "Come on, kid, let's find some— Well, fuck me standing."

Dog sprawled on the recliner with the kid damn near lying on top of him, doing one hell of an imitation of a blanket. The kid was out. Lycos pointed a finger at the animal. "I fucking told you not to get attached."

The dog lifted his lip in snarl before he arched his back and stretched out, nearly obliterating the kid from view.

*Whatever.* Lycos rubbed his face as he left the bedroom. He needed to clean the kitchen, activate the alarm system, and then he needed a couple hours of sleep. Maybe the nightmare would be over when he woke up, and he wouldn't have to play caretaker to a couple of city slickers.

It took five minutes to clean and lock up. He stopped in his office and glanced up through the skylight. Snow obscured the view. He took a chance and deployed his antenna. It took a few minutes, but the signal acquired. He pulled up the National Weather Service's radar imagery and studied the storm heading their way. He pulled up the projected forecast and groaned, actually groaned, at the prediction of two feet of snow by morning. By week's end, they could have close to four feet. He had to go around the mountain to the cabin again. He needed clothes and shit for both of his unwanted visitors, plus their food. He had plenty for him, but... dammit, that meant he'd need the truck. He glanced at his watch. It was going to be a long, long, fucking night.

## CHAPTER 8

Her mouth was so damn dry. Bethanie rolled from her side to her back and groaned. Every muscle in her body ached. She pushed against the... fur?

"Ethan!"

"I'm here, Mom."

Thrashing frantically at the folds of material that confined her arms, she snapped her head toward his voice. "Are you all right?"

"I'm okay." He padded across the floor, and she grabbed him, pulling him onto the bed with her.

"Are you sure?"

"Yeah, I'm fine. You're the one who was in trouble. The man was pissed when he brought you here."

"You mean he brought *us* here," Bethanie replied, distracted. She remembered the man, kind of. Bits and splashes, words and snapshots of things, really, but she knew they had a savior.

"Nope. Dog brought me. The man said I'd slow him down, and he had to get you to shelter fast because the cold is a sly motherfucker, and you could have died."

Bethanie stopped all efforts to break free from the bedding that twined around her. "*What* did you just say?"

Ethan sighed. "You were too cold, and I told you that you shouldn't have given me your coat. The guy had to move quick to get you warm. I couldn't keep up with him. It was okay though. Dog got me here, just like he said he would."

Bethanie blinked at her son as the rest of his words registered. "Wait, he *left* you?"

Ethan frowned. "Mom, did you listen to me at all? You could have died. He had to get you someplace warm—fast! He told me Dog would lead me here, and Dog did. He wasn't going to leave me..."

"Dog?"

Her son turned and pointed. Bethanie followed his finger, grabbed Ethan and dragged him further up onto the mattress with her. "That *is not* a dog!"

"I know, he's a canis lupus lycaon. He's a wolf, but he's cool, and he's really warm. He slept with me last night. His name is Dog."

The animal stared at her before it turned its head and fluidly poured itself out of the chair. The animal padded out of the room without a backward glance. The lights overhead turned on as the animal walked away, just like the lights in the cases of the frozen food department of their local grocery. She pushed herself up and slowly swung her feet off the bed. God, her body hurt. She patted her sock-clad foot against the flooring. Her forehead scrunched. It was warm, like toasty warm.

"The man said you'd be thirsty. He brought this for you last night." Ethan handed her the thermos styled mug.

She reached for the cup and screwed off the top. A thin vapor of steam rose from the surface of the water. Bethanie smelled it and cautiously took a sip. The warmth soothed her dry throat. The water hit her stomach and spread, absorbing much as rain soaks into sun-baked soil. She drank the entire cup. Ethan took it from her when she was finished and put it on the bedside table.

Bethanie looked around what she could see of the darkened room. "What time is it?"

"I dunno. The man is asleep down the incline in the big cave. I didn't wake him up."

"The big what? Cave?"

"Mom, are you sure you're okay? I mean, rock walls and ceiling." Ethan waved his hand toward the wall and then pointed up.

Bethanie dropped her head back slowly and blinked up at the ceiling... which wasn't a ceiling, but rather a... She closed one eye as she turned to face her son. "We're in a cave."

"Kinda, but it's a really cool house, too." Ethan pushed into the side of the bed.

Her body ached like she had the flu, but she didn't have a fever. She could so use a couple of over the counter pain relievers. Her eyes traveled the expanse of the room.

"Where's the bathroom?"

"Through that door." He pointed behind her.

"Okay, I'm going to go use the bathroom. Please don't leave."

"Okay." Ethan flopped onto the bed and burrowed under the mountain of blankets she'd been rolled up in.

Bethanie stopped for a couple seconds as the lights turned on when she walked forward. She looked up and narrowed her eyes at the lights. *Freaky.* She moved and waited for the next light to turn on.

"Motion sensors! Cool, huh?" Ethan called from the bed.

"It's something, that's for sure." Her feet ached. Each footstep sent a jarring pain through the arches of her feet and up her legs. She made it to the bathroom and pulled off her socks. There was nothing wrong with her feet. She pressed the toe of each foot and watched the blood fill the white space as she let go. Her feet had gone numb last night. The pain she was suffering today was probably due to stumbling around in the cold.

Bethanie took care of business and used her finger and the man's toothpaste to scrape and rinse the Sahara Desert out of her mouth. She found his medicine cabinet and helped herself to two maximum strength pain relievers, using her hands to scoop water into her mouth and chase the tablets down. The haggard reflection in the mirror made her wince. She could fall back into that big bed and sleep for another week or so, but she needed to get Ethan and leave. The warm tile under her feet held her attention until she stalled in front of a massive stone wall. Something was missing? There was the wall, and there, that was a drain... toilet over there, two sinks. Her eyes flew back to the stone wall. *That* was the shower? Where was the showerhead? Oh, what she wouldn't give for a hot shower, but her feet ached enough that stepping closer to examine the curiosity was off the menu. Instead, she shuffled out of the bathroom. She could shower at the cabin.

"Mom, I'm hungry." Ethan's lament was proof positive that her son had survived the ordeal in the woods without lasting physical injury, but she still needed words with the guy who *left* her son with a *wolf* and taught him how to say *motherfucker. Seriously, what kind of jerk did that?*

"Okay. If you walk really slow with me, we can go find the man and then maybe the kitchen." Most people wouldn't mind her feeding her child. Most people didn't leave said child in the middle of the forest with a wolf or say vulgar cuss words in front of them either.

"I know where it is." Ethan held her hand as she trundled alongside him.

"Do you?"

"Yeah. I had soup last night." He chuckled. "It was pretty good. I even ate the carrots." He smirked at her look of disbelief.

*Okay, well maybe the man wasn't a complete loser as an adult.*

Bethanie took her time moving down the arched hallway comprised entirely of carved stone. The floors stayed warm under her feet as she passed a closed door about halfway down the hallway. Almost at the end of the hall, she peeked into the last door. Illumination bloomed to reveal a massive office with a bank of computers and a desk phone on the far wall, but that wasn't what stopped her. The walls, from ceiling to floor, were covered in shelves that held thousands of volumes of books.

"Wow." The word fell from her lips in a small whisper.

"He's sure has a lot of books."

"He sure does." That was the understatement of the day.

"The kitchen is this way." The hallway they followed was wide enough to allow six people to walk side by side. As it curved to the right, the floor started a gentle, but noticeable, slope. Turning the corner, she released a soft gasp. A vast cave stretched in front of her. A massive fireplace roared against the far wall where a conversation pit formed a living area. To the right, rows of natural pine cabinets filled the walls over what seemed like acres of speckled white and black granite counters. The largest farmhouse sink she'd ever seen broke up the long run of granite. A stainless steel hood descended from the ceiling over an eight burner cooktop, complete with pot filler. Underneath the cooktop, double ovens and what looked like a built in microwave broke up more wood cabinets. A kitchen island with eight upholstered chairs obscured the lower cabinets past that until the stacked washer and dryer ended the march of cabinetry. No walls separated the rooms, just... space.

"Wow." That seemed to be her go-to word today.

"Yeah, it's cool, huh?"

"Cool, yeah. Really cool. Where's the man?"

Ethan swung his head toward the fireplace. His eyes darted from place to place. "I don't know. When I came out before you woke up, he was asleep on the couch."

Right, well then. Food. The lights in the living area slowly went dark. Okay, so something had been moving in that area recently. The lights in the hall behind her were still on. Apparently, they must stay on for a period of time unless they detected movement. Maybe?

"The bread is in that wooden box on the counter. Do you think he has peanut butter?" Ethan headed to a small wooden box on one of the long countertops. He lifted the little tambour door and pulled out a bag of baguettes.

She glanced at the array of cabinets. "Maybe. If

you were peanut butter, where do you think you'd hide in this kitchen?"

"Uhhh..." Ethan spun from right to left.

"I'd probably hide right by the almond butter and hazelnut spread in that cabinet."

At the low male voice, Bethanie gasped and spun so fast she lost her balance. A hand caught her elbow, steadying her. "Oh, you scared me."

"I wasn't expecting you to be awake yet." The man released his grip on her arm and walked across the expansive kitchen to open the cabinet. He pulled down a large plastic container and handed it to Ethan. Her son smiled and toted the container to the table where he'd placed the bread.

When the guy returned, he stood in front of her and crossed his arms over his chest. His eyes traveled over her. Exposed and vulnerable under his hard stare, she extended her hand. "Bethanie Clark."

The man glanced at her hand and leaned back. Her hand dropped like a lead weight. All right, *so much for introductions*. Her tongue wet her hot, chapped lips. "Ahh... thank you for... ah, last night."

"What in the hell did you think you were doing?" Anger laced the man's question. Ethan's head whipped toward them from where he was digging peanut butter out of the container.

"We got lost when we followed some rabbits. We couldn't find the markers we'd left." The feelings of helplessness, despair, and fear lanced through her again, as sharp, unrelenting and vicious as they were last night. They'd been so close to... No, she couldn't think about it. The helplessness was too fresh, too raw. Her arms wrapped around her waist, and she glanced at her son. He'd put the knife down and sat, watching the exchange with narrowed eyes.

The man's eyes bored across the distance. She could feel it as she turned her eyes back to him.

He shook his head, his stare holding her in place. "Stupid, that's what you are."

"We didn't mean to get lost." *Stupid. Worthless. A waste*. The memories of taunts flowed like blood from a lanced vein through her mind.

"Screw the getting lost scenario. Giving him your coat? Pure, unadulterated idiocy. How in the flying fuck were you going to take care of that kid if you froze to death? Did you think that would keep him alive after you froze to death? Why didn't you start a fire? Find a place out of the wind? Shelter of some sort? Here's a crazy idea, get some kindling going and snuggle together to use your joint body heat to stay alive?"

Her mouth dropped open. "What? How was I supposed to start a fire? I didn't have any matches! And he was freezing! I had to get him back to the cabin. I'd give him every stitch of clothes on my body to keep him warm! And what about you? You left him with a wolf!"

"The kid was fine. You, however, *Miss I'm going to be the stupidest thing God put on the planet while pretending to be selfless*, were going to die if I didn't get your ass into shelter and warmed up."

Ethan flew from the table and inserted himself between Bethanie and whoever this asshole was. He straightened and glared at the man. "Don't call my mom stupid, you jerk. She's smarter than you'll ever be. Just because you found us doesn't give you the right to call her that. You don't know us, you—"

The man pointed to Ethan without dislodging that cold stare. "Shut it, kid, this is an adult conversation."

"Oh, no, this is not happening! Do not talk to my son that way!" Bethanie limped forward and pushed in front of Ethan. This condescending piece of shit could berate her and treat her any way he chose, but he would not, *ever* treat Ethan like that. The man towered over her, but she'd be damned if she was going to back down. She loved her son, and she was a damn good mom. He was all she had in this life. Nobody would take that from her. Nobody.

"Lady, let me set some things straight for you right now. One, *you* have no fucking clue how to exist in this country. I would love for you and your kid to leave even knowing you'd probably get lost all over again. *Believe me, I do not want you here.* Just my fucking luck, leaving isn't an option. There's a blizzard of Biblical proportions going on, and nobody is getting out of this cave any time soon. You go out there now and it's tantamount to suicide. They wouldn't even find your body until spring. Two, that protective momma bear shit you got going on is doing that boy zero good. Life is full of hard fucking knocks, lady. He made it last night. He's stronger for it. He was never in danger, but you were. Three, as soon as I can get your ass out of my life, you're gone."

Her eyes filled with tears. Tears that were born from anger. She held out her hand and Ethan grabbed it. She spat the type of words she'd prayed she'd never be forced to say again past her gritted teeth and clenched jaw. "His name is Ethan. I'm sorry we inconvenienced you. I'll do my best to make sure you won't know we're here."

Hard, dark eyes stared back at her. His face contorted in a snarl before he spun on his heel and left.

"Mom, don't let him talk to you like that. He doesn't have the right. Nobody has the right."

She met her son's troubled stare. She cleared her throat and sniffed back the tears that threatened to fall. "It's okay, baby. Finish making your sandwich."

"I'm not hungry anymore."

"Okay. How about we make a couple sandwiches anyway and we'll eat them later." She didn't want to be anywhere near that man. That vicious, horrid man. They could make sandwiches and fill cups with water and find a place to... hide.

She shuffled to her son and helped him make four sandwiches before she cleaned the knife and put away the peanut butter. She looked through the cupboards as quietly as she could until she found a drawer with plastic bags. She took one out and placed all four sandwiches in it. Her search also yielded two large plastic cups. She filled both with water and then gazed around the cavern. There was an empty space by what looked like the storage area. She nodded in that direction, and they made their way across the vast expanse.

"Look, that's our stuff, isn't it?" Ethan pointed to their suitcases.

She nodded and set the cups on a cabinet. She opened hers and then Ethan's suitcase. They were full of the winter clothes the man had brought them. Why had he gone to their cabin? Her eyes tracked to the furthest bag and beyond. She hobbled forward and blinked when the lights turned on. The dry food that he'd brought to their cabin was sitting on a long countertop that led to a door and what appeared to be a silver panel about three-foot-high and two-foot-wide set into the stone wall.

A sink, food and their clothes. Plus, a washer and dryer. Two freezers punctuated the cabinetry. Closer to them was an open shelf that held a sleeping bag and several backpacks. Okay. They'd stay back here, out of the way. They could be very quiet. She'd learned early in her life how to make herself scarce and unseen. It was something she prayed Ethan would never have to know. Maybe she could make an adventure out of it. She coughed and grimaced at the phlegm in her throat. Wonderful.

"Here's my backpack." Ethan lifted it up.

"Good. Okay. That's good." Bethanie nodded her head up and down, giving a mental confirmation to her plan.

"What's good?"

"We'll stay here. Look, see that shelf where the sleeping bag is?"

"Yeah, what about it?" Ethan looked up at her. "James has one like that."

"Right, well see how far the bottom of the shelf is from the ground?"

"Yeah?"

"We are going to become invisible. Let's put the sleeping bag on the floor, and we can drape something down and... I don't know, hide from the world."

Ethan slid his eyes up to her. "So, he won't see us and get pissed again?"

She shrugged. "Something like that. Let's make it now, and we can have a sandwich when we're done. Okay?"

"Okay. Dude cusses a lot. I mean, a lot."

"Boy, don't I know it. But just because he said them doesn't mean we can, right?" Bethanie pushed her curls back from her face, tucking the longer strands behind her ears before she untied the knots in the strings that bound the sleeping bag.

"Oh, look!"

Bethanie heard the whir of something motorized and glanced toward the sound. The wolf stepped through the silver panel. He was covered in snow;

well, he was for about five seconds. He shook, dislodging the ice from his coat. The animal walked up to Ethan and stood beside him.

Ethan laughed, "He's really wet."

"He really is, and he smells like a dog."

Ethan took a deep breath, "Wet wolves stink."

"They do." Bethanie opened the zipper of the sleeping bag and pushed it under the shelf. She glanced around. Three towels that had obviously seen better days were folded and waiting close to the back door.

"Will you get those towels for me, please?" She handed a towel to Ethan. "See if you can get some of the water off him. Umm... will he bite?" "

Ethan shrugged. "He won't bite me." He draped the towel over the animal's back and rubbed his coat in a completely ineffective way.

Bethanie slowly walked on her knees toward the animal. She grabbed half of the terry cloth and carefully dried the dog's fur. He tilted his head back, and his tongue lolled out.

"See, he likes it." Ethan dropped his portion of the towel and scratched the wolf between the ears.

Bethanie kept a wary eye on both of them as she wiped his paws and then the floor where the animal had entered the house, err... cave. She draped the wet dog towel over the sink and leaned against the stainless, exhausted.

Her throat was raw. Probably from breathing all the cold air last night. "Ethan, will you grab the water? We can have our sandwiches and then, maybe, we'll watch a movie."

"Sounds like a plan, Mom."

Maybe she could nap while he watched. The wolf-dog curled up next to Ethan when he sat down. He watched them eat the food but didn't beg. He'd been well trained.

Her mind flitted back to the man. He was so angry and... big. A dark scruff covered his face. Not a beard yet, but it looked like he hadn't shaved in a couple days. He was tall and powerfully built. His legs were long and just as thick as the rest of him. What she remembered best about the man was his utter rage at their presence and the worthlessness she'd felt at his accusations. Those emotions she knew. The question was why was he so angry, and why did he turn his rage on her? She'd done the best she could.

"Okay?"

Bethanie blinked and cranked her head to see her son. "What?"

"I'm going to watch *Avengers,* okay?" He held up his portable DVD player and the movie.

"Sure, but let's use the earphones, too."

"Time to make like a ghost?" Ethan smiled at her and dropped to his knees beside the draped off area.

"No time like the present." She watched him slide in and followed him under the towels, careful not to move the sleeping bag into bunches as she pushed into the confined area. She was able to lie on her side and watch him get his movie started. The dog's head popped in their space before he crawled half of his body onto the sleeping bag. The smell of damp dog permeated the small area.

"He's a good boy," Ethan said as his sock-covered foot tucked under the animal's neck.

"He seems to be." She agreed, although Ethan couldn't hear her. She could hear the movie through his headphones, small tinny sounds drifted toward her.

Careful not to startle the dog, she turned onto her other side and pulled the towel away from the floor. The heated floor and confined quarters made it very warm in their little space. Cool air flowed in and washed against her. After several minutes the lights in the storage area clicked off. The dog groaned and rolled onto its side. Silence prevailed in the vast expanse of the cave, except for the muted noises from Ethan's headphones. She closed her eyes and said a small prayer that the snow would end soon, and they'd be able to leave.

Ethan glanced over at his mom. She was sleeping. She was always scared. Just like James' mom. Why did grown up men have to be such assholes? He cut his eyes up to make sure his mom was still asleep. She didn't like him to cuss, but all the kids talked that way and he had enough problems fitting in, being 'his' kid.

His father wasn't liked by many of the parents at his school. He knew because parents talked and kids repeated that shit. That's why he and James were friends. James' father worked for his. The other kids banded together to act tough. He learned that his father was feared, and one of the kids in his class said his father was a mob boss. He had no idea what that meant, so he looked it up. Organized crime. He read everything he could about that and then Googled his dad. Some things didn't match up, but he understood enough to know his classmates' parents thought his dad was a criminal. Maybe that was why his mom was so afraid of him. He had so many questions he wanted to ask her, but he didn't want her to be even more sad. His dad scared him so bad he had nightmares. He couldn't tell his mom though. His dad was mean, and not the type of mean that you could stand up to. He protected his mom the best he could. He kept his mouth shut and did what his dad told him, when he told him. If his father demanded good grades, he got them. If he said Ethan couldn't be weak. Well, he wasn't.

James protected his mom, too, but in a different way. Only James ended up with huge black and blue bruises from his dad's fists. James said it was better for him to have the bruises than his mom. He hated seeing those marks on his friend. James said his marks were on the outside, but Ethan's were on the inside. He supposed that was true.

He rubbed his foot against Dog and looked at the wood above him. If he had to stay here until they could leave, he could do it. He wouldn't let that man hit his mom, or yell at her again. Men shouldn't act that way. Why was it okay to be mean to girls? His mom and James' mom didn't deserve to be treated the way their dads treated them. He knew his father threatened to hurt his mom. He'd heard him. He'd heard it all, even though he pretended he didn't. Maybe he wasn't old enough to work and take care of his mom right now, but someday he'd get a good job that made lots of money and take care of her. He'd buy her all that stuff for her gardens and she'd be happy. Some day.

But right now, he had something to do.

# CHAPTER 9

Sitting in the dark confines of his office, Lycos listened for sounds of the woman and her kid. Bethanie and Ethan. He hadn't heard anything in over an hour. He was such a stupid son of a bitch. Guardian had fucked up royally expecting him to be a caretaker. They had his psych eval. They knew better. He didn't do people. Oh, he could blend in to a crowd, become whomever he needed to be, but the one-on-one shit when he wasn't assuming a cover? He sucked at it.

The lights on the incline turned on. The illumination sliced through the darkness of his den. He shifted in his chair, pushing it around. The motion automatically illuminated the darkness of his den.

The boy stood in his doorway. Lycos leveled a stare at the kid and damned if the boy didn't meet it and hold it. "There is a right way and a wrong way to treat people. She was doing the best she could. She's smart, and she's a better person than you'll ever be."

The kid's voice wavered, but he stood firm as he spouted his speech. Vulnerable as hell, but full of courage, enough to take on a full grown adult. The boy was scared as shit, but willing to face off with him to defend his mom.

"I have no doubt about that kid. She is a better person than I'll ever be." Lycos leaned back in his chair.

"Then why were you such an ass?" The kid's fists clenched at his sides.

"You allowed to talk that way?"

"You've said worse."

"Doesn't make it right. You have a good mom and I'm sure she's told you not to say words like that. I didn't. You have a fuck-ton of shit in your favor that I didn't have. Take advantage of that, kid."

"What kind of advantages?" The little fists loosened and the kid lowered his chin.

Lycos shrugged. "I won't call her my mother, but the woman who gave birth to me decided getting stoned was easier than raising me. I ended up fighting to live in some hell holes." Lycos leaned forward. "How old are you, kid?"

"Eleven."

"Yeah, and do you go to school?"

"Yes, sir. Marchdale Academy."

"Huh, that's a private school, with uniforms and fancy classes for smart kids, right?"

"I guess. It's a private school."

"When I was eleven I was stealing food to survive. The money my mom made went to her pimps and drugs. One day she went out and never came back. I ended up in the system. The first couple that took me in beat the fuck out of me. I told a teacher, and they threw me in a group home. There the motto was get tough or get fucked. I got tough. When I turned eighteen they gave me a black plastic bag with my shit in it and told me to get out."

Ethan leaned into the doorjamb, his eyes were wide. "What did you do?"

Lycos shrugged. "I went to work for a guy who sold drugs; a lot of drugs. I moved around and drifted. Ended up in jail charged with murder."

"You killed someone?"

"Nah, but the cops thought I did. I work for the good guys now. Guardian Security."

"How did you get out of jail?"

Lycos leaned back in his chair. "An angel, I guess you could say. An Archangel." He stared at the wall of his office, awash in memories.

*The group homes were where he discovered the usefulness of masked retribution. Accidents happened to the motherfuckers who hurt him. Nobody could blame him, but every one of those sons of bitches knew it was him, and they learned not to fuck with him.*

*He left foster care at eighteen with that damn black plastic bag containing five t-shirts, two pairs of jeans and a windbreaker. Three months later, he was doing work for a mid-level drug-king-wannabe. The bastard cheated him out of his money, and Lycos was tossed out of his apartment by the slumlord who ran the hovel. All his belongings, his clothes and the few things he had, were gone. That drug-king-wannabe laughed at him. Told him to find an alley, curl up, and die. The bastard was found dead the next day—apparently from an overdose. Funny how that shit happened.*

*Lycos survived and found other opportunities. He existed for three years before he landed in jail. Which was fucked. The cops had nothing to hold him on. He'd joined forces with a local hitman. He gathered intelligence for the killer until the man died, and the D.C. cops roped him in as a suspect in that murder... because he was a known accomplice, not because they had evidence. He was fished out of general pop and hauled into an interview room, where he was handcuffed to the table.*

*After an hour of twiddling his thumbs, a man in a three-piece suit walked in and sat down across from him.*

*"I have no money for a lawyer, and by the looks of that suit, you cost." The suit was damn fine.*

*"I'm not a lawyer. I'm your way out."*

*"Nah, see, I didn't do anything. The cops have to let me go in less than twenty-four hours." He was such a cocky son of a bitch back then.*

*"Wrong." The man reached in his pocket and placed picture after picture on the table. He finished with a mugshot.*

*Sitting in that jail, cold steel encircling his wrists, he felt a wave of relief push through him when he saw the pictures. It was a stupid feeling to have. He should have been worried, scared shitless even, but he wasn't. Every last one of the men in those photos were bastards. Their crimes ran from drugs to prostitution, and gee golly, let's not forget the gangbangers and mafia hangers-on. Whatever, they were all abusive cocksuckers; vile, evil people and he'd made the world a better place by getting rid of them. He glanced up at the man in front of him. "Who are they?"*

*No trace of emotion showed on the man's face, and he was good at reading people, even back then. The suit leaned forward.*

*"This man was someone we were watching closely. Very closely." He tapped the picture of Lloyd Fontaine. He'd watched the man kill one of his whores at a party. The girl couldn't have been twenty years old. He watched the son of a bitch choke her to death as he whipped out his cock and fucked her in front of everyone. He filmed it, too. From behind, so his face couldn't be seen. Laughed about snuff porn selling for big bucks on the internet.*

*When he realized what the bastard intended, he'd lifted away from the couch to help the woman, but the hitman he was working for pulled his ass back down. "Move again, and I'll kill you before his guards do."*

*The bastard was, in fact, surrounded by a small army. Lycos held in his rage. Rage at his boss for not helping the woman, and rage at the motherfucker who was laughing as the woman died slowly by his hand. The hitman died two days later of an insulin overdose. Imagine that. After all those years of shooting up, the bastard got the dosage wrong.*

*Fontaine? He died in a tragic bathtub accident. His television fell off the wall and plunged into the water while good ole Lloyd was bathing. Fried the fucker. If he remembered the rumors correctly, it took a long time for the son of a bitch to die. He wondered if Fontaine's death would sell on the internet. Lycos sure as fuck didn't film it for posterity.*

*He leaned back as far as the cuffs would allow him to lean and considered Mr. Suit. "What does any of this have to do with me?"*

*"I'm here with a proposition, an opportunity that will only come once. If you pass our entrance requirements, we may have a place for you within our organization."*

*"And if I don't?"*

*The man stood up. "If you don't, we'll do humanity a favor and end you." He picked up each picture.*

*"Who are you?"*

*"I am your guardian angel."*

*"Have a name, angel?"*

*"Archangel."*

*"Well, Archangel, I accept your proposition, but be forewarned, I don't work well with others."*

*"A lone wolf." A smile split the angel's face. "That's what we're counting on."*

When he glanced up again, the kid was gone. Just as well. He closed the gate to memory lane and returned to the drawings for some other improvements he wanted to make to his new home. He anchored his toe on the ground and pushed his chair from side to side. The motion reactivated the light in his office. He glanced at the clock. Fuck, two hours since his meltdown and convo with junior. Still no sounds in the house. He knew they hadn't left. The security system had recorded when Dog came back in, but no other doors had been opened.

He hadn't lost his cool like that in years. Hell, decades. Why now? He glanced at the computer screen. Displayed in the center was a picture of the woman and her son. It was an image he'd captured off the surveillance system. They were both laughing. He traced her happy smile with his eyes. The boy's face was so fucking innocent, and he had a joy that radiated from the picture. They deserved to be happy. He knew why he freaked out and pushed that woman hard today. He didn't want to admit it, but it was a fact he couldn't ignore. He'd been scared. He'd fucking developed some kind of feelings, or maybe a bond with them, and wasn't that some serious *what the fuck* thinking?

He toed the ground again and let his eyes search the vast library he'd accumulated. He thought of the secrets behind the shelves. Guardian had tapped into his potential as an assassin, and in return, they'd given him the world. He was provided education and training in any area that interested him, and he devoured the annals that lined the walls of his office.

His intelligence was off the charts... his Guardian appointed shrink's words, not his. He knew so damn much, but he had no clue how to explain to the woman why he'd treated her like a smudge of rancid raccoon shit.

He glanced at the computer monitor and then the phone. Lifting a middle finger, he saluted the phone with a terse jerk of his hand. Moriah had fucked him hard with this little witch. The woman's way of getting him back for his words about her freelancing, no doubt. No matter how they'd left it at the club, she'd have been pissed he hadn't supported her. It would be just like her to push this sticky mess up his ass and laugh while he dealt with... fuck him... feelings.

Dammit. Going back and explaining his rude behavior to the woman—Bethanie—sucked sweaty bison balls. *Sorry, lady, I was pissed and yeah, okay, worried, so I yelled at you.*

Which was true. He was pissed she'd made mistakes that could take her out of that boy's life. Every kid deserved a good parent, and that woman was good to her son, no matter what he'd said earlier.

Fuck it. Manning up was the only solution, and letting more time pass would only make the crow he had to eat tougher. If that was possible. He headed down to the main cavern but stalled at the top of the ramp. He'd expected them to be on the couch, but the fading coals from the fire cast a glow over the furniture. They weren't there. No lights were illuminated downstairs. He craned his neck searching the darkness of the hallway. There was no way they'd be able to come up without him knowing.

He walked down to the lower level of the cavern, the lights shining before him. The kitchen was as dark as the living room. He spun on his heel and let out a soft whistle. The damn dog was in the house, that much he knew. He heard a thump and a scurry of nails. A light in the storage area turned on before the dog appeared at the entrance.

Lycos strode over to the area. He saw two plastic tumblers on the counter and a bag holding two peanut butter sandwiches. His eyes dropped to the shelving under it. *What in the actual fuck?*

The woman was asleep on his sleeping bag. Her cheeks were red, and her lips were chapped. Not good. Being exposed like she was last night wouldn't give her a cold, but if her body had been fighting off a virus, her system could have weakened to the point that she'd succumbed.

"Here to yell at my mom some more?"

Lycos damn near stood on his head to see the kid. Yeah, so they were hiding from him in the storeroom. Fuck, he was a monster, wasn't he? *Well, yes, in a very literal sense, he was exactly that.*

He drew a chest full of air, hoping the action would somehow produce the words to prove he wasn't a complete dick. Yeah, no such luck.

He ignored the kid's question and tapped the woman on her hand. She roused slightly and settled back into her slumber. "Hey... you need to wake up." The blonde head snapped up. Lycos winced at the resounding thud her skull made against the pecan wood shelving. "Damn, that had to hurt."

Her hand covered her forehead. Those blue eyes narrowed to slits and glared at him for a fraction of a second before she glanced away. Okay, the attitude was understandable, and deserved. Lycos ass planted on the floor as Dog burrowed into the little cubby they'd made.

"Look, about earlier. It won't happen again." No need to go into the reasons he'd popped off like a fucking rocket. He hadn't compartmentalized correctly because he'd never been in a caretaker role. So, shit got wonky. Now things were straight. They were an assignment. Nothing more.

Her eyes lifted to him. No words, no acceptance, just a blank stare before she dropped her gaze again. Yeah, whatever. That apology was more than he'd given anyone in the last forty-three years. He wasn't going to do it again.

"Yeah, well, don't worry. We'll stay out of your way." The boy's voice slid out from further under the shelves.

"That right?" Well, he could understand that.

"Yes. That's right."

He fought to hide a smile at the kid's belligerent tone. "You can stay here if you want, no skin off my nose. I've said what I came to say." He wasn't going to beg her. Fuck that.

He headed to the fireplace, stoked the coals and dropped a heavy armful of wood on the grate. Flames blossomed and eagerly licked up the dry wood, hungry for fuel.

His stomach growled, empty and pissed at the lack of attention. He stalked into the kitchen and pulled out a venison roast he had in the refrigerator. Potatoes, carrots, and onions joined the roast in a baking pan. He mixed some red wine, stock, thyme, sage, salt, and pepper and poured it over the roast. Because the venison had no fat, he laid three strips of thickly cut pork belly over the top of the meat. The rendering fat would keep the meat moist and flavor the vegetables underneath. Plus, it would make one hell of a gravy. He'd use what was left to make a stew.

Dog's claws ticked across the flooring, accompanied by the padding of the kid's stocking feet. He turned to the entrance of the kitchen where Dog now sat. The kid hadn't shown himself, but he was on the other side of the cabinets. "You can come in." Ethan rolled around the corner and stared at him. Scared? No, probably cautious. "Where's your mom?"

"She's straightening what we messed up."

"Messed up?"

"Uh huh. The towels and sleeping bag."

Lycos shot a glance across the cavern's ceilings. The lights in the storage area were active. "Got it."

"Is it snowing bad?"

Lycos nodded his head. "Worst I've seen it in years." The forecast was for thirty inches, but they'd surpassed that estimate before 5:00 a.m. He'd been damn lucky to get all their shit up the mountain.

"How can you tell?"

"I went out to get your clothes and the extra food from your cabin. Didn't figure you or your mom needed to be out in the cold again so soon. The temperature has fallen even more since I found you."

"So… I guess you are going to let us stay here?"

"Right."

Lycos listened to the uneven shuffle step as the woman approached. He leaned over and gaged her progress.

In one arm she carried the boy's backpack and a small stack of clothes. Without looking at him, she extended her hand, and Ethan immediately grabbed it with his. The young man was almost tall as his mom. She was maybe five feet. An inch or two over, perhaps. The kid had big hands and bigger feet. He'd tower over her soon. Damn good thing the kid was well mannered.

Her eyes stayed on the ground, and she asked, "May we please use your bathroom to clean up?"

Lycos ran his hand around the back of his neck. Fuck it. "Look, you can go anywhere in the house. With the exception of my office, everything is fair game. The office is off limits. Period. But, there is a smaller bedroom next door to mine. I'll move some of the stuff I have stored there, and you and the kid can have that. It has its own bathroom. Give me ten minutes."

He stalked out of the kitchen and up the incline. The spare room was sparse as far as furniture. A bed and a dresser. He stacked his boxed overflow of books against the wall and glanced at the space. The queen-sized bed should work for them. He would need to pull clean bedding and towels from the storage area and bring them up, but the space was now habitable.

A scuffling behind him drew his attention to the hall. The duo appeared at the door. "Bathroom is through there. Kid, come back down with me, and I'll fix you up with bedding and towels."

She stepped back out of his way, dropping her son's hand. The boy kept pace beside him all the way to the storage area. Kid was kinda like Dog in that respect. Trailing right along.

He stood silently and held out his arms as Lycos dropped sheets and blankets into the the eleven-year-old's hands. He eyed the kid and nodded toward the incline. "I'll bring the rest."

The boy nodded and cinched his arms around the mountain of fabric before he headed up the incline. Dog fell into step with him. It was almost as if the animal refused to let the boy be alone.

Lycos grabbed towels, a bar of soap and a bottle of shampoo. He didn't have anything special, didn't need it, so they were going to have to make do with his bar soap and biodegradable shampoo.

He mounted the incline again and dropped the stuff on top of the dresser. "Food will be ready in about an hour." That was as close to an invite as he was going to give. They could stay up here and starve or eat with him. Didn't matter to him. At all.

# CHAPTER 10

"Why do I have to stay in here?" Ethan struggled to pull his thermal shirt over his head as he asked.

"We don't want to make him mad."

"He said we could as long as we stay out of his office. I wanna go see where Dog is." Ethan's head popped through the neck of the white long-sleeved shirt. His hair smooshed down in awkward angles.

"Go comb your hair and brush your teeth."

"Got no toothbrush."

"Wrap a washcloth around your finger and use toothpaste." She needed to go down to the supplies he'd brought from the cabin and see if he'd thought to bring their bathroom supplies.

"That's gross."

"Ethan."

"All right." His sigh preceded him into the bathroom. Bethanie wrapped her arms around herself.

She had the chills. A hot shower would do wonders for her, physically and emotionally. She didn't know how to take *this* version of their hostile savior. Instinct told her to be wary. He'd already lashed out at her for no reason. His reticent attempt at an apology spoke volumes. The man didn't like to admit he was wrong. She glanced at the smaller room he'd given them to use. The term smaller was completely wrong. The room echoed. In fact, it was an antechamber of the upstairs cave. Or that was how she was rectifying it in her mind. Downstairs cavern and upstairs caves.

She listened to Ethan humming in the bathroom as he combed his hair. He bounced out of the bathroom and looked at her expectantly. "You can go find the dog, but you stay away from the man and don't talk to him unless he talks to you."

"Okay. May I watch another movie?"

"If you use your headphones."

"Thank you!"

She cringed as Ethan's words echoed in the room. "We need to be quiet."

"Sorry," Ethan sighed and pulled the door open. Apparently, everything was dramatic at eleven.

Shuffling through to the bathroom, she shifted out of her clothes, folding each piece neatly before she turned on the water and slid under the soft fall. The white noise buffered some of the emotional baggage that had been flitting around her brain. For the time being, she and Ethan were stuck here with a volatile man. Until he proved differently, she planned on being a very quiet, compliant, ghost.

She shivered and closed her eyes. Years fell away as her mind catapulted to the time after she'd been taken away. Keep your mouth shut, and do exactly what you are told, when you are told. Those lessons had been burned into her. When Harvey took her, she'd acted the same way. In her heart, she'd believed the way she acted had saved her life and afforded her the opportunity to raise Ethan. But in the eleven years since she delivered her baby, she'd learned. Learned that life wasn't a constant bow and scrape. She'd made friends. Friends Harvey had vetted, but still, that small privilege had opened so many avenues. She learned she could grow things! A small herb garden given to her as a present one Christmas from one of the mothers on the playground opened her world in ways she'd never imagined. She knew her situation was not normal. Harvey's patronage of her and Ethan came at a price. However, she took advantage of the small privileges he allowed. Bethanie copied actions and emulated the mannerisms of the mothers at the park. She smiled at people, engaged in conversations, she *learned*.

Harvey had never seen her other persona. She'd been careful to keep her eyes downcast, her mannerisms meek, and her answers concise. She'd protected Ethan from her meetings with Harvey. He saw his father so infrequently, and Ethan didn't seem to notice the changes in her when Harvey was at the apartment. Or at least she didn't think he had. She now suspected he'd seen far more than she gave him credit for.

Harvey never changed. He constantly reminded her of his indulgences. He'd detail her purchases, the seedlings he'd allow her to buy, the equipment and nutrients to grow the plants she adored. He also reminded her he could take everything away with a snap of his fingers. On several occasions he had. He'd arranged for James' mom to watch Ethan and summoned her to The Residence. Those weekends away from Ethan had been hard. Her remedial training... Bethanie closed her eyes and shivered at the horrendous memories. She thought she'd shielded Ethan from that, too.

But, since being here on the mountaintop in the middle of nowhere, she'd learned that Ethan had felt or seen all that she'd thought well hidden. The fear, the uncertainty, and the anxiety she'd tried to shield him from had found him, and it made her soul ache.

Bethanie soaped her body as her memories cascaded, matching the water's flow. She'd made so many stupid mistakes, but she'd found role models. James' mother for one. Learning to live was hard. Learning to live chained to a controlling monster was almost impossible. *Almost.* But she'd clawed forward, always looking over her shoulder. Always wondering if Harvey knew what she was doing. Excuses for her actions were ready and at hand. She played scenarios a thousand different ways before she made a decision. Sometimes the decision was to do nothing, not to reach for the opportunity in front of her. Risks to her, she could tolerate. When the risks involved Ethan? No. The gain would never be worth the price Harvey would extract.

A thread of white shampoo formed in her palm and she replaced the container of shampoo. The suds formed around her fingertips. She sighed then coughed. Along with the current situation, her chills, chapped lips, and cough weighed her down. She couldn't afford to be sick.

Her tired brain flicked from the past to the present. Their situation could be dangerous. Their nameless host had already exploded, and all she'd done was thank him. He tolerated Ethan. Fed him, kept him from the elements. She was thankful for that. She turned off the water and pulled a towel into the shower stall with her. Her best course of action would be to keep out of his way. Thankfully the bedroom and bathroom were large.

The warmth of her clean clothes hugged her tightly. She used the towel to dry as much water out of her thick curls as she could before she tossed it onto the rack to dry. After she brushed her teeth and combed the knots out of her hair, she took stock of the room. The boxes in the corner were open. She peeked in. Books. The titles she could see were in foreign languages. Or she assumed they were because they made no sense if they were in English. She moved to the next box, more of the same, although several titles were in English. The third box held several medical journals, a pharmacology book, a physician's desk reference, and several books on genetics. She picked one up and flipped it open. There were dog-eared pages. She scanned the high-lighted passages. The man was obviously researching the effects of a genetic defect.

She carefully closed the book and replaced it. Was he sick? Was that why he lived out here alone? She glanced at the door. No, she wasn't going to presume. She knew two things about that man. He didn't want them here, and he thought she was stupid. The first she'd rectify as soon as the storm abated. The second she'd use to her advantage. Tucking herself back into the shell she'd so recently shed wasn't difficult. She'd do anything to protect Ethan.

She opened the door as quietly as she could and checked the hall. The lights in the office were out, but a beam of light from his bedroom could be seen under the small crack of his door. Bethanie edged out of her room at the same time as he opened the door.

She immediately retraced her steps, trying to stay out of his way.

"Don't do that." His voice carried to her in a sharp, deep command. Even though he hadn't spoken loudly, the words arrested her.

She stilled and cast her eyes to the floor. Waiting. *Don't move, don't talk, don't assume.* She felt the cloak of her past lessons flow over her. She didn't know what the 'that' was he didn't want her to do, and she wouldn't endanger them with another outburst asking what he meant. So, she waited.

"Holy fuck, woman, I'm not going to beat you." He moved forward and she, from years of programming, shied away sharply.

"What in the hell happened to you to make you like this?" He stopped about three feet from her. She could see his feet.

"Life." She regretted the word as soon as it escaped her. She flinched and glanced up at him. Those dark brown eyes were hard as flint.

"Your life sucked that bad? What kind of bastards taught you to fear like this?"

She sent him a quick look. The 'like you' she wanted to include was left unsaid.

"Look, I'm not going to hurt you. I don't want you jumping at the fucking shadows. You act like I'm going to swing at you at any second. I've done nothing but raise my voice, so you need to regroup. If nothing else, think about your kid."

Bethanie lifted her chin. "I am thinking about my son; he is the only thing I think about. You don't want us here. We'll stay out of your way until we can leave."

"Fuck me standing, woman. I was half out of my mind! I'm supposed to be taking care of you, and you get lost on my watch. You could have *died*. The decisions you made put your life in jeopardy. You could've died and left that kid alone in a blizzard. No kid deserves to be alone. Ever. You feeling me?"

She watched him pull his hands through his hair before he dropped them in defeat. "I'm not going to hurt you or the kid."

She blinked at him. Words were wonderful weapons. They gave hope and cut brutally straight to a person's soul. Her ears had been filled with glorious promises and horrendous threats. Words meant *nothing*.

He nodded toward the big cavern. "I'm putting dinner on the table. Join me or don't. I'm through trying here."

She waited a moment, debating her next move. When a soft thud of a cabinet door followed by the rattle of pans told her he'd made it to the kitchen, she followed him down the incline. Ethan and the dog snuggled together on the big couch by the fire. The animal was curled, lying down, and Ethan's head was propped up on the dog as he watched his movie. Delicious aromas of roasting meat and onions filled the gigantic space.

Bethanie edged into the kitchen and cleared her throat. "May I help?"

He nodded to the far row of cabinets. "Silverware is in the second drawer, next to the dishwasher. Plates and glasses above. Everything else is in one of the cabinets or the fridge." He waved purple oven-mitted hand toward the cabinets next to him. That touch of domesticity disarmed her. It was hard to think him a monster with purple oven mitts on his hands.

She gathered what she needed and ensured she and Ethan were on the same side of the table. She opened the massive refrigerator and found the butter. There was a gallon of milk and several sodas in the door. "Ethan, what do you want to drink? Milk or water?"

"May I have a soda, please?"

She glanced at the man. No, Ethan didn't need the soda. He could have water. "Okaaay, water it is."

Ethan rolled his eyes.

She moved to the other cabinets to look for the salt and pepper. The man dropped the knife and serving fork he was using to carve the roast and headed to the refrigerator. He whipped open the door, grabbed a can of soda, and plopped it down on the tabletop.

"Get your kid whatever he wants. I told you, I'm not going to hurt you or him. If it is in this house, it's yours." He turned back to the stove. "Except for my office, you and the kid don't have any restrictions."

Bethanie deposited the salt and pepper shakers onto the table and filled Ethan's glass with ice and soda.

"If he needs more, I have about ten cases of those in the storage room closest to the back door."

Bethanie glanced at him as he fished out the roasted vegetables from the pan. "Thank you."

"No problem. Go grab the kid."

"His name's Ethan. I'm Bethanie." She offered the tentative olive branch again.

"Ryan Wolf." The man didn't look up from his task as he spoke.

Bethanie drew a deep breath as she walked across the expanse to the living room area. Her feet were still sore, but not as bad as they had been this morning. She slowed as she approached, taking in the comforting solitude the far end of the cave provided. The logs in the fireplace had burned down. The coals that remained cast a golden hue toward the couch.

Dog tracked her movements as she approached. He lifted his head as she reached toward Ethan, not threatening her, but watching carefully. She grabbed his toe and shook it gently. "Time to eat."

"Okay. It smells good, doesn't it?" Ethan pushed off his headphones as he spoke.

"Indeed. Our host's name is Mr. Wolf, by the way."

"Really?" He looked up in surprise.

"Yes, sir." Ryan Wolf was a problem because she really didn't understand what he wanted from her, but until she did, she was going to be very, very careful.

"Cool."

"Go wash your hands."

"I didn't do anything to get dirty."

"Did you pet the dog?"

"Well, yeah, but he isn't dirty."

"Ethan."

"Yes, ma'am."

The sighed words stretched back to her as he and the dog headed up to their newly assigned room. She smiled despite the circumstances. That sigh. Ethan had a broad vocabulary of sighs, each eloquent with different meanings. She waited at the end of the incline as her son, and the dog, trotted back down the ramp. The animal's massive head was almost at Ethan's shoulder, but its tongue lolled out of its mouth resembling a smile. Something about the sight lightened her heart for a moment.

"Gross, Mom... Dog drank out of the toilet!" Ethan laughed, and the dog cocked his head.

Bethanie shook her head. "Um, okay then, from now on we leave the toilet seat down. I don't think he's supposed to drink out of the toilet."

"I wish I could break him from that." Ryan's voice behind her spun them both. He pointed at the animal. "Go on, go outside, take a break."

The dog turned and walked away. The lights illuminated as he traveled. The slight whir of his dog door sounded.

Ethan turned. "Can't he freeze out there or get lost in the blizzard?"

"No, he's smart."

Ryan's reply drove a verbal spike into her. The dog was smart enough to stay alive outside but she wasn't. He thought she was stupid. *His* words shouldn't matter, but in a conditioned reflex, she bowed her head and lowered her eyes. She leaned forward and nudged Ethan toward the kitchen. Ethan glanced one more time at the dog door before he entered the kitchen.

Ethan caught her shift in mood. She could see it in the way he looked at her. She smiled at him and nodded toward the plates in front of them. Ryan had served the meal along with crusty bread and a bowl of deep brown gravy. All three sat down and unceremoniously dug in. The scrapes of knives and forks against the dinnerware were the only sounds in the cavern. If she and Ethan had been alone, they would have been chattering away, but he'd learned to follow her clues. She could tell he was doing the same now. He put his fork down between each bite and chewed his food completely. He even ate the despised carrots.

When she'd finished what Ryan had served, she sat quietly with her eyes down and her hands folded in her lap. Ethan arranged his fork and knife on the plate the way she'd taught him to indicate he'd finished. "May I please be excused, Mr. Wolf?"

Ryan sighed and nodded his head. Ethan watched him for a moment longer before he stood, slid his chair in, and carried his dishes to the counter. He glanced at her and waited for her to nod before he quietly walked out of the kitchen.

"That son of a bitch did a number on you two." Ryan forked more meat onto his plate and poured gravy over the slices.

Bethanie didn't respond. There was no need to confirm what was obvious. She cleared her throat. "May I be excused?"

Ryan fell back against his chair. "Why in the hell

do you not get that I am not going to hurt either one of you?"

She swallowed hard and stood with her plate. In a stroke of immense folly, she replied, "Probably because I'm stupid." She whispered, but it felt so damn good to throw his words back at him, even if she ended up paying for it.

"Yeah, okay, whatever. You go ahead and use my words to beat yourself up some more. You enjoy being a victim."

She stared at the floor as tears filled her eyes. "You're a bastard. Just like he was."

"I am, but that was established when I was born." Ryan crossed his arms as he stared at her, still seated, with no indication he was moving any time soon.

She lifted her eyes and struggled to keep her gaze pinned on his. It was hard when you knew your words would be used to punish you, your actions would be evaluated, and retaliation would always follow. "You do not get to judge me. You have no idea what I've lived through," she hissed.

"You're right, I don't. And here is a news blast for you, sweetheart, I'm not ever going to know unless you tell me. I admit I fucked up. I yelled at you. *Get. Over. It.* I also rescued your ass. I could have left you both out there to die, but I didn't. I am not your ex-husband. I am not going to hurt you, and I'm sure as fuck am not going to change who I am so you will stop walking around here like I'm going to backhand you for breathing."

His words, delivered in a calm, even, no-nonsense tone deflated her offense like a pin pricking a balloon. The righteous indignation hissed out of her in a steady stream. She wrapped her arms around herself and looked up at the rock ceiling. The suspended lights bounced eerie shadows over the rock formations. "He wasn't my husband. He bought me from the people who stole me from my family."

She couldn't look at him, but the words had started, and she was no more able to still them than she was able to stop breathing. "I was a sixteen-year-old, pristine, womb to provide him an heir. He didn't want Ethan until he turned twelve, but prior to that, he would allow me to raise him. He demanded Ethan possess impeccable manners and politesse so he could present Ethan to his contem-poraries as an acceptable reflection of Harvey." She'd memorized that statement because when Harvey had first said it, she'd had no idea what he meant.

"Please, come back and sit down." Ryan's voice hadn't changed. His tone was still level and almost kind.

She swiped at her cheeks and dropped her chin. Her curls fell into her eyes. "Why?"

"Because I have a feeling you need to talk to someone."

"No offense, but I don't need to talk to a stranger—especially one who thinks I'm stupid."

"Sometimes talking to a stranger is the best

course of action." There was a pause, and he said more quietly, "I don't think you are stupid."

She shook her head and glanced toward the living area. "He doesn't need to hear this."

"I'll know if he comes back. Right now, I can see the reflection of his DVD player against the wall. You can talk." He stood up, took his plate to the counter, and set it down. He reached over her and grabbed two tumblers before he turned and reached to the cabinet over the refrigerator. He pulled down a bottle of dark, amber-colored liquid.

"Is that whiskey?" Harvey didn't allow her to drink, although she'd sipped alcohol at some events she and Ethan were allowed to attend.

"This is port wine. A... a friend of mine sometimes liked a glass when she'd had a stressful day. She's never been here, but I bought it in hopes she would show up."

"A girlfriend?"

Ryan shrugged. "Not really, but someone in the same line of business as I am. She was easy to be with. No pretenses."

"You don't see her anymore?" Bethanie accepted the tumbler and sniffed the contents. It wasn't acidic.

"No. She ended it. She, like you, didn't like my honesty."

"Did you call her stupid, too?" Bethanie flashed him a quick smile.

He barked out a laugh. "Nah, I called her on a personal agenda that wasn't in line with the company's vision for our work. She disagreed, with prejudice, it would seem." Ryan sat down at the table again and motioned toward the chair. "You said you were *bought?*"

Bethanie took a sip and nodded before she sat down. "I have memories of my parents and my sister, but I can't remember exactly how I was taken. I vividly remember some of the places we were held. The things that happened as I got older are crystal clear. Some of the girls were taken away immediately. They were the age I was when Harvey bought me. Those of us that were younger were moved around from place to place. You learned to keep quiet and do what you were told, when you were told." She stared at the dark amber liquid and swirled it, noting how it stuck to the sides of the glass like a thinned-out version of syrup.

"You were *sold* to Harvey?"

"Hmmm... I'd just turned sixteen, and I was a virgin. I assume he paid for me. That is what the woman who held us talked about all the time. Don't damage the merchandise. We were the merchandise."

She watched as Ryan stared down at his own tumbler. "This Harvey, was he... did he hurt you?"

Bethanie felt her face flush, but he was right, she'd never spoken of any of this before, and she found she wanted to let go of some of the weight that seemed to bury her. "Hurt is a relative term, Mr. Wolf. Considering my circumstances versus what our keepers said would happen if we weren't purchased? No, I wasn't hurt."

"Why didn't you go to the police?"

She shook her head and took another sip of the port. "Because he would have killed me and then after Ethan was born, he threatened to kill both of us."

"Did you think he'd actually do that?"

"I knew he would. Two weeks after giving birth to Ethan he summoned me from my room at his residence. I held Ethan in my arms as I entered his office. He told me to watch." She looked away, her mouth a tight line as the contents in her stomach revolted. When she was certain she wouldn't lose her dinner on Ryan Wolf's kitchen floor, she turned back to him. "Some little kid knelt in front of Harvey's desk, handcuffed and sobbing. 'His father thought to cheat me. His wife and daughter are already dead.' Harvey walked around behind the young man and...." She stopped and fought back the horror of that night. Clearing her throat she continued, "He turned to me and smiled. 'And now his son. Cross me and this will be you and the brat.' No, Mr. Wolf, I had no doubt Harvey would kill me and Ethan as quickly as he'd killed that child."

"He would have killed his heir?"

"He said producing another wouldn't be a problem." Bethanie took another sip. A warmth started to bloom in her stomach.

"And now his enemies are trying to find you?"

She sighed and drained the small portion of port from her glass. "That was a shock to hear. I came home from taking Ethan to school and these two women were in my front room. I was terrified, but Jewell King and the other one, the one who gave me the combination of the lock box, Joy—someone, I didn't get her last name, were very convincing. They had enough evidence to suggest we could be in danger and arranged for us to come up here."

"You just believed them?" Ryan tipped another small portion of port into her glass.

Bethanie lifted the tumbler and took a sip from her drink. "I've been living under Harvey's threats for a very long time. I saw the way that man hurt people. It wasn't much of a stretch to realize someone would want retribution. So, yes, Mr. Wolf, I absolutely believed those two women when they said Harvey's enemies were a threat to me and Ethan."

"It must have been hard to leave everything."

"More so for Ethan. I just had my garden, my herbs and such, but he and his friend, James, were pretty much inseparable. James is the son of an associate of Harvey's and goes to the same school. I'd always thought the two boys were ignorant of what their fathers did, but Ethan has made a couple comments lately that challenge that belief. I think he knows far more than he's ever let on, but I'd do anything to protect him. So, after my talk with those women, we made a plan. I didn't wait, I left that night, like they suggested. I woke Ethan up in the middle of the night, and we left, using the route they gave me. I drove through the night to get here. You scared me when you pulled up. I thought we'd been found by Harvey's enemies. The supplies were nice, but I didn't realize we needed more than what we'd brought. I had hoped to be here a few days; at maximum, a couple of weeks."

Ryan nodded and poured a small splash more into his glass. "When I checked in with Guardian, they were talking a couple months. From what I gathered, Harvey's enemies have gone to ground, and Guardian is trying to figure out what the threat is."

Bethanie understood that, to a degree. Emboldened by the port, because she could think of no other reason, she asked, "What do you do for Guardian? I mean, you live on a mountain, in a cave. You obviously have money; this is beautiful and secluded."

He chuckled and shrugged. "I have nothing else to spend my money on, and yes, I do well. For the record, I take care of accidents for Guardian."

"I'm sorry, but what does that mean?"

"They call on me when they need me. I have a specialized talent. I am able to determine ways accidents can occur and provide a solution to situations they have encountered with minimal disruption to the normal ebb and flow of... life."

Her brain worked furiously to decipher his meaning. She frowned. "I think you just said you kill people and make it look like an accident."

Ryan raised his glass to her in affirmation. "Like the way I phrased it better, but, yes."

She stilled and stared at him. "You kill people for a living."

"I kill only those who have been targeted by my country and are a septic wound infecting humanity."

She glanced down at her hands. "You're an assassin."

"I am. A highly skilled assassin. I am paid to make evil fucks like your Harvey go away."

Her head snapped up. Could that have happened to Harvey? "And Guardian needs this talent?"

"Indeed. I have worked for them for twenty-three years."

"But you live here, alone."

"Dog and I make out okay."

"He's not really a dog, is he?"

"Hybrid, probably. Wolves in this region aren't as big as he is. I think he's got some Mastiff in him."

They sat in silence for a moment. She glanced at the leftover roast and started to stand to clear the table and wash the dishes. Odd as it was for her to act so normal when she'd just found out her savior is actually a killer. No, he was an assassin. Harvey was a murderer, a killer. Vicious, horrible and unconscionable in every aspect of his life. She paused and took a breath to steady herself. "Do you ever say no to an assignment?"

"I have that ability, but I also have the background

on each and every one of those bastards I put down. Animals, like your Harvey."

"Have you ever killed a child?"

"No. And if your Harvey wasn't dead already, I'd track him down and make him pay for what he did, to you, to that child, to other innocents."

"With Guardian's knowledge?"

"Absolutely. I do not work outside the lines."

Bethanie sat on the hard kitchen chair and carefully detailed her current situation. Fact, Ryan Wolf could have killed her and Ethan, but he'd done the exact opposite. He'd gone out of his way to protect them. Fact, he was abrasive, loud and rude, but he'd never lifted a hand against her or Ethan. Fact, he'd been honest with her. He didn't hide what he was or what he'd done.

She had only one option that she could see. She would trust the women of Guardian and Ryan Wolf to protect her and Ethan. Her hand shook a bit as she grabbed her dinner plate and stood.

He spoke, stilling her halfway out of the chair. "What did you do in New York besides raise Ethan?"

She took her plate to the sink. "Do? I was allowed to do very little. Harvey had us watched. He monitored everything. I was allowed to participate in all of Ethan's school functions, take him to the playground, and visit with the other mothers. Other than that, I had a garden and read about gardening. Harvey had to approve each of my Kindle purchases. He allowed me to purchase books about gardening."

"You enjoy gardening?"

"I enjoy growing things and learning about the different qualities of plants. It is so interesting. Before all the pharmaceuticals we have now, people used herbs and plants as remedies for many ailments. You can produce or find remedies for so many things, naturally, without chemicals. Things like ginger, garlic, turmeric, feverfew, St. John's wort... I could go on and on, are effective treatments for a variety of common complaints. I even started a small hydroponic garden in our spare room. It was a hot mess until I learned what nutrients to put in the water and the actual requirements of growing a plant's root system without soil. But like I said, Harvey allowed me that liberty." It had taken her a long two years to perfect her hydroponic system—two mind-numbing, soul-destroying years that she'd paid for with her body and her submission.

"I'm sorry."

She turned on the tap and grabbed a sponge to rinse her plate. "For what? You already apologized."

"No, I really didn't, but it's more than that. I'm sorry for what happened to you. Evil like that bastard shouldn't be allowed to exist in this world."

Bethanie stared at him. She could see the sincerity in his eyes. "As sad as this sounds, it was my normal. He gave me limited freedom to raise Ethan. I pushed that boundary, and I learned everything I could about life, about my plants, and most importantly, being a good mom."

"And... so you grew what in your hydroponic garden?"

She laughed. "Vegetables, mainly."

"Ah. By the way, you are that you know—a good mother—but what happened to you... shouldn't have."

Lifting a shoulder in a shrug, she returned for the platter on the table. "Thank you, but if I am completely honest, I wouldn't change a thing, Mr. Wolf. If I did, I might not have Ethan, and I could never picture my life without him."

"Ryan. My name is Ryan."

Bethanie nodded and worked beside him to clean the kitchen. For the first time since she'd realized they'd gotten lost, she could breathe.

# CHAPTER 11

One glanced at the names on her monitor. Three's candidates were the same as hers, with one exception. The similarity of the names on their lists wasn't surprising. The overall goals of the Fates were the driving force of all decisions.

Her monitor chirped. She glanced at the clock in the upper right-hand corner and allowed a small smile. Three was prompt as usual. "Greetings, Three."

"Your list is almost a mirror image of mine."

One nodded. Three would never win any points for politeness. "My first candidate is also yours. Let's begin with her. What operations has she been involved in?"

"Many, as you can see from her resume. Currently, she is at the forefront in Venezuela. The OPEC mission she completed two years ago netted us over a hundred million in profits. That is when I started to take an interest in her abilities. She worked the Cuba situation."

"Ah, yes, the dirty bombs. That isn't a mark in her favor."

"It was handled so none of our primary assets were identified. Other than a few guards and two ignorant scientists, we lost nothing."

The Cuba project had been one of Three's babies. She'd been volatile for weeks after it became obvious Stratus must abandon it.

"The CIA operative has taken the fall for everything?"

"Yes, as planned. He won't speak, or his family dies."

"Hmmm... Your vision for the bombs is still on track even with Homeland and Guardian's interference?" There had been a setback in the manufacture of the weapons, but it had kept the investigating agencies busy which allowed the Fates, and through them, Stratus, to move in other directions unobserved.

"I have two bombs neither Guardian or Homeland discovered. When the time is right, we will utilize them." A vicious and expected smile spread across Three's features.

"Indeed. Let's get back to the candidate. Her qualifications are beyond reproach. Oxford. Old money. Ties to the Royals through lineage and her uncle is a member of the House of Commons." One ticked off the blocks that were advantageous to them.

"Acknowledged. There is one concern."

One nodded. "Her involvement in the recent New York debacle."

Three sighed and dropped back into her chair. One's attention followed the pen that dropped from her counterpart's fingers. Dropped, not thrown, which was an improvement for Three. "She wasn't up front; her connection was twelve years ago. The chances of her being remembered are negligible."

One leaned forward. "I disagree. All ties, no matter how faint, must be eradicated. There can be nothing to connect her to any operation with which we have been involved. The fact I have to remind you of that edict is troublesome."

"Twelve years, One. Twelve years since that woman has seen her if she saw her at all."

"Have we interviewed the candidate to find out her exposure by other people?"

"She is being contacted. Venezuela is in chaos at the moment. She will call in as soon as word reaches her. The Simmons boy and his mother are on the list to be erased. This is a nonissue." Three leaned forward at the same time as One. They both clicked the file that updated with each kill.

"They have not already been eliminated?" One shot Three a glance as she examined the list.

"As expected, the woman was not a priority, and her involvement wasn't a factor. Simmons was going to kill her eventually. They are on the list because the boy is Simmons' only living heir. With the child out of the way, we can assimilate his fortune using the same process we have in other American estate inheritance dealings. Easy money."

"In order to elevate our candidate, they must be eliminated."

"Concur. I'll reroute assets."

"Agreed. What is the status of Two?"

Three grabbed a bottle of water and took a drink before she responded, "Two was not at any of the locations we identified."

"This is unacceptable."

"Noted. I'm working it."

One stared at Three through the computer screen. The woman failed to meet her eyes for several long seconds. "She won't break."

"She might not have a choice. The drugs are very effective."

"I'm using all my assets."

"Are you?"

"It isn't time for that play."

"If she isn't located in the next twenty-four hours, you will use all means necessary to locate her."

"I understand." Three nodded to herself and cleared her throat. "We have several updates to go through." The woman's Slavic accent became pronounced. One lifted an eyebrow as she lowered her eyes to the agenda. To see cracks in Three's facade was not good. Not good at all.

## CHAPTER 12

R yan heard Dog coming down the incline. That meant Ethan wasn't far behind. The two had been inseparable all day yesterday, and the dog had never spent so much time in the house. Granted, there was at least forty inches of new snow, but still, Dog preferred to be outside. The only thing that had changed was the addition of Bethanie and Ethan. Dog had adopted the kid. No doubt about it.

"You can come in. Do you want some breakfast?"

Ethan rounded the corner. Dog padded forward and sat down beside him. "Yes, please."

He nodded at the carton of eggs on the counter. "Eggs?"

"Scrambled?"

"Sure. Add a couple pieces of toast to the toaster." Ryan cracked three more into the frying pan and stirred the fuck out of the over easy eggs he'd been making. Whatever. Eggs were eggs.

"Mom said not to bother you." Ethan got a knife out of the silverware drawer and fished the butter out of the refrigerator.

"Did she? When was that?"

"Yesterday. Am I bothering you?"

"Nope. Where's your mom?"

"Sleeping. She's really tired."

"I would imagine. She had a rough go of it in the snow the other night." Ryan took the eggs off the burner and grabbed two plates while Ethan buttered the toast.

Ethan fell on his food like a starving animal. Growing boy. He'd always been hungry growing up. *Shit.* He got up and grabbed the milk out of the refrigerator. He snagged a plastic tumbler and filled it up for the kid.

"Drink that. After we square up the kitchen, I'm going out to remove the snow from the solar panels and clear it away from equipment on top of the mountain. You can help."

The boy stopped with his final corner of toast halfway to his mouth. "I can?"

"Yep. Plenty of work to do."

"Can Dog come?"

"Dog goes where he wants, but you'll need to listen to me. There is shit up there you can't touch, or you'll get fried." The storage batteries and inverters were off limits. He'd make sure the kid didn't go anywhere near them.

"You cuss a lot." Ethan scooped up his plate and fork and took it to the sink.

"No shit? I hadn't noticed. Rinse those and put them in the dishwasher."

Ethan's eyes got big before a belly laugh echoed around the cavern. "Yeah, you do. Mom doesn't like me to cuss."

"Listen to your mom, at least until you're an adult. Then you can make your own decisions," Ryan said as he finished his eggs.

"Yeah, like having soda instead of milk," the kid groaned the words like having milk was torture.

"You like soda?"

"I do. Hey, where's the dishwasher?"

"See those two big drawers? Pull the top one out." He'd opted for the pull-out drawer version. It was smaller, took less water to run, and for one person, it was perfect. He'd installed two on the off chance the shit with Moriah worked out, but he'd been building this house for almost fifteen years. When he'd planned the kitchen, she'd been in the picture. Then she wasn't.

"That's cool." Ethan carefully placed his plate and fork in the dishwasher and shut it.

Ryan took care of his own plate and threw the frypan and spatula in the dish drawer. He wiped down the stove and headed toward the storage area.

Shit, they should probably leave a note so Bethanie didn't worry.

"Ethan, run up to my office. On my desk, there are pens and sticky notes. Write your mom a note and tell her we will be back after we get done clearing snow."

"Okay."

He watched the kid tear across the open space with Dog loping beside him. He hadn't actually meant the kid needed to run. *Note to self, the boy functions at a literal level.* He turned to the clothes he'd bought for them and picked through the garments until he had suitable layers for the kid.

He'd just pulled on his outer jacket when Ethan slid to a sock-footed stop in front of him. "Done."

"Where did you put the note?"

"On the bathroom mirror." Ethan grabbed a pair of snow pants that Ryan handed him and hopped around on one foot as he pushed one leg through the material. Talk about comic relief.

"Good call on the location. She'll be sure to see it there."

Ethan smiled. "Thanks." He put on the outer clothes Ryan handed him and finally the boots, gloves and stocking cap. "Crap, it's really hot in all these."

"You'll cool off soon enough." He hit the code on the back door and opened it. Dog bounced out the door, activating his own doggie door as he passed. The rear approach was clear until about three feet from the entrance of the tunnel Ryan had expanded and reinforced.

"Wow, that's a lot of snow!"

Snowdrifts crested in brilliant white caps consuming trees and leaving only the tops peeking out of the glittering virgin expanse. Light puffy clouds dotted a clear blue sky. The grey folds of the stormfront no longer hung low over the mountain. Unfortunately, the good weather wasn't forecasted to last.

"Okay, I'm going to lead the way up. You stay in my tracks. Got it?"

"Got it."

Ryan broke a path through the waist-deep snow, not concerned about exposing his location, but cautious nonetheless. One set of footprints, minus whatever tracks Dog made, would be hard to pick out. Hell, in order for anyone to see the tracks, they needed to be on top of the mountain or have an aerial view. With drone technology, that could happen, but with the snow forecast for tomorrow morning, the chance of exposing his home was slim to none. Not that anyone was looking for him, but he had no idea what the actual danger was to Bethanie and Ethan. Whatever it was, Guardian considered it sufficient to send them to him. Bengal's woman had called them "family". Repeated it, actually.

Twenty-seven minutes later, he broke through the last snow drift and drew a deep breath. The camouflage netting had collapsed under the weight of the snow. He gripped the end of the tarp and pulled. It didn't budge. They'd need to dig it out.

He heard heavy breathing behind him and glanced back over his shoulder. "You going to live there, kid?"

"Yeah, sheesh this stuff is hard to walk in."

"You didn't play in the snow in New York?" Ryan grabbed the kid under the armpits and sat him on top of the drift at the face of his equipment mesa.

"Crap you're strong. I'm heavy. The snow in the city isn't like this snow. It's all gray and gross, and the cars splash you when you go outside to play."

"No parks?"

"Some. We made a snowman once. Me and James."

"James your friend?"

"Yep. Mom let us use her scarf, and we found rocks for his eyes and mouth. He was really ugly, but it was fun."

"Sounds like it. Okay, here's what's going to happen. You are going to sit right here for a couple minutes. I need to go get my snow blower out of the back cave. When I get it out and started, I'm going to make my way over here, and then I'll let you run it while I dig out the buildings. We'll get this all cleared and then slide the snow off the solar panels. Sound like a plan?"

"You're going to let me use a snow blower?"

"Yeah, after I explain how to run it. It isn't hard to do."

"But you mean by myself, right?"

"Yes. Why? Is that a problem?"

"No, sir! I'll do it."

"Good. We all need to pull our weight around here. Right?"

"Right!"

Bethanie checked the oven timer and stirred the pot of stew she'd made from last night's leftovers. Her bread had finished proofing—thank you very much, Ryan, for having a warming drawer with a 'proof' setting on it— and it was almost finished baking.

While she waited for the oven's timer to ring, she ventured out the back door and stood in awe of the snow drifts that feathered out like waves down the mountain. The way Ryan and Ethan had gone was obvious. She craned her neck and shielded her eyes against the glare coming off the snow. Standing in the shadow cast by the cave opening, she didn't linger in the cold.

Galloping paws echoed around her. Bethanie turned and laughed as a canine snowball punctuated with a lolling pink tongue, black eyes, and a black nose, hurled down the entrance. The animal skidded to a stop at the door, its tail flailing wildly, before he scrambled and darted out of the cave again. Three more times the dog sprinted from snowbank to the door acting like a puppy, frolicking and writhing in happiness. Her laughter seemed only to incite his craziness. When she opened the door to go inside, the dog shot through it and skidded to a stop. She grabbed a towel from the shelf she'd discovered yesterday and rubbed the animal down, making sure to wipe its paws.

A wet tongue plastered against her cheek and pulled upward. Cringing at the slide of saliva, she leaned away from the animal. If a dog could smile, the animal was doing his best Colgate impression. "You look fierce, but you're just an ole marshmallow, aren't you?"

The animal's tail swung back and forth, leaving a wet arc on the flooring. "Yeah, between you and Ethan, I'm going to be mopping a lot, aren't I?"

The animal tried to lick her again. Thankfully, she managed to avoid the bath. After draping the wet towel on a hook, she headed back to the kitchen and her meal. She had no idea how long they'd been gone, but it was well past lunchtime. She took out the bread to cool and would keep the stew warm until they came back. Having nothing else to do, she wandered the confines of the cavern. The skill and effort it took to enclose, heat, and power this remarkable house was awe inspiring. If it was like the little cabin, it was solar powered. She'd seen the panels on one of her many excursions with Ethan last week.

The entire home was a construction marvel. She had no idea how to measure the effort it would have taken to haul all the materials up the mountain and plan, plumb, wire, install, build, and weatherproof the cave. The thoughts were mind-boggling.

She wandered over to the huge sectional. The fireplace had hot coals in the bottom that danced with small yellow flames at irregular intervals. She'd never put wood on a fire before, but how hard could it be? The log she grabbed weighed enough that she needed to use two hands to pick it up, and it was the smallest piece in the stack. With careful, slow movements, she sidled closer to the fire and set the log on the coals. Heat instantly flared. She backed away from the fire and watched as the flames started to lick up the side of the wood.

Thinking was a byproduct of having time on her hands. The last hours without Ethan had been the first time she'd had time to herself since she'd dropped Ethan off at school that Monday morning—the Monday the women from Guardian had reached out to her. So much had changed. She sat down and pulled her feet under her as she watched the fire consume the fuel she'd placed on it.

Her life was upside down. Her son's father was gone. That was a fact. Even if she discounted the hovering possibility of some unknown specter of danger that loomed over her and Ethan, she had mountains of obstacles to scale. How would she support Ethan? New York City was impossibly expensive. Everything they had needed, Harvey had provided. He'd purchased clothes, paid the rent, arranged for food deliveries, paid Ethan's insurance and tuition. He'd controlled everything. She had no idea how much money she'd need to pay the rent on their midtown apartment. None.

She had no marketable skills. She did have her GED, as Harvey had required it. She knew how to count and make change. Computers were easy, so maybe she could find a job in a coffee shop, or a local market. She had two green thumbs, but no land to grow crops. She'd need to be off when Ethan was out of school, and he'd have to enroll in a public school. Private education was off the table. She could look for a place around here. The Smoky Mountains were beautiful, and the prices of gas were half what she paid in the city, so one could assume the cost of living was cheaper here. But smaller communities meant fewer job opportunities, too.

Dog walked in and plopped down in front of the fire with a groan. Bethanie's eyes floated from the dog to the fire, to the expanse of the cavern. Every detail of the home screamed wealth. The fixtures, lights, flooring, furniture, everything was well cared for and maintained. Ryan Wolf was an extraordinary man. What he'd created was incredible. She shivered a bit and chuckled. He was incredibly sexy, although it was only last night as she lay down with Ethan that she'd allowed herself to admit that fact.

His dark brown eyes flashed when he was angry. She'd seen that first hand. His hair was a bit too long and curled at his neck. At times he spoke like a trucker, and then he confused her with words of deep concern and caring. Thank goodness he'd given her some port last night, otherwise she might have suffered whiplash from the different tones and feelings of their conversation. In the end, she remained confused. Their conversation while they cleaned up after dinner had drifted from her circumstances to the house he'd built. He'd retired to his office while she took turns playing a game with Ethan. When they went to their bedrooms, she'd had enough nerve to say goodnight as they passed. His surprised smile made her daring worthwhile.

Dog lifted, instantly alert. He darted to the back of the cavern. The whir of the doggie door told her he'd let himself out again and then she understood why. She heard Ethan long before she could see him. His excited voice chattered a mile a minute. She pulled herself out of the warm corner of the couch and headed to the back door to help with wet clothes and wet werewolves.

"Then it stores in the batteries, right, until we turn on something down here?"

"If we are using electricity during the day, the power pulls straight from the panels, and after it converts into electricity, we use it. When we aren't using power, it stores in the batteries so we can use it when it is cloudy, or the panels are obscured."

"Like by snow."

"Right, or darkness."

"That is so cool. Mom! Ryan told me all about

solar energy. He showed me everything, but I can't go inside the battery and hook up shelter without him. It was amazing. I got to run the snow blower. I did good, didn't I, Ryan?"

"Damn straight. One hell of a little worker you got there."

Bethanie blinked at the cuss words, falling a little speechless at the easy way Ethan was talking to Ryan. Admiration shone from the boy's eyes. She helped Ethan hang up his jacket but swiveled her attention to Ryan. "What were you doing?"

"Busy work. I had to clear the solar panels, and make sure the pump house was working. I've wrapped the exposed water lines and insulated the ones close to the surface. This is the first big snow of the season, so I needed to make sure everything was okay. Plus, my satellite uplink is up there. Had to ensure there was no snow on top of it so I can raise and open it. It is my only link to the outside world.

"What about a cell phone?"

"They don't work in a cave. I have voice over IP so I can call out when I have the antenna expanded. I'll show you how to do that so you can call out if you ever have a need."

"Mom, you gotta go up there with us. You can see forever! And we're going to build a sled! You should see the slope, and the snow was so deep. After today there's going to be an ice crust–"

"Ice cap, the crust that is formed is called a cap." Ryan corrected as he slipped out of his snow boots.

"Right, ice cap on the snow so the sled will fly down the hill." Ethan held his hand flat and swept it rapidly in a downward motion.

"Really? Is that safe?" She glanced from her son's animated face back to Ryan.

"Sledding? Perfectly safe."

"Yeah, but we need to make a sled this afternoon. Can I, Mom? Please?"

She sat back on her heels and stared at her son. The absolute joy on his face mesmerized her. "Sure, if it's okay with Ryan."

"It's okay. He's the one who thought it up. I've never been sledding, so he's going to show me what to do."

She turned to confirm that was actually what transpired. Ryan winked at her and smiled.

"Well okay, then. That sounds like a plan. Why don't you go get into some dry jeans and wash your hands? I have lunch ready."

"Okay, c'mon Dog!" Ethan started to run.

"Walk in the house." She called after him.

"Okay!" Ethan slowed down until he hit the incline then raced up the slope.

His feet started pounding against the flooring, and she winced. "Sorry."

Ryan looked up from hanging up his wet clothes. "For what? He's having a blast."

"Yeah, but he can get really wound up."

"He's fine."

Ethan's laughter echoed down from upstairs.

"Thank you for that, by the way. I mean taking him with you. He could have stayed inside."

Ryan ran his hands through his thick brown hair as he smiled. "He's great company, and he worked hard. I figure once we get some food in him, he'll realize he's on empty and pass out. Did you bake bread? It smells delicious."

"Ahh... yeah, I did. I took what you said last night as gospel. I rummaged around and made bread and something out of the leftovers for lunch."

"Perfect, I could seriously eat. That snow's damn heavy."

They strolled toward the kitchen in companionable silence until he asked, "Are you feeling better today?"

"Better. I'm not as sore, but I think I may be coming down with a cold. I have a low fever and chapped lips."

He stopped and put a hand on her arm stilling her. She turned toward him, and he placed his hand on her forehead. "Not terrible. Have you been drinking enough water? You need to push the water. Drink at least ten glasses a day."

"Huh?"

"This cave is over five thousand feet high. You came from the city, and that's maybe thirty or forty feet above sea level. You could be suffering from a bit of altitude sickness. It would explain the lethargy and your chapped lips. You need to make sure you drink a healthy amount of water, rest, and it will pass."

"But I've been here for almost a week."

"It can take anywhere from three to six weeks to adjust. I'll make sure you take care of yourself."

His fingers pushed her hair off her forehead in a tender sweep. His eyes held hers, and a shiver ran down her spine. And because she was suddenly struck stupid, she sighed, "Okay."

"Your curls are soft." Her hair fell out of his fingers. His eyes dropped down and he smiled at her. "Such a contradiction."

"How so?" His eyes captivated her and that smile... His focused attention felt like the warmth of the sun after a winter's freeze.

"So strong, so determined and yet, so soft and feminine." He ran his fingers through her hair again.

"Mom! Dog's got my wet sock!"

Ryan dropped his hand and headed up the incline without a backward glance. "Dog, drop it!" His deep voice echoed in the cavern.

She blinked after him. Did that just happen? Bethanie spun on her heel and headed into the kitchen. She grabbed the serrated knife from the butcher block and sliced through the loaf of bread she'd baked. Her hushed rant spilled from her lips, "Don't be stupid. Don't you dare think he likes you. Life isn't easy. It never has been, it never will be."

A rumble of Ryan's laughter interspersed with Ethan's giggles rolled through the cavern. She smiled despite her concerns. Her son could use a positive role model, even if for a short period of time. And she could admire him from afar, like in the romance books she read. She could have her secret fantasies of being swept away by a knight in shining armor, and nobody would be the wiser. Her eyes bounced around the kitchen and up to the towering ceiling above her. She closed her eyes and pleaded, *please let this be good for us. Please.*

# CHAPTER 13

In his office, Ryan glanced at the dead drop message again. *0-3@2000.*

Moriah was going to call him at eight o'clock tonight. Laughter floated up from the cavern. Ethan was trouncing his mother in a game of War. He could hear them slapping their hands on the cards. He moved back to the office door and shut it, blocking out the lighthearted sounds.

He sat back against the chair and waited for the phone to ring. Bethanie and Ethan had been with him for two weeks. They'd settled into a routine. He and Ethan would clear snow every morning. They'd sled or work on the ice fort they were building in the afternoon. Bethanie remained hypersensitive to the cold. A brush with frostbite would do that to a person. So, he and Ethan spent hours together every day. The kid was smart, and for the most part, he wasn't obnoxious. He had his moments when he didn't get his way or was tired, but overall the kid was okay.

At night after the kid went to bed, he and Bethanie would read or visit, mostly a combination of both. The woman's knowledge of botany, the medicinal uses of herbs, barks and edible plants was extraordinary. He had several volumes of books that described the botanical properties of assorted flowers and plants. He'd used them to work up a natural poison for Anubis. The books had been buried in one of his boxes. He'd pulled them out and you'd think he'd given her the crown jewels. Hell, she treated those hardback books as if they were more valuable than all the gems in the Tower of London.

Bethanie was bright and funny, but to his surprise, he'd found she had unexpected areas of innocence in more ways than one. From their conversations, he'd learned she'd only ever been with Ethan's father and their relationship was severely deficient in warmth or affection. That bastard had done a number on her, of that he had no doubt. Still, she was a romantic and believed everyone deserved to be loved. Ethan was a lucky kid. If Ryan's mom had an ounce of Bethanie's compassion, maybe his life would have turned out differently. Not that he would change anything, but the possibility of having that kind of love lavished on you? Damn, it made a person think.

And brother, did he. His thoughts alone in his bed

at night were about the things he could teach her, the pleasure he could show her, and then he'd jack himself back into reality. Literally. She didn't need someone like him in her life. Life for both of them was complicated enough.

Ryan clicked on the weather forecast and smiled. More snow over the next ten days. Fuck it, he was looking forward to another two weeks of baked goods. Bethanie knew her way around flour and sugar.

He'd be a fucking liar if he didn't admit he wanted her. He'd found reasons to be near her, to casually touch her. There was a mutual attraction, that wasn't in doubt. Her responses to his carefully timed and carefully constructed caresses were proof positive he affected her. She never shied away. In fact, lately, she'd been initiating the contact. He wanted her in his bed, here in his cave and yeah, he even wanted the kid to be here. Ethan was a kick in the ass.

The light on the desk phone illuminated. He picked up the phone, turned the key to encrypt his end of the conversation and waited for the subsequent clicks from her end.

"You there?" Moriah's deep, sexy, voice came across the connection.

He felt an odd disassociation. The reality of talking to Moriah wasn't the intimate sharing he'd once anticipated. There was no urgency. A subtle sense of resignation set in. "I am."

"Yeah, about your safe house. Wasn't personal. Needed to protect the kid and his mom."

"So I was told. Explain to me what the fuck is going on."

He heard her sigh. He wouldn't push because that got a person exactly nowhere with Moriah.

"Between us and no farther."

Like she needed to preface the conversation. "Care to insult me again?"

"Aw, fuck you, very much. Touchy, aren't you?"

Obviously, he was, which bothered him more than he cared to let on. "Do you have information for me or not?"

"Kid's father was deep in Stratus before he was nixed. We captured one of the Fates, at least we believe we did. I'm not sure if that's been validated."

Ryan leaned back in his chair and closed his eyes. "And?"

"Word on the street is there is a sweep going on. People who were associated with Harvey Simmons are being eliminated."

"Hold the fucking phone. What last name did you say?"

"Caught that, did you? I said Simmons." Moriah almost chuckled.

"Well, fuck me standing."

"Nah, been there, done that." Moriah was laughing now.

"Give me a minute here, you knew all this time? She introduced herself as Clark."

"Wouldn't you? Who would want to be related to that son of a bitch."

"Related..." Ryan closed his eyes and dropped his head onto his desk. "Harvey Simmons, he's the father of those two guys on Alpha Team. The pilots, the ones that work at the ranch in the middle of nowhere."

"Ah, see, gossip does travel even to the remote regions of South Carolina."

"*North* Carolina."

"Potatoe, Patotoe." Moriah singsonged.

"Thanatos was talking about the ranch. Mentioned they worked out there now, but I thought one of them was killed?" He pulled in a deep lungful of air and sat back up. "So that is why Guardian considers them family." Bengal's wife's words made sense now.

"I heard both of them were killed. Then again if you believe what is being spread, we *are* dead, so this conversation isn't actually happening."

"Never believe what you hear, and only half of what you see."

"Amen." Moriah agreed.

"So Stratus took out Simmons to cover their tracks. That makes sense." He could see the logic in the play.

"Yeah. So those two with you need to stay low until Guardian figures out the why of the eliminations."

"Again, makes sense. Are you out of the op now?"

There was a long pause. "Yeah, about that. I'm out of the op and, hey, surprise, I'm married."

Lycos leaned forward, the small scratch on his desk became very interesting as his mind dealt with that little bombshell. "Since when?"

"A week or so ago."

"Must have made an impact if you don't know the exact date. Was this by choice or did someone knock you up?"

"Fuck you, asshole and yes by choice."

"To whom?"

"A dead man, figuratively speaking."

"Care to explain that?" As she'd mentioned earlier, as Shadows, they were all dead. Had she married a Shadow?

"Can't even if I cared to share, and I don't."

"Right. So, you've walked away?"

"Nah, I'm going to keep working."

"Then he's one of us." His mind flashed to Thanatos and Tempest. Surprisingly, there was no jealousy attached to the thought of her with one of the Shadows.

"Nope, he's a Guardian, but not one of us."

He could tell by the way she spoke; this guy was special. That tone was not one she'd ever used around him. *Time for a change of subject.* "I get that the woman and kid need protection, but seriously, why did you give up my safe house?"

She laughed, that deep sexy sound came across the line. "Hell, that's easy."

"Spell it out for me, as you noted, I'm being particularly dense today."

"You'll take care of them."

"What would make you think I'd want to take on a woman and a kid?"

"Ryan, I know you. Those two need you, and besides, this is what you've always wanted."

"Excuse me? What I've always wanted?"

"A family. A traditional family. A wife, kids, and a future."

"With my career, you and I both know that isn't a possibility."

"Things change."

"For you, maybe. Congratulations, by the way. I don't think I said that."

"You didn't, but I didn't expect it. We left things..."

He chuckled, "Awkward?"

"Dead." There was no laughter in her voice.

"True." His voice fell. When she walked out, all hope of any kind of continued relationship had died.

"We were never meant to last. We were..." She hesitated.

He filled in the blank, "Convenient."

"Ha, yeah, sucks but it was what it was. If it matters, I was sad it ended."

He couldn't believe she'd admitted that much. Feelings weren't her strong suit. Or his, for that matter.

She added, "You deserve someone you can love. Someone who needs you to take care of them."

"Unlike you." Lycos chuckled when she growled.

"No shit. I'd cut your balls off and hand them to you if you tried that shit on me." Moriah tossed that out there. Funny thing was, he didn't doubt for a second she would try.

He stared at the wall in front of him. "It can never happen. Not for me."

"You don't deny it."

He blinked and shook his head although she couldn't see it. "Deny what? What we had was over? It is. It was. We both knew it wasn't right."

"Yeah, no... I meant you didn't deny a wife and family was what you've always wanted."

"With my past? Yeah, I'm father of the year material."

"They would never need to know about it. Start fresh. Walk away from everything. Don't deny it's your dream."

He rolled his shoulders. "Would it do any good to deny it? But enough about shit that isn't going to happen. Are you happy now? With your Guardian?"

"Completely. Strange as fuck, too, since we are speaking of shit we never thought was going to happen. Proof that it can."

He ignored the last comment. "But you found him?"

"I did. He... he makes me want to be a better person, and if you give me any shit about that comment, you'll wake up with your throat slit."

He laughed at her threat. She'd have to find him first. Not that she couldn't if she searched long enough, but it was an effort she wouldn't make because he wasn't that important to her. "I'm happy for you." As he said the words, he realized they were the absolute truth.

"I need you to do me one last favor. Consider it a wedding gift."

"What? My safe house wasn't enough?"

A short chuckle preceded her words, "No, I need you to open your eyes, my friend, then if you have enough balls, open your heart. I've learned letting people get close it isn't as lethal as we once thought."

"At least for you."

"Promise me."

"If I could make that promise to anyone, it would be you."

"Think about it."

"Probably won't. Goodbye, Moriah." He placed the phone in the cradle and turned the encryption key to the off position.

Without a conscious effort, he collapsed the antenna and powered down his computer. Moriah was married. He was... well, hell, he wasn't sure what square he was landing on right now, but one thing he did know, he was okay with it. They were done. His lingering hopes of reuniting with her were distant desires that stemmed from memories of their time together and not born of need, or desire, but... familiarity. He chuckled to himself and scrubbed his face with his palms. Oh, hell yeah, familiarity was a fucking firm foundation for a relationship, wasn't it?

He shook off whatever feelings Moriah's call had cast over him and headed down the incline. Dog's head whipped in his direction. For the last two weeks, the animal had been a permanent fixture in the house. He was Ethan's shadow, companion, guardian, and playmate. They'd built a rope out of old towels braided together. Dog would play tug of war with Ethan; however, the animal was so strong he literally pulled Ethan across the hardwoods. Ryan hadn't laughed that hard in years.

"Hi! Are you done with your work?" Ethan hopped up from the couch, bouncing in anticipation.

"I am. You can go get it."

"Yay!" Ethan charged to the back door with Dog on his heels.

"You spoil him." Bethanie's soft words made him turn.

"Nah, snow ice cream is a necessity."

"I've never heard of it." Bethanie pulled her sweater around her slight frame. She smiled up at him. He loved the unguarded openness that had appeared over the last two weeks. He sat on the arm of the couch next to her and tucked the flop of unruly curls behind her ear.

"I don't doubt it. Not much of a city thing."

"That world seems so far away." She leaned into his touch for a moment. Their eyes met and held.

Ethan slammed through the back door with a grunt. They both turned their attention to the back of the cave. Ryan patted her hand. Hers found its way on top of his. He smiled over at her. "Then you are in for a treat, too."

Bethanie chuckled and marked the page of the book she was reading before leaning back against the couch. "The fireplace is hypnotic."

He diverted his attention from her to the flames that consumed the wood. She set the book down next to her and they sat in companionable silence.

"What are you reading?"

"One of your botany books. I love the descriptions and the sections about known homeopathic remedies. I'd give anything to see this mountain in the spring and summer. The natural bounty literally at your doorstep is mind-blowing."

He smiled at her, but it was hollow at best. Damn, he'd really like that. To have her and Ethan here in the summer. He'd love to take her through the foliage and show her the wonders of the mountain. The woman was an information sponge, just like her son. She absorbed the books, and they discussed the things she'd discovered. Intelligent? Hell, if the woman had access to education, there would be no stopping her. She was... bewitching. He was enchanted by her, which was dangerous and, only a few weeks ago, he'd have said it was incomprehensible. He should not have these thoughts about her. He shouldn't care about the kid, either. He wasn't supposed to care about his charges. Yet...

As he gazed at the fire, Ryan couldn't help noticing the total lack of discord, a discord he'd anticipated when the assets had been dropped in his lap. It had never fully materialized. Minus that one blow up the first morning, they'd coexisted. Hell, they'd even had fun. In fact, their time together was pleasant. Bethanie was vivacious, smart, witty, and sexy as fuck. He'd tried to shelve that last observation, but in close proximity, he couldn't help noticing the way her tight little body moved, the flash of her smile, or the glances she gave him when she thought he wasn't looking.

He'd thought it was him at first, but he'd noticed that she always seemed to be too close. But no, it was intentional. The soft brushes of his skin against hers were engineered, *by her*, and fuck him if he didn't like it. He wanted to have her near. Wanted to touch her. She'd allowed him to see her interest, and fuck him if he didn't return it. She was like an energy force under his skin. He knew when she was close by, felt her presence when they worked together, and missed her when she wasn't with him and Ethan.

This need was a problem, actually, but one that would be resolved soon enough. They'd leave, and his life would revert to the solitude he loved. So why the little niggles of discontent every time he considered them leaving? He glanced back at the ramp leading to his office. He could picture his life going back to the way things had been for the last twenty years, returning to the isolation and insulation which prevented emotions from playing a role. In his line of work, emotions were weaknesses he had used to manipulate his targets.

He was in the business of killing people. To drag innocents like Bethanie and Ethan into that world would be unconscionable. Moriah and Bengal were unusual. They'd found a spouse in the business. Ryan sighed. Lightning rarely struck twice, and never three times. Bengal and Moriah were damn lucky.

He wasn't. He'd been fucking precise and careful, until the advent of Bethanie and Ethan. Now his brain was teased with ideas he shouldn't consider and desires he couldn't afford to act on. Whatever. He'd chalk up his weird mood and idle thoughts of shit that could never be to the lingering effects of being happy for Moriah.

Ethan staggered forward with a five-gallon bucket full of snow. He lifted it three steps and put it down, waited a moment, and lifted it, shuffling three steps before he set it down again.

Ryan shook his head. The kid had determination and grit. He walked over, reached down, and took most of the bucket's weight, but allowed Ethan to continue to help.

"Okay, grab a chair. Put it over here on my right." Ryan hefted the bucket of pristine snow into the deep kitchen sink.

"What do we need?" Bethanie hovered by the refrigerator.

"Two cans of sweetened condensed milk and vanilla extract." The look of doubt that crossed her face was almost comical.

Ethan stood next to Ryan as he grabbed a spoon and opened the pop top on the milk. "Okay, this is how we make snow ice cream. Take that can and slowly pour it on top of the snow while I stir." He watched as Ethan dribbled the thick milk over the top of the snow.

"Perfect. You keep doing that while your mom adds a teaspoon of vanilla, and I'll keep stirring."

He stirred the concoction, reaching down into the bucket to gather up some of the hard-packed snow into the mixture. After a couple minutes, he nodded to the bowls stacked by Ethan. "Hold them out, one at a time."

He filled each bowl and Bethanie took them to the table. Ethan pushed his chair to the table and sat down. Okay, maybe he levitated instead of sat. The kid was excited.

"Can I try it now?"

"Sure." Ryan planted his ass in his chair and gave it a try. *Not bad.*

"Oh, my goodness, this is fantastic! Just like ice cream." Bethanie's surprised exclamation received a full-bodied head nod from her son.

"Do you like it?" Ryan spooned in another mouthful after he asked Ethan.

He shook his head and swallowed the ice cream. "So good. Can we make this every night?"

"No."

"No."

He looked at Bethanie and laughed at their perfectly timed answers. Her eyes sparkled, and the smile she gave him was radiant. She turned to Ethan. "This is a special treat, so we should only have it on special occasions."

Expecting blowback, Ryan shifted his gaze to Ethan. The boy narrowed his eyes and stared at his mom—spoon suspended in the air—before he visibly deflated in his chair. "Okay."

"Finish up, then it's time for bed, mister. We've had a long day." Bethanie stifled a yawn.

She probably was tired. She'd bundled up and helped Ethan dig out a portion of the snow fort they'd been building while he'd made supports for the plywood ceiling. He'd made sure the thing was safe. He'd be damned if the kid was going to end up buried under a ton of snow.

"May we go out to the fort tomorrow?" Ethan asked.

"In the afternoon if it isn't snowing too bad. According to the weather service, you will have snowblower duty in the morning." The forecast was for another foot of snow.

"Awesome." Ethan scooped the last of his ice cream into his mouth, excused himself, rinsed his bowl, and put it in the dishwasher.

"Shower, pajamas, and bed."

"Okay. Night, Ryan. C'mon, Dog."

"Night." He chuckled as the dynamic duo headed up the incline to the upper rooms.

"Thank you for showing us this. How did you learn to make it?" Bethanie pointed to the quickly melting snow ice cream in her bowl.

"You're welcome, and that's a story of necessity. I was up here, man, maybe two years ago, and I was Jonesing for something sweet. As you know, I don't bake. So, I got online and entered the ingredients I had in the cupboard. Presto, snow ice cream shows up on my feed, and there you have it. Necessity, thy name is sweet tooth."

"Well, thank you to necessity and the internet." She laughed softly and stared down at her bowl for a moment. "I also wanted to thank you for everything you're doing for Ethan and me. He's never had a positive male role model before, someone he could look up to, you know. It's nice for him to finally have that."

Ryan's gut dropped south and settled somewhere near Antarctica. *Him*, a positive role model? *Ah... no.* He set his spoon in the bowl as Bethanie got up to rinse out her dish. *Him as a role model?* Oh, yeah, that was laughable. He could start by showing the kid how to use a hypodermic needle. So many uses. Air bubbles in the bloodstream, undetected loss of brake fluid. Creating an insulin overdose or mimicking a fatal heart attack with an untraceable drug.

Then, of course, there was the mixed bag of martial arts he could show the kid. How to kill by shoving the cartilage of the nose through the brain while making it look like the person fell down the stairs. Oh, and fuck, let's not forget drowning in a bathtub, or accidental electrocution via household appliances. Roadkill? No problem! He had that covered, too. Amazing how many accidents happened on solitary roads with no guardrails. Yeah, he was one hell of a role model, wasn't he? "I want to thank you for taking care of us. I can't tell you the last time I felt safe, but I feel that way here, with you." She gave him a small smile and walked out of the kitchen.

Bethanie felt safe? Well, yeah. She was isolated, and she knew what he was. She should probably take Ethan and run as far away as she could. That thought brought a wave of desolation along with it.

He glanced at the bucket in the sink. He'd enjoyed the hell out of the last two weeks, which sucked on multiple levels. Memories made in this house would haunt him when they left, but there was no question in his mind. When Guardian sorted the situation out, Bethanie and Ethan would drive down the mountain and leave. That was the best-case scenario for everyone.

There wasn't a crystal of ice left in the sloppy mixture at the bottom of his bowl when Ryan finally shook himself out of the thoughts in his head. He needed to man up and cast off the stupid thoughts that Moriah's call had dredged up. He'd play babysitter for another couple of weeks and then resume his life when they went back to theirs. End of story. Period.

# CHAPTER 14

Bethanie catapulted into a sitting position. *Never again. Never.* She picked up Ethan's leg and pushed it off her. She'd been kicked, hit, and rolled on, for the last hour and a half. Snow ice cream before bed was never going to happen again.

She rolled off the side of the bed and padded into the bathroom. Not because she needed to use the facilities, but because she needed a small bubble of her own space if only for a moment. When she padded back toward the bed, she thought better of it, especially since Ethan was now spread eagle in the center of the mattress.

She pulled the bedspread off the bottom of the bed and wrapped it around her. The couch was calling her name. With the bedspread draped over her head and hiked up in her arms so she could walk, she headed to the door. Dog moved away from the threshold as she approached. She stopped and watched the dog trot over and hop up onto the foot of the bed. "You're going to get kicked," she muttered, and the dog huffed in response and made a circle three times before he lay down. The animal was wicked smart, except in this. He *was* going to get kicked. "Don't bite him, and don't say I didn't warn you."

She yawned so hard her entire body shook. Shuffling down the ramp, she made a beeline to the couch only to pull up short.

"What are you doing up?" Ryan set aside a notebook and patted the cushion next to him.

"I could ask the same question." Bethanie shuffled over to the couch and settled into the seat.

"I'm working on a design for that chamber." He motioned to an area past the fireplace that was walled off from the rest of the living areas.

"What are you going to make?" She'd walked into the isolated cave when he was taking measurements the other day. It was bigger than her New York apartment.

"I was thinking maybe a hydroponics garden."

"Really?"

He smiled at her when she jumped up on her knees. "See, there is this woman in my cave who knows a shit-ton about plants, how to grow vegetables and herbs, the medicinal uses for them, and the practicality of raising sustainable produce. For a person in my situation, that's useful knowledge, so I started to do some research."

"*Really?* Oh, I'd love help you. I have three books on my Kindle about hydroponics. The system doesn't have to be elaborate to function well, and you could mix the plantings to allow maximum yield. Wait! You could use the hot spring because the minerals would help feed the roots!" Never had she put her ideas forward with such enthusiasm. With Harvey, she'd learned never, ever, to put her ideas forward at all. *Oh, God.* All the old knee-jerk feelings of vulnerability and self-ridicule swallowed her excitement. She snapped her mouth shut. Crap, she needed to shut up. This wasn't her home.

"What? What just happened there?"

Bethanie deflated against the back cushion of the couch. She shrugged and gave him a weak smile. "I'm sorry. This is your project. You really don't need help from someone like me." She had no formal education on the subject; besides, she had no idea if he even wanted her involvement.

He shook his head and gave a laugh before he smiled at her. "The hell I don't. Listen, I have no idea how to grow the shit. I'm more interested in the engineering of the operation. I'm building a list of things we'd need. Grow lights, tubing, tracts to hold the hanging gardens. The list is far from complete. So, please, help a lug out and set me on the right path."

Bethanie sat down and hugged her knees again. "I'd love to help. Thank you."

"You're welcome. Now you know what is keeping me awake, what are you doing down here?"

She rolled her eyes. "Ethan is dreaming he's *Adonis Creed* or something. I feel like I've gone nine rounds in the latest *Rocky* movie. No more snow ice cream before bed. He's sleep boxing." She rubbed her face as she dropped into a heap against the back of the couch.

"Noted. Next time, we'll give him a chance to burn it off before bed."

"Hmmm... sounds like a plan." She smiled at the thought of the next time. "Was your call tonight bad news? You seemed kinda up in your head when we were making the ice cream."

He opened his mouth and then closed it as if he'd changed his mind. He shrugged. "Remember that friend of mine, the one I bought the port for?"

"Yeah, an old girlfriend who wasn't exactly a girl-friend. The one who broke up with you. I remember."

"She got married."

*Wow, okay.* "Oh. That's why you were upset. That's understandable." She drew up her knees, wrapped her arms around her legs, and stared at his profile as he gazed into the fire. He was such a wonderful man; she had no idea why someone would walk away from him.

"No, actually, I wasn't upset, or jealous, or any of the things I thought I should have been."

"Because you're over her."

"I don't think that was it. If I'm honest, I think I

wasn't upset because I didn't love her to begin with. I liked her a lot, but mostly, she was convenient." He winced. "And doesn't that make me sound like an ass." He shook his head.

The question seemed more to himself than to her, but she found herself wanting to answer it anyway. "No, it makes you sound as if you've thought through the past. She's married now, so it's pretty obvious she felt the same way, true?"

He chuckled and nodded, still staring at the flames of the fire. "True."

Bethanie watched the flames lick the logs, dancing as they consumed the fuel. She wondered what it was like to have a relationship that you mourned. "I think I would miss the intimacy. I'd miss the solace of having someone to talk with, someone to comfort and hold me. That's what I would miss the most, I think... Not that I've ever had someone like that." She dropped her head against the back of the couch, content to just sit next to him. His presence next to her in the darkness was so... right.

"To be honest, I never thought about what I needed in any real sense. I thought if anyone could put up with me, it would be her."

Bethanie snorted out a laugh. "Put up with you? Please, there are school moms I know who would pull out each other's hair to get your attention. You have to know you're like a catch, right?"

He laughed and shook his head. "Believe me, I'm not."

"Right. Imagine your picture in *Vanity Fair* underneath the caption reads: 'Handsome, rugged outdoorsman with the body of a Greek god, great with children, will do housework, is funny, engaging, and extraordinarily smart.' I'm telling you, you are every woman's dream come true." Bethanie laughed at his shocked expression.

"Yeah, well, I'll beg to differ. You, on the other hand, *are* a catch."

Bethanie snorted and pulled the bedspread around her tighter. "Yeah, okay. 'Penniless single mom, without a job or prospects for a job, being followed by people who want to kill her and her son.' Hell of a caption."

He turned toward her. Their knees touched, and he leaned back on the couch, almost matching her position. "That's not the caption I'd use."

"No?" She looked away from his steady gaze. Meeting it hurt because she could imagine the one he'd use. Stupid, city-slicker, single mom, with no sense of direction, no job, and no prospects for a job, seeks a wealthy sugar daddy.

His fingers traced the edge of the bedspread, bringing her attention back to him and he shook his head. "The caption I'd place under your picture is beautiful, smart, sexy woman, fierce mother, and all around wonderful person."

"You think I'm... fierce?" God, she wanted to ask him if he thought she was smart and sexy and beautiful, but she'd changed her mind midstream.

He nodded and pulled the bedspread toward him, closing the space between them. "Beautiful, smart, sexy and fierce."

"You do?" she whispered, because she didn't want to wake herself up if she was dreaming. She'd been trying to show him how much she would welcome his attentions, but she didn't think he returned her feelings.

"I do." *Oh, God, he did.* His lips were warm, and when they made contact with hers, an electric sizzle jolted through her. She sighed and leaned forward. Yes, this she needed this from him. His attention, his focus, his warmth and God help her, his touch.

His arm wrapped around her and tugged her forward. She caught herself against his chest, her hands connecting with the hard muscle under his shirt. Those muscles had driven some pretty wonderful daydreams. Her breath caught in her throat. This was happening. They were happening. If this was an ice cream induced dream, she never wanted to wake up.

His chest moved under her palms as he pulled her closer and changed the angle of their kiss. His tongue swept her lips, and she opened for him. The sensations, taste, touch, and scent of the man holding her warmed her deep inside. Her hand palmed his jaw as they kissed. The feel of his stubble scraped against the skin of her palm and sent a shiver through her. Her skin prickled as sensation washed over her. His chest vibrated as he made a sound of approval when she chased his tongue with hers. His hands held her secure against him.

He lifted his head and, in the firelight, she could see the desire in his eyes. "Beautiful." He pushed her hair away from her face. "Fucking perfect."

She wanted to be with this man so badly, but... "This is probably a mistake."

"I know." He dropped a kiss on her lips.

"We should probably stop."

"I know." Another sweep of his lips against hers.

"Ryan?"

"Yes."

"I don't want to stop." God help her, she wanted this. For her. She wanted him for selfish, covetous reasons. She wanted to know she could affect a man, make him need, not just be used. She didn't need forever, she'd settle for right now. She couldn't stop. Wouldn't. The ramifications be damned.

He lifted away. His eyes held hers, and she read a multitude of emotions, many of which she couldn't categorize, but he was here with her in this moment. That she could see. He leaned down and kissed her lips gently, breathing, "I need you, too."

He consumed her. There were no other words to describe the terrifying, thrilling, free fall she was experiencing. There was nothing she could do to stop herself even if some cautionary warning had made its way into the rational part of her head.

He maneuvered her easily. One moment she was held against him, the next she lay on her back on the couch. The bedspread fell away, forgotten in a rush to find skin. Her skin, his skin, it didn't matter. He kissed down her neck and showered sensation through her body.

She tugged at the buttons of his shirt and growled in frustration. He lifted up and, not bothering to unbutton it, whipped his shirt over his head. She splayed her hands against his pecs. The hard muscles moved, rolled and bunched under her hands as he undid his belt and jeans. He was fearsome and yet gentle. Powerful enough to take what he wanted, but she didn't feel threatened. She felt safe, wanted, desired. Her hands traveled over his chest. He pulled her hand to his mouth and kissed her palm, sending a shiver through her entire body.

"Are you sure?" His words were breathed against her palm and wrist as he kissed her.

"Positive. Please, don't stop."

"I won't. Take off your pajamas," he growled as he stood and dropped the denim. *Oh, my God.* He was beautiful and big. His erection was long and full, weighing his cock down where it lay against the two nestled weights below. He reached for his shaft and wrapped his hand at the base. "Bethanie, it's your turn. You need to get naked before I die here."

She slid her hands down the brushed cotton of her sleep shirt and slowly undid the buttons. Her hands shook, but she wasn't going to deny herself this. She hadn't had sex except for Harvey. She hadn't wanted it then, but she did now. God help her, she wanted Ryan with an ache that echoed deep in her belly.

She let her sleep shirt fall open. He kneeled on the couch and worked his way between her legs. His fingers trailed from her knee to the vee of her hips. "I'll be careful. I don't have any condoms here, but I've been tested, I'm good to go."

"I've had several physicals since the last time Harvey... We don't need condoms. I can't get pregnant."

Ethan's delivery had been very hard because he was such a big baby and she'd been little more than a baby, herself. She wasn't able to have children again. Harvey had been explicit about that. In his eyes, her only value lay in his occasional use of her for his sexual pleasure and her raising of Ethan.

He dropped down over her. His dark brown eyes holding hers. "Tell me you want this as badly as I do."

"No." She watched his eyes flare in surprise, and his body froze against her hands. "I want this *more* than you do."

A slow smile spread across his face. "Not possible." He lowered and kissed her until her mind melted and ran out her ears. Harvey never kissed her. This, what was happening now, was beautiful and everything she'd hoped it would be. His hands and fingers sought every part of her, and she was just as greedy. She was desperate with need and desire by the time he brought his leg up and moved hers, opening her for his sex.

He held her head in his hands, carefully cradling her, making eye contact as he slid his cock into her. He was so thick he had to work his way in. It was too much and not enough. His massive body lowered over her as he dropped to consume her. His kisses distracted her from the discomfort of his size until there was no more tightness. His hips rocked back and forth with small movements, gradually gaining momentum. Her body joined him, meeting his thrusts with her own. The sensations that radiated from her sex amplified. Her belly tightened with each union, pushing her toward something massive and extraordinary and so very necessary.

She clawed at his back in an effort to get to that place she sensed just out of her reach.

"Shhh... I got you." He lowered his lips over hers and only then did it register she'd been begging. He shifted, bringing up his knees, and thrust into her. Surprised at the power, she gasped. He drove in again and again, harder and faster. *Yes! Oh, God.* Her body clenched against him. The rapture of the sensation warped through her in waves, and she bucked her hips, grinding against him as her insides tightened. An explosion of white, red, and black danced behind her tightly closed eyelids.

He sped up, and his arms tucked her into his chest. His hips stuttered, and he bowed, his back arching as he held inside her. She felt his cock jump and watched as his neck muscles corded. A forced, almost soundless groan erupted from him moments before he relaxed over her. She allowed herself to cling to him, afraid to let go and even more afraid he would require it. She needed to be held right now. She needed to know what tenderness and kindness after sex could be like, and she hoped Ryan would give her that gift. She said a small prayer and promised to cherish the memory forever if it was granted, but braced herself for reality.

He dropped his head and blinked to bring Bethanie into focus. She held onto him, and her eyes betrayed the fear her carefully constructed expression tried to hide. He had no intention of disappointing her and withdrew from her beautifully tight heat only to drop behind her on the couch. He reached across her and flipped the bedspread over them. Easily positioning them, he lifted her head to his shoulder. Her soft sigh of contentment did a pump job on his ego, inflating it until he was ready to burst. He brushed a kiss to her temple and waited. She was practically vibrating with the need to talk. He could sense it, as he could sense he'd raced across a divide he shouldn't have breached. His inner voice was still calling him a fucking idiot, although he'd stopped listening to the fucker when he'd initiated that first kiss.

He was going to be alone in this house with his memories of this woman and her son, and he was going to suffer. Self-flagellation was one of his many talents, just one he didn't share with others, not even Moriah.

"So... we just did that." Bethanie's eyes caught his for a fraction of a second.

"I'd say we just did that well." He chuckled when she rolled her eyes at him.

"This can't get weird for Ethan."

"Weird? As in?"

"He really likes you."

"Okay, I like the little shit, too." Ryan leaned down and kissed her shoulder.

"That's not what I meant."

"Exactly what did you mean?" He nuzzled her collar bone and licked the teardrop indentation at her throat. A shiver raced through her. A self-satisfied smile curled on his lips as he worked his way down her chest.

"We can't..." Her gasp when he took her pert nipple into his mouth silenced her objection.

"We can't...?" He trailed his tongue between peaks to her other nipple, giving it the same attention he'd just laved on the first.

"What?" Her hands threaded through his hair, and she held him against her breast. Not that he minded, he'd stay here for a while. Fuck if he wasn't hard again. She made him as horny as a teenager. He lifted over her and centered himself between her legs, supporting himself on his elbows.

Her legs curled up and wrapped around the back of his thighs. She arched into his ministrations, needy and open. Bethanie offered no agenda, no battle for dominance, just pure, sweet, submission. He lifted and fused their lips together, entering her in one slow, languid, push. He was big for her, but her body had adapted and gloved him in tight, hot, velvet. He wasn't rushing this time. This time he wanted to hear every sound she made, take note of what touches left her shivering and which ones lit her on fire. He wanted to know how to please this woman, how to make her explode and how to put her back together, kiss by heavenly kiss. She was addictive, sexy and for the moment... his.

He knew the moment she orgasmed. He felt her body tighten, watched her gasp when her eyes popped open then shut tightly. He could feel her undulate in her climax, and it was all he needed to bust through his own orgasm. He dropped his head to her shoulder and closed his eyes, fighting back an unwanted realization. He'd fucked too many women to count. He'd had a relationship and steady sex with Moriah, but he'd never "made love." Fuck him. Almost forty-four years old, and it was a distinct possibility tonight was the first time he'd ever made love to a woman. Sex with emotions attached was a powerful motherfucker, and it had reared back and kicked him right in the nuts. When this woman left, he was going to be fucked in a completely different way.

CHAPTER 15

One glanced at her computer screen and lifted a precisely manicured eyebrow. The video request from Three pinged once again. An unscheduled communication from Three flagged disorganization and mayhem. They kept to a schedule for a reason. She maneuvered her mouse and engaged the encryption for the video chat software and waited for the connection to make its way to Three's system.

"I have the Candidate online. Her connection in Venezuela is tenuous but holding at the moment. I knew you'd want to hear firsthand her accounting of her involvement with the New York players. Our images will be blocked, and our voices have been modified. The line is secure."

One nodded her head, her ire at the unexpected interruption waned, albeit only by a modicum.

The screen split in two. Three's image was

replaced with the picture of an iceberg. How appropriate. The woman was an ice-cold killer. She chuckled at the image. "Do I dare ask what image you put in to represent me?"

The picture dissolved and Three flashed a rare, honest smile. "A picture of the Milky Way." The ice reappeared.

"Ah, acceptable." Indeed, she made sure all things orbited as they should. It was her position to ensure the Fates regulated themselves and Stratus with precision and ruthless efficiency. She identified the chaff, and Three eliminated it. The position Two had held was that of counterbalance to the duties One and Three performed. Of the three of them, Two, unfortunately, was... disposable. One pasted a stickie over her camera. She trusted Three, but accidents did happen, as well as calculated risks. Three calculated risks very well.

"The candidate is being patched in now." The image of a middle-aged woman flashed on the screen. High cheekbones, full lips, dark hair and blue eyes. A unique and striking woman, but the thing that struck One was the attitude oozed from the woman. Confidence. Complete and utter surety of herself. A strong attribute and one needed as a Fate.

"This conversation will be short. Frame your answers accordingly. What was your connection to the recent situation in New York?" Three's question cracked like a whip through the mechanically enhanced voice software.

"I worked intermittently in the state for almost two years. It was one of my first international assignments. I studied the transportation, training, and monetization of our assets."

One nodded to herself. The line was secure, and yet the woman did not divulge information that could be understood or used against them. In reality, the Candidate had been learning the human trafficking business, the income stream the prior, incompetent and warring, Fates had lost to the Russian Mafia. A waste of effort and monetary benefits.

"Did you come into contact with the merchandise purchased by this person?" Harvey's picture flashed on the screen.

"Many times, and for extended durations. He had specific tastes and purchased several of our more expensive models."

"Several?" Three asked for clarification.

"Indeed. Two were reported defective and disposed of. I took matters into my own hands and ensured the third was compliant enough, and I believe the product met his needs."

"Could you be identified by the third model?"

The woman's eyes narrowed, and she nodded. "Indeed. The model needed extensive modification and training. I believe the purchaser's intention was to remove the model from his collection when it had served its purpose."

"That did not happen."

"Unfortunate." The woman cocked her head.

"Even if the product was to identify me as having a part in this event, there is no proof."

One spoke for the first time. "The slightest connection to any events that would cast interest in your direction would not befit the position for which you are being considered. Are there any other stumbling blocks from past missions? Any direct contact?"

The woman sat still for a moment before she shook her head. "None. With the exception of the training I did in New York, all my activities have been thickly screened. The former individuals who held your position were less than cautious with our care and upbringing. I took matters into my own hands and shielded myself.

One agreed wholeheartedly with her need for caution. The old regime drove the organization into the ground, but One's thoughts on the matter weren't for the Candidate to know.

The woman's video feed went blank. "The connection was cut by me." The icy expanse evaporated, and One watched as the yellow paper over Three's webcam disappeared. She reached up and removed hers as well.

"I have taken steps to eliminate the woman who can identify our candidate. I find no fault with this candidate except for this burr. When she takes her place as Two, she must be untouchable."

"Where are we with that endeavor?" One lifted her heavy gold pen and rolled it in her fingers.

"We have the date she left. We know she left New York in the middle of the night with her son. We found her vehicle thanks to our assets in law enforcement. She abandoned her car and cell phone in a parking garage in Allentown, New York. We were unable to view security camera feeds of the facility. They claim the system malfunctioned, and we were able to validate the system was down for three days. However, we were able to access traffic cameras and sift through the vehicles that entered the street in front of the garage and did not exit that street past the garage. That totaled one hundred and fifty vehicles over a three-day period. We've tracked down all but ten. When we bumped those ten against rental cars leased and new cars purchased during that time frame with the same make, we came up with something very interesting."

One sighed heavily. She honestly didn't care how they found the woman. The details were minutia and, at her level, unnecessary. "Get to the point." She had so many other duties to complete. This waste of time was usually absorbed by Two. How she missed that buffer.

"A car was purchased the day before that matched the make of one of those ten."

"And?" One prompted when it was obvious that Three was being obscure on purpose.

"A shell company purchased it. After days of exhaustive searching, we still do not know who owns the company or the vehicle."

"Which means it is a cover for a federal agency." An obvious assumption.

"I don't think it was federal... I believe it was Guardian."

One lifted a brow. "Why?"

"It makes sense. Simmons' heir, the one we killed on Capitol Hill, was once employed by Guardian. He had an identical twin brother, whom we also terminated. At the time of his demise, he was an asset of Guardian."

One leaned back in her chair. "How does either death connect Guardian with this woman?"

"Her child is the half brother of the two deceased. Maybe it isn't the woman Guardian cares about."

"So, you assume Guardian is protecting the family of dead operatives?"

"Seems logical."

"It also seems logical the US Marshals would spirit her away and put her in protective custody because of what she knows about Simmons' businesses."

"I disagree; she was insulated."

"She was alive and remained alive. Simmons favored her." An obvious conclusion to draw, as she was not included in the string of dead bodies the man left in his wake.

"I want to continue to look for the vehicle." Three leaned forward. "Regardless who is hiding her, we will find her."

"Do as you please, but first, tap into our assets

with the US Marshals. They would know if she is in protective custody."

"I will." Three held up a finger, and her screen went blank. She heard Three talking in a low muffled voice before her image reappeared.

"I can confirm that Two is dead. She was being held in a detention facility used by all US agencies. An armed incursion of undetermined origin eliminated Two and all but a few detainees and one guard. The collateral damage was intentional to ensure no one knew Two was the target."

"Finally. Let us make haste on the New York situation and proceed with the sanitation effort on our Candidate." At last things could move forward.

"Our next call is scheduled in one week. Do you want me to contact you if we eliminate the problem before that?"

"To what end? Eliminate the woman and the problem is solved." One disconnected the call and unhooked the encryption from the video software. Three was becoming an effort to deal with. The new Two was needed posthaste.

ethanie sat on a stump across from Ryan, hypnotized by the fluid, graceful movement of his upward swing, the downward thrust of the double-headed ax blade, and the violent crack of the wood splitting as the sharp wedge tore the log in half. Granted, her focus was the man rather than the process. He'd stripped out of his coat. The flannel shirt lifted as he raised the ax, and his ribbed abdominals flashed before he lowered the ax. The downswing exposed the small of his back. His arms stretched the fabric as he set another log on the massive stump he'd rolled in front of the wood pile.

"Mom?"

"Yeah, honey?" Bethanie snatched her attention away from the man who'd made her ache so wonderfully last night.

"Are you sure I have to do school work?" Ethan watched Ryan and waited until Ryan reached for a new log before he darted in and hauled the split logs over to the quasi-sled Ryan had built to tug large quantities of wood up to the house.

"I'm positive. Ryan got online this morning while you were playing with Dog. We've found one that looks good." It had advanced placement. Ryan also calmed her concern about putting Ethan's name into the system. They'd use Ryan's last name and have Guardian make up a similar but fake school record to submit. Ethan's grades could be transferred back to his record when things settled down.

"Are you going to be my teacher?" Ethan grunted as he stacked the wood on the sled. "C'mon, Mom, it's full."

She stood up and grabbed the rope with him, and they tugged the sled to the wood pile by the back of the cave.

"Yes, I will be your teacher, and anything I can't answer, Ryan will help with." She handed Ethan a log, and he put it on the stack.

"He's really smart, isn't he? He built the house and everything." Ethan turned back for another log.

"I think he is." She handed him a log and turned to pick up another.

"Do you like him?" Ethan took the wood out of her hand and turned away.

Bethanie felt a warmth spread across her cheeks and chuckled. "I do like him."

"He's cool. He cusses a lot, but he's cool. I'm glad

he's not still mad we're here, and I like when he teaches me stuff."

They worked in silence for a little longer and emptied the sled. They headed back to the sound of wood being chopped when Ethan said, "I wish he coulda been my father."

"What?" Bethanie froze in her tracks, and the front of the sled bumped into her snow boots.

Ethan looked at her and shrugged. "I know it can't happen, but sometimes I think that." He tugged on the rope. "Mom, you hafta move."

She stepped out of the path of the sled and watched as Ethan trudged ahead and positioned the sleigh for more wood. Ryan smiled at him and helped him load the wood that had been chopped while they were gone. Ethan's look of adoration must mimic her own. She pushed back the fears learned at the hands of ruthless people; fears conditioned into her from twelve years of controlling abuse. She drew a deep breath and squared her shoulders. Here, on this mountain, there was no need for fears. The man in front of her was kind and self-disciplined. Ryan wasn't the monster Harvey had been. She was finally free of that malice, free to unlearn the fears formed in her past.

A hawk or an eagle cried in the sky drawing her eyes heavenward. *At this moment, she felt as free as that bird.*

❧

"He's asleep?" Ryan lifted the heavy mink blanket in invitation. Bethanie dropped her robe and slid out of her sleep shirt before she tucked herself into his side. He dropped the blanket over them as he rolled on top of her.

Her arms snaked around his neck, and she smiled. "Your fault. You got him all wound up."

"What?" He reared back and laughed, "I won that game, fair and square."

"You cannot win Trivial Pursuit unless you land on the center circle and answer the question correctly."

"I did!"

"You didn't." She laughed and imitated his deep voice, "The answer is right because I said so, and it's bedtime."

Okay, so maybe he was in a hurry to be alone with her tonight. Bethanie had been teasing him all day with touches and shy looks when Ethan wasn't in the room. The woman had driven him insane. He couldn't get enough of her and hated that they couldn't touch when Ethan was around. It felt… wrong.

He shrugged off the truth and settled between her legs. "Well, dammit, why don't I get to play the adult card? You do it all the time."

She tugged him down and threaded her hands through his hair. "You can play adult with me anytime."

"Yeah?" He dipped down and ran his nose up her

neck, stopping to tenderly bite her earlobe. She shuddered under him. "You like that."

It was a statement, not a question. They'd been sneaking time together after Ethan fell asleep for over three weeks now. He'd cataloged her body's responses to his touches. He knew how to drive her to the brink within minutes or how to churn a slow, deep burn within her. She wasn't the type to take the lead, but she'd follow him, trust him, and fucking make him combust with her reactions.

He rolled and brought her on top. Her eyes widened in surprise. "What are you doing?"

"We're going to do something different tonight."

"We are?"

"Mmm hmmm." He lifted his hips and ground against her core.

"What do you want me to do?" Her blue eyes were heavy with desire. She pulled her bottom lip into her mouth when he rolled his hips again.

"Scoot up." She moved slightly, and he shook his head. "Hands on the headboard, scoot up over my face."

"What?" Those eyes popped wide open.

"Trust me. I'll make it good for you."

"But..."

"If you don't like it, tell me, but I think you'll be happy you tried." He ran his hands up and down her back, easing the stiffness that had invaded her once languid body.

She lifted her eyes to the headboard and looked back at him. "Are you sure?"

"Believe me, I'm sure. I want to taste you. I've wanted to since that first night." His hands ran up her back, and he pressed her down to his lips. He did his best to make her forget her reservations, to melt her hesitation, and abolish her doubts.

She pulled away, panting in fresh air. Her lips were puffy, wet, and rose-colored as she stared down at him. But there was concern in her eyes. She was vulnerable, so fucking exposed, and she was trusting him. Even though that mother-fucking bastard had used her, he'd never shown her the pleasures her body could enjoy. Ryan had made it his mission to teach her what intimacy between a man and a woman could be. The emotional connection between them, fuck, it made it sweeter. Hotter and so fucking addictive.

Slowly she reached up to the headboard and inched forward until he lifted one of her knees and slid his arm through her legs. She lifted the other, and he moved his shoulders, so her knees were on either side of his head.

A soft gasp fell from her when he turned and kissed the inside of her thigh. Her legs trembled. "Beautiful. You are so fucking beautiful, Bethanie."

"I…" Her words were cut off when he licked the inside of her thigh.

She was an open blossom in front of him. So close and so damn perfect. "Don't. Don't tell me you're not.

You are. To me, you are." And he meant every fucking word. Damn him to hell for eternity, he meant Every. Fucking. Word.

With his arms wrapped around her thighs, he pulled her down to him. He kissed the inside of her thigh again before inching up her hot skin. Her trembling became more noticeable as he got closer.

"Ryan…"

He hummed his response. Words were not possible at the moment. He moved his hands and spread her sex with his fingertips before he licked a strip through her and paid particular attention to the hard nub at the top of her cleft.

She trembled against his mouth. "Oh! God, that's… Oh, do that again."

He smiled and slid his lips against her skin. "Believe me, I wasn't going to stop." He adjusted his arms and opened her.

"Ryan! This is… oh, yes, there, please… please…"

He opened his eyes. Her head had lolled forward, her eyes were closed, but her expression, hell, she was nearing heaven, and he was going to be the one to get her there. It took all the willpower he possessed to go slowly. What he wanted to do was lollipop her with three licks and get straight to the candy center, but he also wanted her to enjoy the buildup, and understand how good he could make her feel. He fucking needed her to explode so he could taste her. His cock throbbed, hard as a fucking diamond and weeping with need, but he didn't care. This moment, this was for her.

He knew exactly when his slow licks and playful teasing flicks weren't enough. Bethanie's hand found his hair and her fist curled tight as she rocked down onto his mouth with a low moan. It was the most wonderful sound he'd ever heard.

Ryan pulled her even closer and sucked her clit into his mouth. She bucked against him. An anguished sound of delight moved through the room. Okay, *that* was the most wonderful sound he'd ever heard.

He redoubled his efforts, and she shattered over him. He feasted on her, consumed her, and he fucking loved it. When she slumped over him, he helped her down his body, rolled her over and entered her, slowly easing in, making her give way to his size. She was tight, so fucking tight, and she was perfect.

He rested his head on her shoulder when he was balls deep. He was so worked up, he'd lose control if he moved.

Her hands trailed down his back, and she dug her nails into his ass. "Finish, I know you want to."

He groaned and moved. It took six strokes for the white-hot pool at the base of his balls to explode through him. His body arched hard against her, and he rode out his orgasm. He'd climaxed so violently his arms shook with the effort to keep himself from suffocating her with his weight.

"That was wonderful." She placed a tender kiss on the inside of his bicep.

He shivered at the warmth of her lips and opened his eyes. He lifted his head so he could see her. "Just for the record, from my point of view, that was better than wonderful." He pulled out of her and rolled to the side, tucking her into him as he dropped.

"What's the word for better than wonderful?" she asked as she burrowed into his side and propped her head up on his shoulder.

"Stupendous?"

She countered with a laugh, "Stellar?"

"Phenomenal."

"Spectacular."

Ryan turned and adjusted her on his arm so he could see her. "Perfect. What we just did? That was perfect."

Her eyes searched his face. He saw the doubt, the fear, the trepidation, and knew there was nothing he could do to alleviate any of it.

He tucked her into his side. Her sigh of contentment sent a white-hot knife of guilt through his soul. This beautiful, gentle woman had risked her life to remove herself and her son from danger. And where had she ended up? Sleeping with a minion of Satan, a killer of unequaled skill. He was an assassin. A paid harbinger of death. Did the abominations he hunted deserve to be expunged from the face of the earth? Hell, yes. Did that make him any less of a monster? Not in the slightest.

How could he ask her to stay with him and put her life and Ethan's at risk? He couldn't, and what's more, he wouldn't. When Guardian cleared the situation up, and he had no doubt they would, Bethanie and Ethan would have a chance at a good life. Not isolation on top of a mountain with a soul damned to burn in hell for eternity. There was no way he could change his past. What he was. Fuck him, he wished he could, but wishes were just like dreams— apparitions that disappeared in the harsh light of day.

There was nothing he could do except treat her like the treasure she was and try, somehow, let her know what a grave impact she was making in his life. A tall order when he had zero to offer her.

"I think I'm in trouble." She reached up with her hand and cupped his cheek.

He grabbed her hand and kissed the palm. It was all he could do. He had no words. No way of responding. He didn't know what was happening between them. He'd never felt the emotions she engendered, and was hard up to identify them. He had no direction, no idea where to go with this. Finally, he told her the truth. "I'm lost."

She closed her eyes and whispered, "We both are."

"Are you ready?" Ryan snugged on his gloves.

"Yes, sir." Ethan patted his coat pockets.

"Checklist run down." Ryan put his hands on his hips. "Flint and steel."

Ethan patted the leg of his snow pants. "Check."

"Knife?"

"Check." The boy patted the other leg of his pants.

"Fuel?"

"Two!" The boy held up two protein bars and then shoved them into his coat pocket.

"And why do we make sure we have these items when we go out?"

"Because with the flint and steel I can make a fire. The knife I can use to cut small branches that won't break. I can drink melted snow to stay alive, but the body needs fuel after..." His face scrunched in concentration... "I don't remember the exact amount of time, but I need to eat to keep my body going."

"Right."

"What's in our packs?"

"Emergency blanket, hatchet, string, a water bottle and a plastic bag with matches and kindling."

"Do we need any of that to survive?"

"Nope, but it is good to have. Plus, we are taking the sleeping bags because we are staying out all night."

"Why are we staying out all night?"

Ethan grinned. "Because it's my birthday tomorrow."

"Perfect. Let's go."

Ethan and Dog shot out the door like their tails were on fire, the smaller version of Ryan's pack bouncing on Ethan's back. "We'll be back a couple hours after sun up. I'll teach him how to tend a fire through the night, and I want him to set up a shelter." Ryan stepped over to her and gathered her in his arms.

"He loves going out with you. Thank you for offering an overnight trip as his birthday present." She pushed up on her toes and initiated the kiss.

He palmed her delicious ass and lifted her. She laughed and wrapped her legs around his waist. "We aren't going far." He lowered for another kiss. He couldn't get enough of her taste on his lips.

"Ryan! Come on!" Ethan's shout pulled them apart. Bethanie dropped her legs, and he lowered her to the ground.

She slid her hands across his down-filled coat. "Go. I have to pull down his next assignment and submit this week's grades. I want to do that before it starts to snow again. I don't like going up and fiddling with the antenna."

"It isn't supposed to snow until tonight, and only a couple inches is forecast." Ryan grabbed a knit cap off the hook by the door. "Are you sure you don't want me to bring up the firewood?"

"No, I like the exercise, and the sled you two built makes it easier. Go. I have a birthday cake to make, and you promised snow ice cream."

"Yeah, but we are eating that early. Remember what happened last time." He winked at her, and she blushed. "Seriously, don't overdo it. You know what to do if you need me."

"Blow the whistle and keep blowing it until Dog hears me. Believe me, I've got this. Now go before I have a wet dog and wound up young man back in the house."

"Bossy little thing, aren't you?" He bent down once again to kiss her.

She murmured, "Damn straight," before he captured her lips.

"Mom, you said a bad word." Ethan's voice ripped them apart. "Stop kissing her and c'mon, Ryan."

"What if I want to keep kissing her?"

"That's just gross, and it's my birthday tomorrow, so I get to say! Let's go!"

Ryan winked at Bethanie and followed Ethan out the door.

They walked down the mountainside side by side. Ryan kept an eye out for the perfect place to build a shelter.

"How do you do that?" Ethan pointed behind them.

"Do what?"

"See, here is where I walked, but I can't see where you are walking."

*Oh.* "That is from years of practice. See the pine straw?" Ryan pointed ahead of them.

"Uh huh."

"I step on that; it shields my footprint. Then I look

for the next step. It's automatic now, I've been doing it for so long." He glanced back to his trail. He could pick out his footsteps; he hadn't been mindful of the route, but he could see why Ethan saw the difference.

"Oh." He watched as Ethan cast around and took an exaggerated step to reach a rock. He stepped on it and smiled back at Ryan. "Like this?"

"That's right but do me a favor and don't break an ankle or anything. Take smaller steps. You won't always have a place to put your foot that won't leave a print, and that's okay. Besides, your mom would kill me if you got hurt."

Ethan laughed and hopped onto a fallen tree. He used it as a balance beam, his arms held out to his side as he walked. "Mom wouldn't kill you."

"I don't know, kid. She's pretty tough." Ryan stepped over the balance beam tree and kept going. He heard Ethan jogging behind him to catch up.

"She likes you."

"Yeah, you think?"

"Well, yeah, she *kisses* you." He made gagging sounds, and Ryan chuckled at his antics. "Are you going to marry her?"

*Whoa.* "Say what, now?"

"Marry her. Are you going to marry my mom?"

*Well, fuck, how in the hell was he supposed to answer that?* "Ah... we..."

"Look!" Ethan whispered and pointed ahead and to the right of them.

A deer lifted its head and sniffed the air. They

were upwind, so she didn't catch their scent. Ryan glanced to the sky and thanked the cosmos for the distraction. They watched the doe for about five minutes before something spooked her, and she crashed through the woods in bounding leaps.

"She was neat."

"She was."

"What scared her?"

"Probably something that was stalking her." Could have been Dog, but he doubted it. Dog had been eating leftovers lately. Spoiled animal.

"Would it kill her?"

"If it was hungry enough, sure."

"That's not right." Ethan glanced back over his shoulder to where the animal had bolted.

Ryan debated for about ten seconds before he slung off his pack and sat on it. "Take a load off, Bud, I need to have a talk with you."

Ethan was a quick study. He dropped his smaller pack, and ass planted the same way Ryan had. He positioned himself in the exact same manner.

"Okay, this is the gist of nature, kiddo. Animals, all animals including humans, live in a hierarchy. The top of the food chain feeds on the bottom of the food chain. It is a fact of life. Huge whales in the ocean scoop up whole schools of fish to eat. It takes a lot to keep those big bodies going. In the forest, there are things called apex predators. They feed on animals that are smaller, weaker or can't defend themselves."

"Like the deer?"

"Just like that. A wolf, cougar, bear, bobcat or even man would look at her and see food, a means to exist."

Ethan stared at him with that concentrated narrow gaze for a while. "So, they kill for food."

"Yup."

"Humans kill, but not always for food." Ethan's voice got small. "Wars and stuff."

Ryan waited until he looked up and nodded. "It has been my experience that there are three reasons *animals* kill."

"Three?"

"First reason animals kill is to survive."

"They hunt for food."

"Exactly. That is survival. There are other reasons, though. If a wolf or a coyote contracted rabies, and they were spreading that disease by attacking you or the people you love, what would you do?" Ryan's mind flashed to the twenty-seven bastards he'd put down. They no longer spread their strain of deadly epidemiology.

"Stop them."

"Correct. That is the second reason. *Animals* kill to defend themselves, their young or even their pack."

The boy nodded his understanding. "What's the third reason?

"Believe it or not, some animals kill just to protect their territory."

"Like how?"

"For instance, lions will kill hyenas, because they compete for the same food. But the Lions won't necessarily eat them. In the lion's case, they are claiming their territory and eliminating threats to their existence." *Like drug dealers, cartels, mobs and other assorted scum at the bottom of humanity.*

"So, they don't want the hyenas to take their food."

"Correct. Lions will kill not only for food, not only to defend themselves or others against an attack, but to stake a claim to their territory."

"Huh. It sucks for those weaker animals who can't fight back. They're all just going to die."

*Not if he could help it.* "Not true. There aren't a lot of apex predators in the world. Most of the wildlife around here will die of old age or natural causes. Apex predators generally go for the weak or the sick and lame. They are easier to catch." *Manipulate, black-mail, torture, enslave.* "Anyway, when the apex predators take out the weak ones, they make the herd stronger because only the strongest survive. Nature has a way of taking care of its own."

"Ryan?" Ethan looked up at him, his eyes were deadly serious.

"Yeah, Bud?"

"I'm really glad I'm not an animal."

"Right. Come on, we have a shelter to build and a fire to start." He stood up and shouldered his pack. Ryan glanced around as Ethan put his pack back on, assaulted by an unfamiliar emotion. Fuck him. He wanted to make sure the kid never saw humanity's underbelly. He wanted to *protect* him.

"Ready?" Ethan smiled at him.

"Ready, willing and able." He'd never have that opportunity, would he? Ethan wasn't his to protect, and fuck him if that didn't make him feel as if he were being skinned alive.

# CHAPTER 17

Lycos glanced at the dead drop message again. He'd been staring at it all morning and fuck him if he didn't want to ignore it. *3-Tiger 1100*. Their usual time. Eleven hundred hours. He hated check-in day. He shrugged his shoulders and leaned back in his chair. The check-in was routine. Probably the usual update. Or at least he hoped like fuck it was. He had come to dread the weekly calls. Had come to dread the thought this call might sever the ties that held Bethanie and Ethan to him.

He'd been instructed to call Bengal at eleven hundred hours, his time. He glanced at the clock on his monitor. He leaned over and flipped the switch to activate his satellite dish.

He spent two minutes steeling himself. The conversation was one he'd hoped to avoid. No doubt Guardian had eliminated the threat to Bethanie and

Ethan. He should be happy. He wasn't. He fucking wasn't.

He lifted the receiver and dialed the number before he keyed in his encryption.

"Operator Two Seven Four."

"Sunset clearance, third operative." Lycos dropped his head and rubbed his eyes. He did not want to have this conversation.

"Standby third operative."

"How are you surviving?" Bengal inquired as a way of a greeting.

"Fine." He kept his words concise, clipped.

"Ever eloquent, my friend. We have some information about your current situation."

He braced himself mentally. "Go ahead."

"It would seem the Fates and Stratus are on an all-out campaign to eradicate any connection between the woman we had in custody and any operation she could have provided information about. That would be the why of the deaths of the people associated with Harvey Simmons."

Well, that made sense. "Had in custody? Why the past tense?"

"The facility she was being held in was hit. A small army descended on the building. All but one guard and several inmates were murdered. The guards returned fire and called in backup, but it didn't arrive in time. We can't know for certain the woman we were interrogating was the target, but that is our assumption. The CIA and the FBI are in agreement. The other detainees weren't high enough on anyone's radar to warrant a purge."

"Did you get information from the woman that would help Bethanie?"

There was a pause before Bengal replied. "Not enough."

"Where does that leave them?"

"A couple options."

"Which are?"

"Guardian can enfold them until we eliminate the threat."

"Where?"

"Our facility in the midwest."

Lycos closed his eyes. He'd heard about the South Dakota complex. Asp and Anubis lived there. Yes, they'd be safe, but... "The other option?"

"Federal Protective Custody. Not our preference, but she would need to make that decision."

"Your woman said the boy was family."

"True, after a fashion, he is."

"Where is his family?"

"At the complex."

"Shouldn't someone tell her?"

"Yes, you should. Ethan has two half brothers. They are willing to take care of both Ethan and his mom. Oh BTW, in case no one gave you the details on that, Moriah is married to one of Ethan's brothers."

Lycos dropped his head to the desk. Moriah, Asp,

Anubis *and* a complex full of Guardians. Bethanie'd be safe. Ethan would have opportunities.

"There is a third option, but I'm not sure..."

"What?" Lycos' head snapped up.

"They *could* stay with you."

"That's a pipe dream. Stop smoking chemicals, man."

"Straight up tell me you aren't falling for that woman and I'll shut up."

"How the fuck? Why would you think that?"

"Because, asshole, every check-in I've had with you, you've been a total douche until you find out they aren't going anywhere, and then it's like the weight of the world has been lifted off your shoulders. I know you, man. We grew up in this business together. You've never had a problem doing your job, but once your genius fucking mind caught some education, you didn't *have* to do this job. This life isn't all there is for you. You've paid your debt to society, to Guardian, to whatever ghosts live in your past. Walk away. Find your light. Forget the darkness and the Shadows. You've earned it."

Lycos bounced Bengal's words around for a moment before he shook his head. "I took an oath to Guardian. Whatever it takes."

"As long as it takes, brother. I'm telling you, your obligation is paid in full. You don't have to live by that oath any longer. It took until now. This moment in time. You *can* walk away. No one knows where you are except the two people currently with you, and they don't know your past. You can protect them. You are off the grid. Stay that way."

Lycos stared at a vein of mica that ran through the rock he used as his desk and traced it with his finger. "This location is far from perfect. Ethan won't have kids up here. She'll be isolated. Again."

"Dude, there is a difference between living in an isolated location and being controlled."

"Truth." Lycos conceded.

"Can I ask you something?"

"Since when do you ask?"

Bengal's huff turned into a laugh. "I'm turning over a new leaf."

"You're full of shit."

"I am. I admit it. Seriously, are you going to let them walk away?"

"What I want doesn't matter."

"Not true."

"Absolutely true. They deserve to be happy."

"And they aren't now?"

He couldn't deny the radical change in both Bethanie and Ethan's behavior. They smiled. They laughed. Yeah… they were happy. Lycos thought back over the last three months. Hell, over the years he'd been preparing to disappear without a trace. "What would it take to walk away?"

"One thing."

"And that is?"

"You tell me you're out."

"It can't be that simple."

"It is that simple. You walk. We sever ties. You drift away, and we reminisce about the good old days."

"Bengal?"

"Yeah?"

"I'm out."

Bethanie glanced at the plans rolled out on the kitchen table. The size of the project was almost overwhelming. If Ryan was able to build the hydroponic garden, the mountaintop home could almost be self-sustaining. He had power, water, and with the garden he'd have fresh vegetables. They ate venison that he'd killed. She cringed at the thought of eating Bambi, but as he reminded her, he didn't kill the animals for sport, he killed them to survive. It didn't make it easier, but she understood the rationale, especially since running to the market was, best case, a two-day event.

"Mom, is there more peanut butter?" Ethan held the cabinet door open as if another container would miraculously appear.

"Nope. We are out." In fact, they were out of quite a few things. She'd stretched the staples as far as she could, but they needed flour, yeast, sugar, and obviously peanut butter. She had a list and jotted down items as the supplies dwindled. It was hard to believe they'd been here for three full months. It was almost the first of April. The days warmed into the forties and the snow was melting, although in the shaded areas of the mountaintop it lingered in frigid stubbornness.

"I'm going to starve!" Ethan dropped to the floor and put his arm over his eyes. Dog padded over to him and snuffled under his arm until Ethan laughed and rolled to his stomach. Dog kept nosing him around the neck and ears, and Ethan laughed harder.

"I'm sure you'll survive," she said over the laughter. She stood on her tiptoes, grabbed the last container of chocolate-hazelnut spread and set it on the counter. "Here you go."

Ethan lifted his head and smiled as Dog licked his face. "Cool!" He sprang up and grabbed the container.

"We need supplies. I'll have to make a run soon." Ryan walked in and wrapped his arms around her, dropping a kiss on her lips.

"Gross." Ethan made his normal choking sound when he saw them kiss.

"We do, but we can manage for a while." She glanced at Ethan before she whispered, "What did Guardian say?"

Ryan slid his eyes to Ethan. "Hey, Bud, I'm going to borrow your mom for a minute. We'll be in my office."

Ethan glanced at him and nodded.

"Clean up after yourself and then finish your

homework," Bethanie reminded him before she followed Ryan out of the kitchen.

Dramatics in full swing, Ethan sighed, "Do I have to?"

She laughed and called back, "Yes, you have to!"

She headed up the incline after Ryan. He shut the door behind them, enclosing them in the book-lined office.

"Is it bad news?" She wrapped her arms around herself.

"It isn't good news." Ryan leaned against the deep rock ledge that served as his desk.

"What's that mean?"

"Guardian has tracked a progression of... deletions."

"Deletions? I'm sorry, I'm not following."

Ryan sighed and ran his fingers through his hair before his shoulders sagged. "I didn't want to tell you this, but everyone associated with your husband is being systematically eliminated."

"Eliminated as in... killed?" A ripple of gooseflesh spread across her body.

"Yes."

She didn't want to know, but she had to ask, "Why?"

He looked up at the ceiling of his office. "The current theory is Harvey was a small part of a much larger operation. Guardian believes he was a pawn who knew too much. In order to ensure the people he was working with are not exposed in any fashion, they are cleaning house."

She clutched at her throat, her breath caught, and she whispered, "But we don't know anything."

He reached for her and pulled her into him, spreading his legs so she could stand between them. The immediate warmth and strength of his body against hers became a balm to her fractured nerves. He kissed the top of her head and spoke softly, "I know."

"What are we going to do?" Her hands found his chest, the strength of his muscles and the feel of his heart beating under the palm of her hand grounded her.

"Well, there are a couple options, but no decisions you need to make today. Okay?"

"Options?"

"Yes. First, Guardian is willing to relocate you. They have a place in the midwest where they believe you and Ethan would be safe. How long you'd have to stay there is unknown, but if I had to guess, I'd say it would be a permanent move."

"Permanent?" She dropped her eyes and focused on the button of his flannel shirt. Leave here. Leave him? Permanently? God, she didn't want that.

"I also need to let you know that Ethan has two half brothers. They live out there, and they are willing to take you and Ethan in."

"Half brothers." Bethanie closed her eyes. That meant she wasn't the only woman Harvey had used.

The bastard. But, being related didn't make her and Ethan safe. Not like they were here. She shook her head and spoke to his chest. "But I don't know them. Are they good people?"

"I would assume so. They are connected to Guardian."

She lifted her gaze to his. "You said options. What else?"

"There is the option of the Federal Witness Protection Program. Again, you'd be relocated, but the US Marshals would make sure you're safe. Nobody, including Guardian, would know where you relocate."

Why was it so damn cold in his office? She shivered as she spoke, "Do you trust the Marshals Service?"

He drew a deep breath and nodded. "They are good, but if I was handed the choice between those two options, I'd go with Guardian. They're better."

"Oh." She dropped her eyes to that button at the middle of his chest again. They'd have to leave. She'd been living in denial, playing house as it were. However, reality had just slapped her out of her fairy tale.

She drew a breath, but it didn't expand her lungs. The weight crushing her chest wouldn't let her breathe. She needed to face the fact she'd have to leave the mountain, leave Ryan. Desolation's icy embrace froze her from the inside out.

He closed his eyes and pulled her into his chest.

His chin rested on her head, and his chest rumbled under her ear. "There is a third option. You could stay here, with me. Off-grid. I can protect you and Ethan. It isn't perfect. He has no friends here, and we are isolated–"

She thrust back. "Yes! Yes, I want us to stay here. "She wrapped her arms around his neck and held on to him. He'd become her anchor, her foundation.

"Are you sure?"

She nodded against his chest. "Positive." A sudden, terrifying thought raced through her mind. She pushed back again. "Unless you don't want us?"

His eyes shone as he looked down at her. "I wouldn't have mentioned it if I didn't want you to stay."

"What do we need to do? Do we need to tell Guardian?"

He smiled and shook his head. "I took a gamble and told them I thought you'd stay with me, but we can make it official tonight. I'll arrange a time for you to talk to them."

He pulled her into him, and she practically crawled up his body. He laughed and cupped her ass, lifting her up until she could wrap her legs around him. The kiss they shared was liberating and exhilarating.

She leaned into him and reveled in the warmth and strength that enfolded her. A quiet comfort settled over her. Thoughts of permanence bounced through her mind. What they'd need to do to stay here. Silly things they'd need to get. She needed a hairbrush. The comb she was using was killing her hair, and they'd need more school supplies for Ethan. Oh, they'd need summer clothes. Ethan was growing like a weed. "We'll have to buy some things, and I don't have any money." She didn't need the brush, she could do without it.

"Hey."

Bethanie looked up.

"I have money and investments. I can't imagine we will ever need anything I can't afford."

"I don't want you to feel obligated."

His brow furrowed. "Obligated?"

She nodded. "To take care of us."

He leered at her. "Woman, what I feel has nothing to do with obligation. Absolutely nothing." He dropped another breath-arresting kiss on her that left her panting and clinging to him for support.

"I want you here. I want Ethan here."

"I'm sure I speak for Ethan when I say we want to be here."

"Then it's settled." He tucked her against his chest again. His hands smoothed a pattern across her back. She didn't know how long they stayed like that, holding each other and lost in their individual thoughts before she realized something. "I still have their car. I haven't moved it since we got here. Maybe we should take it down the mountain?"

Ryan squeezed her tightly before he stood.

"Details we can handle later. How about we go break the news to the bottomless pit?"

Bethanie grabbed the hand that was offered and laughed, "He is that, isn't he?"

Ryan stopped at the door. "You really think he's going to be okay with the decision to stay?"

Bethanie smiled up at him. "I know he will be. He adores you; he loves the mountain, and I'm sorry, but there is no way he'd ever leave Dog."

Ryan threw back his head and laughed. "Well that settles everything, doesn't it?"

Bethanie smiled as she walked beside him. The decision they'd made tonight did settle almost everything. Almost.

## CHAPTER 18

Bethanie tried to pull the covers up to Ethan's chin and frowned at the foot of the bed. "Okay, buster, since the elephant masquerading as a dog on your bed won't let me pull up your blankets, you need to scrunch down."

Ethan laughed and scooched down, dragging his pillow with him. "I'm really glad we get to stay here."

"Are you?" Bethanie pushed his mop of blond hair off his forehead. He needed to get his hair cut soon.

"Uh huh. I like it here."

"So do I. What's your favorite thing about living here?"

"Favorite?"

"Okay, second favorite, because I know Dog is your first favorite."

Ethan sat up and dropped his hand on the animal's snout. He stroked Dog's fur and looked at her. "I love Dog. But..."

She lifted his chin so she could see his eyes. "But...?"

"He's not my first favorite. I like that you're not sad anymore."

*Oh, God. How much had her baby actually perceived in New York?* "I'm not sad. I'm very happy, but I want you to be happy, too."

Ethan looked down and watched his fingers comb Dog's coat. "I'm gonna miss James. He won't have anyone when his dad gets mad. His mom should leave and take him with her."

"I know." Bethanie felt a cold chill creep through her. Her son knew far too much about what was actually happening around him.

"Maybe someday we can invite him to come here?"

Bethanie had to smile at the hopefulness in his eyes. "Maybe, but we'll have to wait until Ryan says it's okay." It would never happen. James' father worked for Harvey. He'd use the knowledge of their whereabouts to his advantage. Somehow.

Ethan nodded. "He's really cool. Not like Father." Ethan yawned and lay down, pulling the covers over his shoulder.

"No, not at all. Hey, you know what I found out today?"

"What?" He rolled to his back and put his arms under his head. He was turning into such a young man.

"Well, your father had two other sons. So, you have two half brothers."

Ethan sprang up to his elbows. "I do? How old are they? What're their names? Where do they live?"

Bethanie made a face and bobbled her head from side to side. "Wow, okay... well, I don't know their names, but I can find out. They live somewhere in the midwest. Again, I don't know exactly where, but I'll have Ryan ask, and they are older, I think."

"*Old* like you?"

"*Old?*" She pounced on him and tickled him until Dog got agitated and tried to get between them. "Okay, big boy. I'm not hurting him." She gave the animal a pat on the shoulder and shifted so she could see Ethan. "Probably not *old* like me, but older than you. They said that we could come live with them."

Ethan shook his head vehemently. "I don't want to leave here."

"Neither do I, so maybe we can just go visit someday? Would you like that?"

"Yeah, that'd be fun."

"Good. Now scrunch down and get comfy." She lifted off the bed and waited for him and Dog to settle. Bending at the waist, she kissed his forehead. "G'night, Ethan."

"Night, Mom."

She headed out of the room that had been emptied of books and christened Ethan's room about two weeks ago. Her son had no problem sleeping alone and didn't blink an eye when she and Ryan had given up the pretense of not sleeping together. Kids were amazing. Her kid was phenomenal.

"Hey, Mom?"

"Yes?"

"I lied; Dog *is* my favorite."

She laughed and shook her head. "I knew that. Sleep tight."

She closed the door a bit and headed into Ryan's room. *Their room.* The sound of the waterfall shower obliterated the silence. She turned back and shut the door to their room. Ethan never wandered at night, and he knew to knock before entering their bedroom. According to Ryan, he and Ethan had a 'guy' talk and agreed that most kissing should be done in private. She chuckled as she lifted her night-shirt over her head and padded into the massive bathroom. She paused just inside the door. Ryan stood under the shower, his hands braced against the wall, his head hanging down. His muscles rippled when he pushed off the wall and straightened.

For some reason, he looked tense. She waited until he glanced her way before she walked toward him. His eyes roamed her body as she approached, much like she'd been eyeing him moments before. He extended his hand and pulled her into the cascade of gloriously warm water. He drew her into him, his firm sex trapped between them. "He in bed?"

"He is."

"No bedtime regrets about staying here?"

"Nah. I told him about his brothers. He'd like to

know their names and maybe go visit them sometime."

"I can get that information for him." Ryan pushed her wet hair out of her eyes. "And you? No regrets?"

She shook her head. "None."

He stared at her for several long minutes as if he were trying to reassure himself of her commitment.

"Are *you* having regrets?"

He'd had all evening to think about it, maybe...

"None, but I do want to tell you some things about my past." He ran his hand up her arm and cupped her neck. "I can't tell you everything. Most of what I did for Guardian was classified, but I want you to know me. All of me."

She put her hand on his chest. "Then it is only fair that I tell you about me."

He began to shake his head, but she reached up and put her finger on his mouth. "I want you to know me. All of me." His words echoed back at him. "Let's finish showering, and we'll talk."

He bent down and kissed her once, and then again. Bethanie melted under his touch and would have forgone the talk if he hadn't backed away. "Shower, talk, then adult time." He handed her the shampoo.

She held the bottle in her hands and watched as he soaped up his chest. The suds rolled down his stomach to his–

"Shampoo."

She jumped at his words and reluctantly pulled

her eyes away from his cock. "Right. Shampoo." She blinked and jerked her eyes to the side. "Shampoo."

His laughter reverberated through the cave. They managed to wash and get out of the shower with only minor detours—a couple of kisses and some touches. She toweled off quickly, grabbed the comb she'd been using, and picked up her sleep shirt from the floor.

She crawled to the far side of the bed and plumped her pillow up against the headboard. "What did you want to share with me?" Ryan pulled the blanket and sheet back and slid into the bed, completely naked. Which was not fair because she wouldn't be listening to him now. "Pull the sheet over you, or I'm going to be distracted."

He smiled and lifted his eyebrow suggestively.

She slowly shook her head and motioned to the sheet. "Nope. Talk."

He flipped the fabric over him and turned toward her, propping himself up on his elbow. "When I was Ethan's age, the state of Michigan took me away from my mother."

Bethanie gasped. "Why?"

"Okay, maybe I need to rephrase that. I never knew who my dad was. When I was eleven, my mother left me alone in the room she rented and never came back. She was an addict. She shot up in front of me all the time. Used what money she made to fund her highs. We rarely had food. I learned to beg and steal on the street. An old lady that lived on the first floor caught me stealing out of her garbage can and called social services. They tossed me into a foster home."

Her heart ached for him and for everything the eleven-year-old Ryan had been through. Those beautiful brown eyes of his reflected a misery he didn't speak of, and that tore at her heart. She couldn't comprehend a mother not taking care of her child. It was... so wrong. "I'm so sorry."

Ryan shrugged. His eyes dropped and focused on the sheet between them. "It was all I knew. I grew up hard. Learned how to defend myself, how to protect myself from people who preyed on the weak."

"You must have been so lonely."

"I was alone most of my life, even when she was around. But that isn't what I wanted to talk to you about." He cleared his throat and glanced up at her. The eyes that met hers weren't nervous. He was deadly serious. The gravity of the moment settled on her, vividly focusing her attention to him. "Guardian recruited me when I turned twenty-one."

She blinked at the jump in conversational direction. "To stage accidents? To make it seem like people died in those accidents."

"Yeah, I can't talk to you about the details of what I do for the organization, but I want you to know, I am one of the best in the world at what I do. I am more than capable of protecting you and Ethan should anyone come up this mountain, and I won't hesitate to lay down my life for either of you."

"Oh." Her fingers shook in front of her mouth.

What he was saying mimicked her thoughts. Her life had shifted in the last weeks and months. *Shifted? No... changed...* Her outlook on life had changed because of this man. He'd become the central point of both her and Ethan's lives. Ryan was a gravitational pull they couldn't resist and had tethered them in his orbit. They belonged here, with him. She knew it as certainly as she knew she loved him.

He reached out and trailed his finger along her leg. "It's important you know I want you both here, with me, and that I have the ability to make sure you're both safe."

"I never doubted it. Not once." The man had always taken care of them, even when he didn't want them here. He was kind and giving, the exact opposite of Ethan's father. "Do you think there is a real threat against us? I mean, we aren't witnesses to anything. We don't want anything of his."

He tossed his pillow up to the headboard and moved to mirror her position, sitting with his back to the headboard. "There is a legitimate threat against both of you."

He lifted his arm, and she leaned into him. She relaxed into his embrace and whispered, "For how long? I just don't understand how anyone could think either Ethan or I could be a threat. Can you?"

"People like the ones looking for you don't need a rational reason to do what they do. It is sufficient to know they are after you and Guardian is working the issue. We are safe here. We are going to be okay."

He kissed the top of her head, and she relaxed with the realization she believed him, just because he said it was so. Lord, how her life had changed. "It's hard to believe."

"What's hard to believe?" He kissed the top of her head again, and she smiled at the sweet gesture.

"That I'd find happiness." A sad chuckle fell from her at the admission.

"You've had a hard life."

She nodded. "Like you. We've been alone for a long time. Even though we were around people, nobody knew us or knew about my past."

"Do you ever think about looking for your family?"

"I did. The woman who, I don't know, I guess controlled us while we were waiting for buyers, told me they were dead. She took great joy in letting me know no one was coming to help. I didn't believe her. Later, when Ethan was in preschool and I was allowed to take him to the library for story time, I checked. I used the time he was listening to the stories to research news releases and obituaries. They're gone." Of course, she was listed as a casualty, too. It was surreal reading about her parents, sister and herself perishing.

"I'm so sorry for your loss." He wrapped both arms around her and held her to his chest.

"It all seems like a horrible dream. Before Ethan, I imagined being rescued. I watched as the others with me lost hope, like me. Then Harvey happened. The first thing he did was threaten to hurt me if I was disobedient." The faint scars that lined her wrists were barely discernible to anyone but her. Harvey's eyes as he cut her and watched her bleed still haunted her. He was excited by the blood, by her pain, and by her begging. He'd never cut deep enough to open a vein, but she didn't doubt for a second that he would. She shivered and pushed closer to Ryan.

"And then Ethan happened."

She nodded and leaned away so she could see him. "He was so innocent, and he needed me as much as I needed him. Of course, I knew Harvey would kill both of us if I ever deviated from his demands."

Ryan's jaw tightened, and his eyes flashed with anger. She reached up, laid her hand on his cheek and shook her head. "All of it, my past, Harvey, *all of it*, was worth being where I am today with you and Ethan. I wouldn't change a thing."

"You are a remarkable woman." Ryan pulled her to him and rolled them so they were lying flat on the bed. His lips traveled her body, his hands accented and punctuated their journey. She held him and let herself be consumed by his attention. The warmth of her skin amplified under his tender caresses. She ran her hands over the muscles in his arms and chest. He was so strong, solid. He'd become her foundation.

He centered over her and nudged her core with his erection while holding her attention with his gaze. "I wouldn't change a thing," she whispered as he rocked into her. Sweet heavens, how could this remarkable man be with her. Overwhelmed. That was how she felt. Overwhelmed with gratitude, with happiness, with... emotions she couldn't process, didn't want to examine.

"I don't deserve you." Ryan's whisper caressed her soul.

"You do. You deserve this. Us. We both do. Life owes us." She arched under him as he filled her. So good. So unbelievably wonderful when he made love to her. She knew he wasn't just scratching an itch. Ryan was making love to her, whether or not they'd said the words.

"It does." He rocked into her and settled deep inside her. Their bodies aligned. His hips moved forward and back, stroking sensations deep within her as his kisses fueled the intensity of their union. Neither of them tried to hurry the pace. Her hands traveled his body. Her hips matched his languid strokes.

She memorized the feeling of him under her fingers, his strength, his gentleness, his dominance. He led her through this intimate dance and set their pace to music only lovers could hear. She shattered under him and felt when he reached his own release. His body strained over her; his muscles tightened around her. She smiled as his body weight sagged on top of her, as if being held in her arms was where he needed to be. Being loved by someone as wonderful as Ryan Wolf was a blessing, one she prayed she'd never lose.

# CHAPTER 19

"Are you ready?" The sun had yet to come up. Ryan stood beside the driver's side door of the Guardian vehicle. His truck and the enclosed trailer he used to haul building supplies was parked behind her vehicle.

"Yes. I'm going to go slow, though, I don't like the hairpin curves."

"Slow is best. I'm in no rush. If it gets too late, we'll spend the night off the mountain." He leaned in to kiss her.

"Are you sure Dog can't go with us? He wants to!" Ethan was half hanging out of his truck, petting the animal.

"You're going to fall on your head!" Bethanie admonished. The boy rolled his eyes at her and continued to pet Dog.

"Go on, start out. I'll corral the daredevil and follow you down." Bethanie was right, the kid was going to end up on his head if he leaned out any further.

"Are you sure you're okay with him riding with you?" She shook her head when Ethan overbalanced and grabbed frantically for the outside door handle.

"Whoops!"

"Whoops, my ass," Bethanie muttered.

Ryan's head snapped toward his woman, and he laughed. She rarely cussed. "Go, I've got him. Once we get off the mountain, I'll pass you and lead the way."

She nodded, hit the button to raise the window and pulled out from in front of the safe house.

Ryan trudged over to his 4x4 truck, grabbed Ethan by the back of the coat and lifted him back through the window. "You are going to break your neck."

"But Dog wants to come with."

"Dog can amuse himself for a day without you."

"He'll get lonely."

"He'll be fine." Ryan made sure Ethan was all the way inside the cab before he gave Dog a pat on the head and rounded the cab of the truck to the driver's side door.

"Okay, ready?"

"Yeah! Can we have McDonald's?"

"Sure, for lunch. I thought we'd take your mom out to dinner at a nice place."

"Italian? She loves Italian."

"We can do that." He put the truck in gear, released the parking brake, and pulled onto the road.

"Are we spending the night off the mountain?"

"That depends on how long everything takes. The current melt has cleared up the roads so we can come back up tonight without worrying about ice on the blacktop." There was a worrisome late season storm warning for the states east of them, another reason getting resupplied was necessary.

"We have chains so we can come home even if it snows, right?"

Ryan turned to look at the boy. *Home*. He smiled and winked. "You bet. We can come home."

"Dog will get worried if we don't come back tonight."

"He'll be fine. When I leave for work, he's alone for weeks or months at a time."

"Yeah? What do you do?"

"Ahh..." *Stepped right into that pile of shit, didn't you?* "I worked for a company called Guardian Security."

"Worked? Are you a police officer?"

"More like a trouble-shooter. I helped them keep things running smoothly."

The boy's body stiffened, and he jerked toward Ryan. "You don't have to leave to go to work now do you?"

"Nope. You and your mom have my undivided attention for the foreseeable future."

"How long is that?"

"A long time."

"Cool."

*Cool. Yes, it was.* Ryan tapped the steering wheel in time with the country CD playing in the cab. He listened as Ethan expounded on the excursion he and Dog had yesterday. Bethanie was slowly giving her son more freedom and allowed him to go outside without constant supervision, although she hovered. He couldn't blame her. That was one thing he promised himself he wouldn't influence. They needed to find their own 'normal', and Bethanie needed to learn to trust her son when he was outside. The night they'd spent lost in the woods had scarred her far more than it had her son. Although Ethan wasn't actively rebelling against the tight apron strings, Ryan could see they were starting to chafe the boy.

He and Ethan chatted until they drove off the mountain and passed Bethanie, who'd pulled off the road and waited for them. Ethan waved wildly at her as they passed and took the lead.

They arrived in Charlotte just after nine in the morning, and Ryan drove straight to the mall. Bethanie got out of the vehicle, locked it and climbed into the truck. Ethan slid over the back of the front seat and buckled up in the rear. "Mom, we get to go to McDonald's!"

"Really? For lunch or breakfast?"

"Both!" Ethan grabbed the back of the seat. "Please!"

"Breakfast for now. We'll play it by ear after that.

Okay?" Ryan offered a compromise. Bethanie threw him a smile, and Ethan gave a long-suffering sigh in the back seat. Coming from Ethan, a sigh could mean any number of things. His mind flashed to Moriah and her variety of grunts. Though a decade younger, Ethan was on track to surpass her lack of vocabulary.

$\sim$

"I'm exhausted." Bethanie dropped her head against the back of the front seat. Her eyes closed and she yawned.

"I'm not. Dog is going to love the rawhide bone I got him." Ethan held up the three-foot braided rawhide and brandished it like a sword.

"You are spoiling him." Ryan glanced in the mirror at Ethan. The boy gave him a cherubic smile and laughed.

"I'm surprised we got all the equipment and groceries into the trailer." Bethanie yawned again. The sound was echoed in the back seat. Ryan glanced back again and noticed Ethan had wedged himself in the corner of the seat and had his feet up. Once he stopped moving, he was going to be out. The kid had run circles around them all day. Ryan was amazed he was still awake after the massive plate of spaghetti he'd eaten.

"I broke the order up. I have a pretty good idea what will fit in this trailer. The rest of the system will come in next week." In a different city. He'd run down the mountain and pick it up and anything else they'd forgotten.

"How many times has your truck and trailer made the run up the mountain?"

"Plenty. I've been working on the house for years."

"You must know the Charlotte home improvement and lumber yards pretty well then."

"No, not really. I ordered a lot of the equipment, cabinets, etcetera, online. I have people in a couple of different towns who I pay to accept deliveries, and they place the order in storage units. I get what I need when I need it." None of it was in his name. He didn't make numerous trips to the same location, so nobody took notice of him. Off the grid and out of mind was a necessity for his existence.

"You spent too much money on us." She reached out her hand, and Ryan took it, driving with his left hand.

"You both needed clothes, and Ethan needed some stuff to entertain himself. The movies were on sale."

"Still, I don't want us to become a burden." She squeezed his hand as she spoke.

Ryan glanced at her. Her eyes were shut. His gaze lifted to the rearview mirror and he smiled. Ethan's eyes were closed, too. His head tipped back, and Ryan caught a small snore from the boy.

"You will never become a burden to me." He lifted her hand and kissed the back of it, smiling as he put her hand back down on the seat. She was asleep. He drew a deep breath and settled his view on the horizon, on guard for anything that could jeopardize the perfection he had in the cab of the truck. *His family.*

While the drive back to the mountain was uneventful, there were two or three cars that concerned him, but they turned off or passed him, and he eventually relaxed. At least until it started snowing. Big, wet flakes fluttered down from the heavens. Ryan rolled his shoulders. Based on the forecasts, he needed to get all the food, supplies, and equipment to the big cave tonight or it could be a week or more before he'd be able to reach the truck again.

He pulled into the covered parking area he'd built and woke Bethanie. "Hey, sleepyhead."

She blinked and lifted her head, wincing a bit. "I slept all the way?"

"You were indeed exhausted."

She turned and glanced back at Ethan. The boy's mouth was wide open, and he was snoring, giving an old fashion hand saw a run for the money.

"Is it snowing?"

"Yep. Winter was late this year. There's an old wives' tale around here that winter isn't over until the Mother's Day snowstorm hits. We have another month to enjoy nature's folly. Let's take Ethan up to bed, and then I'll come back and unload."

"What? No. We can help."

"No need."

"No, we need to pull our own weight. Ethan, honey. We're home."

*Home*. Ryan turned to hide the grin that split his face. Indeed, they were home.

Dog sat at the trail's head. His tongue lolled out the side of his mouth as his ass danced on the frozen dirt, waiting for Ethan to get out of the truck.

Ryan pulled the largest cooler out of the back of the truck and waited for Bethanie and Ethan to grab a few bags. They worked for three hours, unloading, unpacking, and putting stuff away while Ryan made trip after trip to the cave. He used a dolly to bring up the heavy equipment. Come morning, any trail they had left would be obliterated by the snow already starting to accumulate.

He locked the truck after unhooking the trailer and putting a boot on the trailer wheels. Other than Shadows, he'd never seen anyone up on the mountain, but he wasn't going to leave his property ready and available for someone who just happened to come along. His truck was locked and alarmed, and he took the long way to the cavern. He stopped and lifted onto the top of a boulder. He heard Dog padding behind him and moved over when the animal's claws scrambled up the large rock. The beast settled next to him.

He reached out and patted the thick, wet fur at the dog's haunches. "Who'd have thought it, boy? We have a family."

The animal lay down beside him, his head on his

paws. His ears helicoptered as he listened to the night noises. Ryan eased back on his gloved palms and stretched his legs out in front of him. The cold seeped through his clothes, but he didn't feel like moving. Right now he, like Dog, watched for threats. The precious contents of the cavern were a responsibility he readily shouldered. The weight of that obligation wasn't a millstone. In fact, the heft of this new responsibility blanketed him in ultimate purpose. He was more than his upbringing, more than his past. He'd tenured his resignation and walked away from an abyss of evil. The ease of that decision shocked him on many levels.

He'd always pictured his future as a solitary existence and a death without anyone knowing he'd left life's bindings. He didn't deserve the happiness that settled around him. He didn't deserve Bethanie or Ethan, but he was fucking going to claim them, and fuck anyone who dared come after them. An evil smile crossed his face. He had a *reason* to kill now. It wasn't a job any longer. This was personal. God help the bastards who hunted his family because Satan's fury was nothing compared to the obliteration he'd unleash on the motherfuckers.

# CHAPTER 20

One answered the incoming video call, noting that Three was precisely on time, as she had been for the last nine weeks. She clicked on the video request and ensured her encryption was activated.

"We found her."

One lifted a brow and waited.

"We have located the vehicle parked at a mall in Charlotte, North Carolina. We've acquired the security film of the parking lot. She was picked up. We have the plates of the truck. They trace back to an octogenarian from Boca Raton, Florida. We are working on accessing the traffic camera feeds for that day."

"One of our best teams needs to be sent to the area."

"Already done. If she's being hidden, she may have protection. I want no excuses for her escape. The ones who remained loyal to us from the remnants of the Colombia mission have been added."

"Indeed. Two's replacement needs to ascend to her position."

"I concur. Other than the update on the woman, we have movement in Venezuela. The factions are fighting, and they have not noticed us, or our agenda. The Candidate is there for humanitarian relief, and her efforts have been reported widely in Europe. The coverage has not made it to the US."

"The woman needs to be put down before the Candidate's efforts are made public here."

"We have confirmed all other merchandise the Candidate worked with in her tenure have been recycled. They are not an issue."

"Then we proceed with all haste. Do you need me to pull my technology assets to encourage access to the information you require?"

"Can you pull your techs without jeopardizing any ongoing missions?"

"I have four who are laboring on the contents of the Russian hacker's hard drives. They can be spared for this."

"The contents? I can't remember when you briefed you had full access to the information on that drive." Three leaned forward and her fingers tapped on her keyboard as she frowned at the screen.

"I briefed it. I'll pull the tapes if you require." One lifted an eyebrow. Three questioning her briefing was unsettling.

"Not necessary. I recall the meeting. I'll be thankful when Two arrives. The balance is off, wouldn't you agree?"

"Assuredly, the harmony has been disrupted. Another reason to double our efforts on the information contained on that hard drive." One was glad Three recognized a lack of synergy.

"Has there been anything new gleaned from the information they are recovering?"

"Unfortunately, no. There is a terabyte of raw information. Making connections and putting things into context is going to take time." One allowed a smile. "When we do, Guardian will no longer be a problem."

"I feel the need to remind you your line of thinking could be faulty. It has been years since the hacker was killed. By now, Guardian could have erected a defense against all the intelligence on the drive."

One's anger boiled. Three was technically correct, but the reprimand did not sit well. "We will go through each piece of information, line by line. If there is a weakness, a way in, we will follow it."

"Of course. Now shall we move on to another item on the agenda?"

Three looked down at her desk and missed the sneer One sent her way. Perhaps it was time to start another candidate listing.

# CHAPTER 21

"Is there anything else we need?" Ryan glanced at the list they'd built over the last week. The snow hadn't abated, but getting off the mountain with his chains wouldn't be a problem. He needed to pick up his orders, and he'd stop for whatever they'd forgotten before he made his way back up the mountain. The trip would take him to Fayetteville and back through Charlotte. He would avoid the areas they visited before, limiting his exposure. The trip had been planned in advance to ensure he wasn't crossing the same areas. Humans were creatures of habit. They drove the same route, ate at the same places, saw the same people. Even the most adventurous of those he tracked had always fallen back on habit. It was how he made his kills. Gambling on human nature was a sure thing.

"Don't forget the peanut butter!" Ethan's voice carried from the front room where he and Dog were supposed to be reading a book for a homeschool report.

Bethanie rolled her eyes and called back, "We have plenty."

"Hey, you can never have too much peanut butter." Ryan chuckled and pulled her to him as he leaned on the counter.

"He needs to eat more veggies."

"He'll be fine. He's strong and healthy." Ryan dropped a kiss on her upturned lips.

"He'll turn into a peanut."

"Perhaps. You know how to reach me if you need anything." He'd gone through the steps over and over, but leaving them alone for the first time was, well hell, it was fucking nerve-racking.

"I do. And I know what to do in case of an emergency. We'll be fine. You'll be gone two days."

"Max."

"Don't try to push it. According to the Highway Patrol's website, the roads are horrible, and I worry."

"You saw that, did you?" He'd been working on his route this morning when she'd brought him a freshly baked cinnamon roll.

"I did. Don't take any unnecessary chances. We'll be fine."

"You know how to activate the alarm. Make sure you do that each evening after Dog comes in for the night."

"I will. We'll be okay. I watch you do it every night."

"We can postpone the pickup." He didn't like the idea of leaving them on the mountain alone.

"Then we can't finish the garden. Seriously, we are going to be okay. He has homework. I'm going to start the seedlings, and we have a bunch of new movies. We will be fine."

Ryan pulled her into a hug. He'd feel better if Bethanie had access to his weapons. Once the weather cleared and he could take them out and train them on safe handling and shooting techniques, he'd feel better about leaving them. *Nah, he really wouldn't.*

He'd checked in with Guardian last night. Even though he no longer worked as an assassin, he was armpit deep in protecting Bethanie and Ethan, and Guardian wanted them safe. So, he still had access, which was a damn good thing. There was no further information, which drove him insane. It could mean whoever was looking for his family had given up, but based on his experience, he doubted it. If it were him, he'd be waiting for some indication of their whereabouts based on the life they left. Thank God Bethanie and Ethan knew not to reach out to anyone in New York. All tendrils of their past life had to be severed, and he'd gone over everything, twice. No online presence. Ethan's homeschooling was cloaked, and Bethanie's web browsing for the things she needed for the garden was done anonymously. She put the items in the shopping cart, and he ordered the items with an alias.

"You better go." Bethanie squeezed him tighter, belaying her words.

"I know." He squeezed her against him as if to graft her into his DNA, and wasn't that some sappy shit. He let her go and grabbed the list of things they'd forgotten on the last trip down the hill.

He pocketed the list and held her hand before he gave a sharp whistle. Both Dog and Ethan came running. The boy, however, didn't stop. He flew at Ryan, and Ryan caught him. The boy's arms wrapped around his waist. He rubbed the kid's back. Fuck him, he teared up. It was the first time Ethan had hugged him. He closed his eyes and held on. He cracked his eyes open at the touch of Bethanie's hand on his arm. She smiled up at him. Words weren't really needed. Although he'd never say it out loud, she knew what the hug meant to him.

Ethan pushed away and smiled. "Don't forget peanut butter."

"I won't. You take care of your mom, okay?"

"Dog and I will protect her."

"Don't doubt it for a minute."

"When are you going to be back?"

"No later than two tomorrow afternoon." He was probably going to have to spend the night in Charlotte. He hated the idea, but it was the smartest course of action. He leaned over and kissed Bethanie again.

"Gross, you guys!" Ethan spun on his heel. "C'mon Dog." They raced back to the couch. Ethan flopped on it and Dog jumped up after him. The ensuing laughter, yips and tussling as they fought over the corner seat were loud and filled the cavern with happiness and life. He'd had no idea what he'd been missing—which was probably a good thing. How in the fuck would he have made it through the first forty years of his existence if he'd understood what he didn't have? Now, he knew, and he fucking coveted every second of his time with the two people who had transformed his life.

With his arm around Bethanie, they strolled to the back door.

"Be safe." She wrapped her arms around his neck, and he dropped a kiss on her upturned lips.

"I will. I'll be back as soon as I can." He cupped her neck, and his thumb traced her cheekbone. The words he wanted to say were at the tip of his tongue, but this wasn't the place or the time.

"We'll be fine." She smiled at him and nodded to the door. "Get gone so you can come back. We'll miss you."

Ryan dropped a final kiss on her lips and walked out the door. This was going to be the quickest trip down the mountain in history.

Or not. Ryan rubbed his neck as he watched the clerks at the electronics warehouse search for his order. For fuck's sake. He glanced at his watch again.

The manager came over, and a new round of fingers pointing at screens ensued.

He'd paid over three thousand dollars for a track system that would rotate the crops around the grow lights, giving them optimum exposure. "If you can't find it, I'm out of here."

"No, sir, we have it, but it was sent to the store on the other side of the city." The manager glanced up at him and smiled. "I'll have it brought over. Will two o'clock be all right?"

"No, it will not be all right. Give me the address, I'll go pick it up myself," Ryan ground out.

The manager's eyes popped wide, and he nodded. "I'll be glad to take ten percent off the purchase price."

"Don't bother. The address?"

Ryan snatched the business card the manager handed him with the address jotted down on the back of it. He plugged the address into his truck's GPS and groaned. Thankfully, he already had all the groceries and supplies. This last pick up would set him back a couple of hours, but he should still make it back up the mountain by two.

"Mom!" Ethan shouted from the front room.

"Stop yelling at me and come in here if you want to talk to me, please!" Her hands were wrist deep in dirt. She'd been labeling containers and filling small egg-crate-sized cups with growing mixture. The seedlings would start in the small containers and then when a root system was established, they'd be moved to the hydroponic cradles. The small amount of soil would eventually wash away as nutrient-enhanced water dripped over the roots.

"Can I go down and wait for Ryan?" Ethan leaned against the doorway.

"No. You need to stay here." She pointed to a bag of dirt. "Would you bring that over here please?"

Ethan rolled his eyes but dragged the dirt toward her. "Why can't I?"

"Because where he parks the truck is too far away for me to see you." She snipped the bag open and used her hands to cup enough soil to fill the containers in front of her.

"But I know the way. You let me unload the truck with Ryan. I was by myself then. I'm not a baby, and Ryan has taught me how to be careful."

She stopped what she was doing and turned her attention to her son. "I know you're not a baby. I'm sorry if you think I'm treating you like one, but, until we know for sure there isn't anyone looking for us, we need to be safe. Ryan asked that we stay in the cavern while he was gone. I think we can wait just a bit longer, don't you?"

Ethan shoved his hands into his jean pockets. "I know the way. I'm not going to get lost, and there isn't anyone else on this stinking mountain."

*Wow.* "Okay, I'm not sure what's going on here,

Bud. I thought you liked living here?" She sat back on her heels.

"I do, it's just... nothing." He shrugged his shoulders and glanced out of the cave.

"It is only an hour or two before Ryan comes back. How about you watch a movie? You can bring it in here if you want."

Ethan sighed. "Mom, I don't need constant supervision. I'm twelve, not two."

"I didn't mean to imply that you were. You can watch it in the front room if you want?"

"I'm going to my room."

"Okay." She watched him turn around and shuffle out. "Hey?"

He turned around and glanced at her.

"I think you're a fantastic young man. You make me proud, every day."

He shrugged his shoulders again. She heard Dog's claws tripping across the hardwoods following Ethan toward the incline.

She sighed and looked at the dirt in front of her. More and more, Ethan was looking for independence. She let him set his own boundaries when it was safe. Was she overly cautious? Perhaps. She dropped her head back between her shoulders and stared at the roof of the cavern. When whatever threat they'd been living under went away, she'd make sure Ethan attended the homeschool functions in the area. It would be an effort, but he needed friends and interaction. Shielding him for the short term was for his own good, although when you're twelve, she didn't suppose understanding limitations was easy. She glanced at the containers she needed to fill and drew a deep breath. She'd finish, wash up, and then maybe they'd both go down to wait for Ryan. The thought brought a smile to her face. It was just overnight, but she missed him. Obviously, Ethan did, too.

She let the soil filter through her hands and pressed it gently into the small cups. Three months ago, she'd never have imagined such happiness. Of course, she was in love with Ryan. In love with the way he treated her, the way he treated Ethan, the way he cared for both of them. She could remember the warmth of her family before she'd been taken. Random feelings that still existed deep inside her hummed when she thought back, but in reality, other than Ethan's love for her, she'd never felt the kind of love and connection she felt for Ryan. They shared a passionate, desperate love that spread from their bed to them as a couple and then continued on to the family they were forming. That type of love transcended what she had been to what they were now.

Granted, his love was buried under a pretty gruff exterior. She'd watched Prepper television shows late at night when Ethan was asleep, and her mind wouldn't shut off. Ryan was obviously of like mind to the people who'd built off-grid, but he wasn't crazy like some of the characters featured on the shows. They were probably cast for ratings only. Ryan lived away from everyone by choice, and thank God he did. If they hadn't come here, she had no idea what would have happened to them.

But they had been directed here, and they'd met Ryan. Ryan Wolf the big, gruff teddy bear in disguise. *Oh dear, his cussing!* She chuckled as she pushed more dirt into the little cups. The words he said. He was trying to censor himself, but it was pretty much guaranteed Ethan now knew every cuss word in the universe. Of all the problems that could revolve around her, limiting Ethan's exposure to R-rated words was one she'd gladly tackle.

Lifting to her knees, she grabbed the last three seedling crates and set them down on the far side of the already filled cups. Another hour and she'd be done. She carefully scratched her nose, trying not to smudge too much dirt. She gazed around the large cavern. Ryan had run the wiring for the lights and was picking up the bulbs and the track system. She'd wait until the grow lights were installed before she started the seeds Ryan would bring up the mountain. She sighed and cupped her hands in the nutrient-rich soil. It was almost spring—a time of rebirth for her, for Ethan, and for Ryan.

# CHAPTER 22

R yan manhandled the truck up through the frozen ruts. It was damn cold and getting colder by the minute. While winter had been slow in coming this year, it was being a tenacious motherfucker, refusing to let go. He pulled into the sheltered area where he normally parked his truck and slammed the brakes on. His eyes fixed on the tire tracks, fresh tracks, smaller vehicle. He threw the truck into park, turned it off, grabbed his forty-five from under the front seat and was out of the vehicle.

He slipped to the far side of the enclosed trailer and moved forward, quietly. He bent down and examined the tracks. Someone had done a K turn. The mud at the edge of the tracks was frozen, but the deeper grooves weren't.

Ryan eyed the trail. There was a profusion of

tracks. He moved forward, careful to scan for threats. He dropped and searched the tracks. *Fuck!*

*Ethan's boots.*

*Dog's tracks.*

*Massive prints. Boots. Men, one, no... two... at least three men.*

*Blood, small drops.*

*Ethan's tracks there... moving to the east.*

*The men had followed.*

*Ethan was running here.*

Ryan pushed on, stopping at another large area of messed up tracks.

*More blood.*

*Drops in an arc. An arm thrown out?*

Ryan's eyes read the scene. Dog had attacked. He could see where he launched from his hind legs, three feet outside the track impacted area. Just there was blood and an imprint of fabric on the ground so the man Dog had lunged for had fallen. Further into the area, the tracks were muddled, but there was a lot of blood. Dog's fur mixed into the tumult of tracks. He saw where Dog had bled and where the man bled. Different patterns. Blood drops scattered in a different pattern for the taller one, the human. Dog had lain here. He put a hand in the depression where Dog had bled. Where was the dog now? He glanced at a bloody trail. Wolf prints only.

Ethan's tracks were no more. Two men returned to the parking area. One carried Ethan, his tracks were much deeper on the return. The other man was injured. From the thick splattering of blood, Dog had punctured a major blood vessel.

He hadn't seen a vehicle on the way up the mountain, but there were numerous roads and multiple options. If you weren't familiar with the mountain, getting lost or turned around was almost guaranteed.

He rose from a squat and quickly worked the trail back toward the cavern. More blood. Fuck, too much blood.

He took off for the cave as fast as he could run. He cleared the ridge and died a little inside. Dog was lying on the trail in a pool of blood.

The dog lifted his head as he approached.

"Its okay, bud. Let me look."

The dog whimpered. Ryan held his gun, his finger on the trigger, safety off as he examined the dog. Two stab wounds. One on the shoulder, the other along the neck. The neck wound was the bleeder. The more the animal tried to move, the more it bled.

He searched the trail ahead. Only one set of tracks. Ethan's and Dog's, going down to the parking area.

Ryan glanced up toward the cavern.

Ice coursed through his veins. His mind processed the scenarios. Everything else receded to the background.

The motherfuckers who dared come here were going to pay with their lives.

He stood and surveyed the area, as Lycos, a killer, an assassin, an apex predator. He surveyed the ground as a father, though not by genetics, as a husband, though not by law. The enemy had brought the war to him.

Ryan put his weapon on safety and tucked it securely between his belt and his jeans, keeping it outside his clothing and readily available. His mind raced with implications as he lifted the animal in his arms.

He put one foot in front of the other and moved as fast as he could with a squirming animal in his arms.

Whoever had come up the mountain had Ethan.

*Bethanie?*

He hadn't seen tracks. The front of the cave... they could have taken her from there.

His breath came in measured puffs. His eyes roamed the rocks, the snow banks, and the crevices, the landscape as familiar to him as the back of his hand. He saw nothing.

The back door was locked. He lifted his knee, propping some of the massive dog's weight on his leg as he keyed in his code. He listened and stared into the depths of the cavern. Lights were on in the kitchen. He heard the tap turn on.

He bent and laid Dog on the floor, grabbing his weapon as he lifted. He tapped the access panel and killed all the lights in the cavern.

"What? Ethan? Did you turn off the lights?" Bethanie's voice carried from the kitchen.

"Bethanie!" Ryan bellowed as he turned the lights back on.

She appeared at the doorway; her eyes huge. "What happened?" She ran toward him.

"Where's Ethan?"

"In his room."

"Go check."

She popped up and screamed, "Ethan!"

He heard her pounding up the incline, her terrified screams of her son's name echoing in the confines of the cave.

"Shhh... I've got you, big boy." Ryan pulled his medical pack off the bench and leaned down again as Bethanie flew down the ramp.

"He's not there!"

"I saw tracks. There was a struggle. Someone has him."

"Has him? Oh my God! No!"

Ryan reached up and grabbed her, forcing her to look at him. "Go upstairs, put warm clothes on. Get a change of clothes for Ethan. Put them in a plastic bag then come back down here. Dress in layers. Like I showed you, remember?"

"What are we going to do? Who has Ethan? Oh my God!" She was gasping for air, and wild desperation had supplanted rationality. She wasn't tracking, and he couldn't let that happen.

He grabbed her shoulders and shook her as he yelled, "Stop it! We have to move. We have to move *now*. Go get dressed in warm clothes. Layers. Get the small pack out of Ethan's room and put clean clothes into it. Do you understand?"

She nodded. He released her. "Go. Now!"

She bolted back up the incline, a keening wail trailed her.

Ryan put his hand on the straining animal, keeping him from trying to rise. "I'm sorry, bud, this is all I can do for you now." He filled the syringe with morphine, guessing at the animal's weight. He'd knock the dog out, keep him from moving and injuring himself more. He injected the sedative and secured thick stacks of gauze with an ace bandage to try to stem the bleeding. By the time he was done packing and wrapping the wounds, the dog was out. He laid his hand on the animal's head for a split second and then raced up the incline.

He could hear Bethanie in the bedroom, but that wasn't where he was headed. He flew into the office. The eighth shelf up, the seventh book in, he popped the lock and pushed the shelf out of the way. It took seconds to enter the vault. He stripped off his jacket and slid on his shoulder harnesses. Twin Desert Eagle, forty-five caliber, automatic loaders were filled with ammo and slipped into the holsters. He slapped a web camo belt around his waist and clipped on three ammo packs. He lifted his leg and strapped a knife onto his ankle before grabbing a small pouch containing binoculars and snapped it into place.

"What is this?"

Ryan glanced at Bethanie. She had her jacket on and the small pack he'd told her to grab. He pulled his jeans down and lifted the other leg. He strapped a small caliber handgun to that leg. "A weapons vault."

"What do you need this for?"

He turned on her and lifted his hands. "We are not having that discussion now."

He grabbed a web belt and clipped a sheathed knife onto it and an empty ammo pouch. "Put this on and go fill that pouch with protein bars."

He didn't wait to see if she'd moved. He jumped up to the top of the cabinet and grabbed a coiled length of rope and a pack containing emergency flares, a hand shovel, a flint and steel, matches and kindling.

He put his coat on, threw the rope across his chest and snapped the pack to the back of his ammo belt. He reached up and grabbed his M-4. He'd built it. It fit him, and he fit it. He secured the vault and headed downstairs.

Bethanie was leaning over the dog, petting him. She stood as he approached. "What happened to him?"

"He attacked whoever has Ethan. They stabbed him. Twice."

"Is he going to live?"

"Don't know." Ryan headed out the door. "We are going up to the top of the mountain."

"Why? Shouldn't we get in the truck and go find them?"

His steps ate up the ground, and he could hear her scrambling behind him. "No. We need to go up. We can see most of the mountain from here. With the snow that has been falling, we should be able to see any vehicle tracks and know where to start our search.

"Who took him?"

"The better question would be why was he outside?" Ryan scrambled up to the very top of the mountain and pulled out his binoculars.

"He asked if he could meet you at the parking area. I told him no. I told him to watch a movie. I thought he was in his room."

"The back door was still locked."

They looked at each other. "Dog's door," Ryan said, and Bethanie nodded her head. Ethan had to have slipped out of Dog's door and gone outside without permission.

He steadied his breathing and started his strip and grid search of the entire fucking mountain.

"Anything?" Bethanie's panic voice asked.

"Working it," Ryan replied as he moved along the road he knew he could see. The snow was wet and clinging. The forecast was for six inches, and at least half of that had fallen in the last hour or so. It would rapidly obliterate any trace of... *There.*

He dropped the binoculars and pulled his weapon off his back.

"Are you going to shoot something?" Fear rippled through her voice.

"No, the scope has better magnification than the binoculars." He pulled the caps off his scope and lifted the weapon into firing position. It took him a few seconds to find the road, but yes, there were fresh tracks, one way, and if they were on that road, they'd find the safe house.

He slung the weapon over his shoulder. "Come on."

"Did you see them?" He could hear her boots clambering over the rocks as she followed him.

Ryan ignored her to concentrate on completing a steep descent without breaking his leg. He wedged his hand between a cleft of a rock, slithered over the edge on his belly and lowered his body all but three feet from the bottom before he released his hold and dropped. They were taking the fastest route, not the easiest. He turned and held his arms up and out to help her down the sheer drop off.

She never hesitated. She was game, he'd give her that. She swung her boots off the ledge and twisted, holding on to the rock. "Ready?" She peeked over her shoulder.

"I've got you. Push back a bit when you drop."

Her back tightened, and then she pushed off the face of the rock with her foot. She lost her grip, but her backward momentum was perfect. She'd pushed far enough away that she wouldn't leave a trail of skin and blood on the rock. He caught her and righted her immediately.

"You didn't answer me. Did you see them?"

"No, only tracks."

"Do you think it is the people Guardian warned us against?"

Her voice elevated and lowered with each hop from rock to rock. He jumped up onto a boulder and extended his hand back to her. "I have no idea who they are."

"Do you think he's okay? Do you think they have hurt him?"

"Don't."

"Don't what?"

"Don't do that. It's counterproductive. What we are doing now is what you need to be concentrating on."

They traveled for several hundred feet down another steep incline. The route was hard, dangerous, and fast. Bethanie remained quiet and soldiered on, which gave him time to think. The safe house would be where he'd go if one of his men were injured. Heat, lights, bathroom, a place to stash the kid, and to make plans. They could continue down the mountain, but unless they applied a tourniquet to whatever appendage Dog had maimed, half of the duo that grabbed Ethan was going to die. The amount of blood loss necessitated fast action, especially if the mission wasn't just to grab Ethan. Given the information he'd had from Guardian, it wasn't. They wanted both Bethanie and Ethan dead, and in order to get to Bethanie, they'd leverage Ethan. His mind snaked over the many ways they could use the child. A sneer lifted his lip. He'd peel the skin off anyone who hurt that boy and make sure they lived to endure the entirety of his revenge.

He turned and extended a hand again to Bethanie. Her focus was on her step, and her brow was furrowed with worry. He wished he could erase it, but this was reality, her reality and Ethan's, and it had come to bite them all in the ass.

The cabin was a mile further up the canyon. He waited at the base of the crevice they'd traversed. Bethanie stopped beside him, her breathing ragged. He examined the ghost of a trail that led between the trees and down below the safe house. They'd have to climb up to the back of the house, but from the house, the trail was almost impossible to see.

Snow fell around them. He could hear the small tinkling noise of the frozen particles hitting each other. Hearing snowfall had always been a miracle. Today, the sound lent nothing but distance to the equation. Distance from Ethan, from safety, and from the person he'd hoped to become.

"There, between those two trees, do you see the trail?"

She nodded.

"I'm going to go down that trail and then up the incline and get Ethan. I need you to stay here." She opened her mouth to argue, and he shook his head. "No, I can't do what I need to do if I'm worried about you." He grabbed her hand and stepped down and around a rock outcropping. The small overhang was clear of snow for the most part. "I'll fix you a quick shelter. If I'm not back in two hours, you activate that cell phone, and you punch that emergency app. There are hand warmers in the outside pocket of Ethan's backpack. If you get too cold, you open them up and shove them inside your clothes, near your core."

"I remember." She helped him set up a quick lean-to, and he put a stack of pine boughs under the overhang. She could huddle into the boughs, and they would keep her off the rock.

He slid his watch off his wrist. "Where is your phone?"

She patted the front pocket of her coat.

"It has a charge?"

She nodded, her eyes large and worried.

"Two hours. If I'm not back, push that alarm."

"Please, bring our boy home." Bethanie looked up at him, pleading.

He grabbed her and clutched her close to his chest. "I'll bring him back. Do not leave this place unless I call you. I can't worry about you and take care of Ethan."

She nodded. He pulled away and started off before he turned and whispered loudly. "Don't activate that alarm because of gunshots. Two hours, no matter what you hear, all right?"

She nodded and stepped back under the shelter. Lycos turned and adapted to the terrain. He knew this land, and he'd prepared for the day he'd have to defend the safe house. He knew the structure's advantages and its weaknesses. He was using the first of many now.

The narrow channel ran along the length of the ridge above the cabin. It curved under the incline, and if anyone looked out over the ledge, he wouldn't be seen. There was a cleft that was scalable about a quarter of a mile past the house, and that was where he was headed.

The snow accumulated, wet and heavy on the branches of trees. As the temperature dropped, small branches would break. He used those same branches to pull himself up the nearly straight climb to the top of the ravine. Darkness was falling now, and that, too, would aid his approach to the safe house.

He pushed himself over the ridge top and froze, listening to the sounds of the forest. The slam of a door drew his attention toward the safe house. A generator kicked in and he smiled. Another buffer between him and detection. The solar panels hadn't been cleaned since Bethanie and Ethan had moved in with him. The power stored in the batteries wouldn't have lasted long. He kneed up and rose up behind a tree before he ghosted forward, being cautious where he planted his feet.

At three hundred feet, he could see through the window into the kitchen. He could see movement, but the snow was coming down hard, and it wasn't clear who was moving. He worked closer to the safe house, being careful to stay out of the line of vision from the windows on his side of the house.

The tree in front of him would be where he split to the back of the house. He leaned against the tree behind his mark and took a breath, steadying his heartbeat. He flattened and low crawled, out of sight from the windows, to the next tree. The rope over his chest scooped up snow and piled it at his neck as he pushed forward. His rifle strap twisted, tightening the weapon to his back. He lifted cautiously and peeked around the tree.

Movement in the kitchen. Two men. Dammit, both appeared to be moving well enough, no impediments or injuries that would hold them back, *unless*...

The trip to the back of the cabin took too fucking long, but he couldn't risk alerting the motherfuckers to his presence. He carefully worked his way up to the back of the safe house. He halted in an uncomfortable crouch against the outside of the home and then slid up the side, making sure his equipment didn't touch the building. Noise would alert the men inside the structure.

Heavy encompassing snow fell, and the wind, which had been dormant, was now driving the flakes sideways—just Mother Nature settling in for a blizzard of epic proportions. That was okay with him. He knew this mountain. The men in the safe house didn't.

He lifted to peek just over the window ledge. There, a man on the bed. Yeah, Dog did some serious damage. The light from the hall illuminated the bed and the man. The blood that had seeped through the sheet covering the man meant they'd decided not to put a tourniquet on the injury, or Dog's damage was up higher on the shoulder/neck area, and they couldn't stop the bleeding.

Lycos dipped and moved to the other side of the window and tried to catch a glimpse of Ethan through the interior door. He could just make out the door to the other room. It was open, and there was no light on. *Where the fuck was Ethan? Front room?* He didn't see the boy in the kitchen with the other men. Where would they have put Ethan? He circled to the front of the cabin. At the corner, he stopped and counted stacked logs. At the fifth log, he let his fingers travel over the wood until he found the seam. He pushed in hard and flinched at the loud click.

Out of instinct he froze and listened. Nothing. He released the pressure and felt the door eject and open to the outside. He'd installed the gun port when he lived in the house, never imaging the future use he would put it to. He was making an assumption the men were still in the kitchen as there were no lights on in the front room. He squatted down and faced the cabin before he slowly allowed the door to open. Six inches by six inches, the square pulled out and then swung out further on a spring that would allow him to shut it from the inside. He controlled the movement.

"He's a fucking dead man, his body just doesn't

know it yet." A Boston accent. Southie if Ryan had to guess.

"He's still breathing. Besides, have you looked outside? We could be here for a while. Which sucks because we are supposed to meet up with Walker and Martin. They are out there somewhere." That guy sounded midwestern, and his voice was close. Ryan pushed the chink back, closing all but the slightest opening. He held his ear close and listened.

"I'm not complaining about being stuck here. We have some food and its warm. That wolf tore the fuck out of Max's neck. I don't know how he stabbed it." Southie's voice was louder as if he'd moved into the front room, too.

"Yeah, but what do we do about the kid? The little fucker was fast." Midwest's voice sounded frustrated.

"He's as good as dead. We'll go back to the place we found him and look for the woman. She's our payday anyway."

"We should have hunted her down when we were there." Midwest swore and said something Ryan didn't catch.

"We had the kid to deal with, and who the fuck knew how bad Max was? Besides, with this weather we wouldn't be able to see our hand in front of our face."

"Bosses are going to want an update."

"Sucks to be them. I'm not reporting in until we have something. Let them freak on the other teams."

"That's a good way to get dead."

"What are they going to do? Come up the mountain, find us, and kill us? I don't think so. They have ten teams out here in bumfuck nowhere, and I can fucking guarantee all ten of us are snowed the fuck in."

"Then we call in and tell them we are snowed in. They get their report, and we get to live."

"Fine, but we ain't mentioning that kid. If we do, they'll send everyone up to this particular mountain, and we'll have to share any money we get from catching that woman." Southie coughed a bit after he spoke.

"Agreed, besides we are going to have to deal with the fucker who was driving the truck. Can't imagine he'll stay off the mountain long. If I had a piece of ass like that woman, I'd be back banging her."

"He's nothing. We get that woman; we'll have some fun with her before we slit her throat, if you get my drift. The least we should get after freezing our balls off up here. Want some more coffee?"

"Hell, yes. It's drafty as fuck in this place."

"I'll report in. Then we need to contact Walker and Martin. I'm going to tell them we searched the mountain and it was clear."

"Yeah, tell 'em we are waiting out the storm, but the whole mountain is clear. We're golden then." Southie agreed.

"I could use a vacation."

"Me too. He dead yet?" Southie's voice softened a bit.

"Nope, still breathing."

"Fuck, it's going to be a long night."

"Nah, he'll die quietly." Midwest's voice was barely audible as they moved toward the kitchen.

Ryan pushed the wood back in place and scanned the darkened forest around him. Was Ethan still in the house? Was he tied up? Unconscious? Dead? He saw the vehicle they'd arrived in. An SUV. *Fuck, they wouldn't leave him in the vehicle, would they?*

He moved to the far side of the truck and approached, using the truck to shield him from view. He lifted from his crouch and searched the interior. Nothing.

Ryan sprinted across the clearing to the back shed. He opened the door and flipped three switches, killing the generator. Darkness and silence shrouded the house. He slipped behind the door and slid along the wall, closing it and leaving himself inside the structure. He eased his rifle and rope off and set them in the corner of the shack before he reached down and drew the knife out of his scabbard. He flattened against the wall and waited.

Indistinct voices sounded inside the house. A slam of the kitchen door and muffled curses preceded the shine of a flashlight. The door slammed open, and a lumbering figure moved into the shed. The flashlight focused on the generator.

Ryan moved. His free hand grabbed a handful of the man's hair. He slammed the man forward, and his face bounced off the generator a fraction of a second before he snapped the man's head back and placed the razor-sharp edge of his knife against the fucker's throat. The big guy's legs were rubber, and he staggered a bit before his brain caught up with the life or death situation going on. At that point, he froze and seemed to stopped breathing. Smart man.

"Where is my boy?"

"I don't know what you're talking about." Southie's denial earned him a slight twist of Ryan's knife. The man's body spasmed as he tried to back away from the blade. Ryan held the point tight against his throat and patted him down with his free hand. He removed an automatic from a holster at the man's waist. He tightened his hold on the man after he secured the weapon in his own web belt.

"My boy?"

"He's in the cabin."

"Which room?" Ryan pushed the knife closer, blood oozed over the blade. He knew it because he could feel it on the hand holding the bastard against his chest.

"Back bedroom."

"You're lying. Do you have a death wish?"

"You think you're going to kill me no matter what? Right?" Southie laughed. A strange reaction to his imminent demise. The man couldn't move, or he'd be decapitated by the blade against his neck. "Who the fuck thought I'd buy it in the middle of fucking nowhere?" The guy laughed again.

"Who sent you here?"

"Fuck you." Spittle flew from Southie's mouth.

"No, fuck you," Ryan growled and flicked his wrist. The man flinched. "I can make you suffer, or I can send you off quickly. Why are you after the woman?"

Southie's teeth clenched, and he snarled and then choked when the blade sliced a bit farther. "They want her dead."

"Stratus?"

The man grunted. "Dude, you're thinking small time. Think bigger. You're in way over your head. Let me go and get out of here. You don't know the wrath that will come down on you if you fuck up their plans."

"Why are they after her?"

"How the fuck would I know, man?" Ryan tweaked the knife again. "Okay... okay. Most of the time we erase people who have seen too much, ya know. We work in the shadows."

"Really?" An evil laugh rolled out of him. "Let me introduce myself, I *am* a Shadow. I *am* the darkness. I *am* a Guardian, and you are a boil on the ass of humanity, not worth my time or effort, but what sealed your fate is that you went after *my* family."

The man deflated in his grasp. "The kid got away, man. Headed into the woods. We tried to track him, but he was too fast. Professional courtesy, man, make the end quick, I've never made them suffer."

"And yet you suggested raping my woman before you killed her." Ryan pulled the knife across the man's throat. Deep enough to kill him, shallow enough to make sure the man had time to contemplate his regrets. The man dropped to his knees; his hands wrapped around his neck.

Ryan walked around him, picked up his coil of rope and rifle. He walked out of the shed and pulled the door shut behind him. He strode straight to the back door and walked into the safe house.

"Yo, Rich, what happened to the..."

The gun bucked in Ryan's hand. The darkened figure of Midwest dropped in the doorway, falling backward into the living room. He made his way into the bedroom and did a quick assessment of the bastard Dog took out. Southie was right. The man was on his way out. Ryan had no desire to expedite the journey. Let the fucker suffer. He spun and left the bastard to to die of his wounds.

On the way out he patted down Midwest and grabbed the man's cell phone, the key ring from his pants, and the handgun that never cleared leather.

He hit the door at a run. Ethan had been out in this weather for almost three hours. Ethan was a quick study, and he was smart, plus he had the basics of survival down, but he was scared and alone. Fuck, what he wouldn't give for Dog's tracking ability. Ryan ran to the road that skirted the area where he'd left Bethanie. It was hard to be sure of his location with the snow coming down and the darkness that surrounded him. "Bethanie!"

"Here!" He heard her from around the curve in the road.

"Come this way." He cupped his hands to his mouth and shouted, "Ethan!"

"Ryan, what's happening?" He could barely see her running toward him, her dark form a small moving object against the backdrop of snow falling on the shadow of the mountain.

He cupped his hands to his mouth again and yelled, "Ethan!"

As Bethanie got closer, he yelled to her, "Ethan escaped. He's running away, and he's got about two and a half hours on us."

"Where would he go?" She spun around her arms outstretched. "Where do we start?"

"He'd head toward safety. He'd head home, but he wouldn't try to scale the face of the mountain." That was the way they'd come down.

"That way?" Bethanie pointed to the long, slow slope that rounded the face of the mountain and would eventually lead to the cavern. Shit, in the dark and snow, the treacherous chutes that littered the way up would be impossible to see.

"Yeah. Let's go." He headed out with her on his heels. "Did you hit that alarm?"

"No, you were only gone an hour."

"Good. You stay on my six. We have to move fast." They didn't need every police agency in the tri-state area swarming the mountain. Not with two dead bodies and one corpse wannabe at the safe house.

"Are they coming after us?"

"No."

"I heard a gunshot. Did you kill them?" Her voice wavered a bit.

"Two of them. The third, Dog took care of."

He wasn't about to deny he'd taken those bastards out. They were paid killers, and they put the people he loved at risk. He suddenly got why Moriah went off script. The moralistic high ground he had previously perched his ass on was impossible to reach from where he currently stood.

Ryan put one foot in front of the other. He moved with purpose and intent, but he heard the echo of Bethanie's silence. He stopped to let her catch up and cupped his mouth again, calling out to Ethan. Bethanie made it to him. "Call for him."

If the boy was terrified, he might not recognize Ryan's voice, but he'd recognize his mom's.

"Ethan!" Bethanie shouted his name. The wind howled around them and snow hit his face. A small sound in the distance. Was it his imagination?

"Again." He pointed to where he thought the sound came from.

"Ethan!" Bethanie screamed her son's name.

"*There*. Keep calling!"

Ryan shook his head as he traveled toward where he thought he'd heard the sound. Bethanie called again. He stopped and held up his hand. She fell silent.

"Again. Only once and then we need to listen."

"Ethan!"

"Momma!"

"It's him!" Bethanie turned and shouted. "We're coming! Ethan, we're coming! Keep yelling, baby!"

Granite outcroppings tripped them as they scrambled in the direction of Ethan's voice. Ryan stopped and barred Bethanie from going further. There was a sheer wall in front of them. There would have been no way for Ethan to climb that surface. Ryan swept the area, looking for... no. *Fuck, no*.

"What? Why are you stopping?"

He lifted a hand "Ethan?"

"Down here!"

Ryan dropped to his knees, pushing snow away from a small hole. "Buddy, are you okay?"

"I hurt my leg. They killed Dog!"

"He was alive when we left him, Bud." Ryan took his rifle off his shoulder and removed his coil of rope.

"He was?" The small voice traveled up.

"Talk to him, Bethanie." Ryan needed to work and work fast.

"Yeah, baby. He's in the cave; Ryan brought him home."

"I'm sorry, Mom. I just wanted to wait for Ryan."

"I know. I know. We aren't going to talk about that now. How did you hurt your leg?"

"When I fell down the hole, I think I scratched it bad. I wrapped up in the blanket like Ryan told me."

"Yeah, did you? Good job. Have you eaten anything?"

"I was saving the bars till I got really hungry. I don't have anything to make a fire with down here. It's all rocks."

Ryan sprinted to a solid looking pine tree and anchored his rope around the bottom. He fixed a quick rig and moved back over to the hole. The edge of the chute was sharp and was going to wear on the nylon rope as soon as his weight dropped over the edge.

"I need a small log." He kicked snow trying to find something that would keep them both suspended and prevent the rock at the ledge from eating through the weave of the rope.

Bethanie pounced on a branch and pulled it out of the snow. "This?"

"That will work."

He moved the entire branch toward the opening. "Ethan, I'm going to pop a flare so I can see how to get down there with you. Close your eyes, okay? The light is going to be so bright it will hurt your eyes if you look at it."

"Okay. When?"

"I'll let you know." Ryan snapped the pack off his web belt and opened it in a practiced move. He fished out a flare, popped the top, and struck the course top against the chemicals on the cap of the flare. Once it flamed, he held it out to his side so the burning chemicals could drop off into the snow.

"Okay, close your eyes, Bud."

"Okay."

Ryan got down on his belly and hung over the edge. "Fuck me." His whisper blew away on the wind.

"Oh, my God!"

Ryan rolled up and grabbed the back of Bethanie's leg. She pushed away from the ledge.

Her hand flew to her mouth. "If he moves, he's going to fall off that shelf."

There were about ten inches between the boy and oblivion.

"He hasn't yet." Ryan needed to get down to the ledge, get the kid piggy-backed and then hand-over-hand it back to the top of the chute.

"Can I open my eyes now?"

"Yeah, sorry, Bud. You need to do me a favor, okay?"

"What?"

"Push back against the wall and stay there until I come down to get you. I don't want to land on top of you."

He heard the boy move. "Okay. I'm back."

"All right, I'll be down in just a minute." He stood and wrapped the rope around his legs. This was going to hurt like a motherfucker.

Bethanie grabbed his arm. He snapped his eyes to hers. "How are you going to bring him back up?"

"He is going to grab on to my neck and ride on my back as I climb back up."

"There is no bottom to that chute! What happens if you slip or, God forbid, fall?" Hysteria tripped through her words just as sure as Tiny Tim tiptoed through those damn tulips.

Ryan stood to his full height and rolled his shoulders. "I need you to settle down. You losing your shit right now will do nothing to help the situation. Keep away from the ledge until you can grab him and pull him onto the ground beside you. Understand?"

She nodded but stopped him as he turned. "Please, be careful."

He nodded. "He'll be okay."

"I need you back up here, too. Be careful. Please."

Ryan heard her, but his mind was focused on the work that needed to occur. He stepped over the branch before he dropped down the chute. The bite of the rope against his thighs was sharp and intense. He slowly lowered himself down. "Bethanie, hold that flare over the opening." A flicker of orange-hued light filtered down the chute.

"Hey there, Bud." The kid was filthy. His coat was ripped to shreds, and he had blood frozen on the front of his jeans.

"I'm sorry, Ryan."

"Yeah, no worries, kiddo." He toed the ledge and winced when the portion he pushed on crumbled under his foot. "We need to get out of here so we can go take care of Dog."

"He was protecting me."

"That's because you're his human." Ryan stepped in between Ethan's leg and the ledge. It held, thank God. He loosened the rope and did a one-legged squat. "This is what we're going to do. You're going to climb onto my back. Piggyback, right?"

"Yeah?" Ethan gave him the same look his mother had given him just a moment before.

"I'm going to climb back up the rope with you on my back. When you get up to the top, your mom is going to pull you out and onto the ground. Don't try to stand up, just slide on your belly and get away from the ledge, okay?"

"You can do that?"

"You know I can." Ryan winked at the boy. "Now stand up, but press against the wall when you do, okay?"

Ethan pushed his back against the wall and stood up.

"Now, your right arm over this shoulder." He helped the boy bring his arm across his shoulder and held it in the middle of his chest. "Give me your other arm." Ethan let him position his arms. "Okay, buddy, this is going to suck, but I need to take off your gloves. I'll put them in my pocket, okay?"

"Why?"

"Because your gloves are made of nylon and they are slippery. You need to be able to hold on tight, and no matter what, you cannot let go." Ryan unwound the rope from his leg that was anchored on the ledge and wrapped the other leg so he could toe it and push himself up. He stuffed Ryan's gloves into his pocket.

"Are you ready?"

"I think so."

"What did I say about that?"

"If you think you can't, you probably can't. If you think you can, try harder, and do that shit like a boss."

"There you go. Now, are you ready?"

"Yes, sir."

"Okay, hold on with your arms and then wrap your legs around me. Lock your ankles together and do not let go. Yeah?"

"Yes, sir."

He waited for Ethan to wrap around him and half pulled, half lifted to a standing position. "You good?" He glanced up. That six-foot climb to the top looked like six miles. He needed to get up, quickly, so the kid's grip didn't slip.

"Do that shit like a boss," Ethan whispered in his ear.

"That's right." He took his gloves off and shoved them into his other pocket. Drawing a deep breath, he reached up and pulled.

Hand-over-hand, straining and hurting, five fucking inches at a time, he pulled his weight and the hundred pounds on his back up the braided rope. His toe slipped, and he hung for a moment. He jiggled his toe, desperate to find the nylon. He felt it slap his calf and worked the rope to gain a hold again.

"You're almost here. I see you." Bethanie's voice was close, but fuck him if it didn't seem like a year had elapsed since he first looked down this damn hell hole.

He felt Ethan move. "Hold still. Don't move." He hissed through gritted teeth. The skin on his hands had shredded, and blood was making the rope slippery. He toed up and moved his arm again. A fucking inchworm process, but he could feel the wind now. They were close. So damn close.

He felt the moment Bethanie grabbed Ethan. The rope slammed into the wall, and his hands slipped as soon as the weight pulled from his back. He dropped three feet before he was able to stop the slide.

"Ryan!" Bethanie reached down. "Let me help you."

He shook his head. He just needed a minute. "Is Ethan safe?"

"He's fine. I need you out of that damn hole."

"You shouldn't cuss." He chuckled and glanced up again. Fuck, hadn't he just done this?

"I'll cuss if I damn well want to. Now get your ass up here."

"Mom said a bad word." Ethan's head popped over the edge. "Why are you still down there?"

"I'm trying, dude," Ryan chuckled.

"What do you say about that?" Ethan asked, mimicking Ryan perfectly.

"If you think you can't, you probably can't. If you think you can, try harder and do that shit like a motherfucking boss."

"How come you get to say motherfucking, and I don't?"

Ryan chuckled and reached up. He pulled and

toed, pulled and toed, pulled and toed until he felt two sets of hands trying to drag him out of the hole, which if he was honest, was more a hindrance than a help, but he made it to the lip and elbowed up to solid ground. He low crawled until he could feel dirt under his feet and flopped over onto his back.

"Son of a bitch." His hands were going to be permanently cupped. He extended his fingers and winced. Yeah, the rope burns hurt like a bitch.

"Yeah." Bethanie flopped beside him, and Ethan fell on the other side.

"Mom?"

"Yeah, Bud?"

"Can we go see if Dog is okay now?"

"Absolutely."

Ryan waited for one of them to get up, but neither moved. They had to be as emotionally and physically wasted as he was. He stared at the sky and watched the white flakes fall for a long minute before he groaned and pulled them both into him. His arms screamed in protest. "Come on. Dog needs us."

They all staggered up. "Bethanie, check his leg?"

She dropped and pushed Ethan's jeans up. "Nasty scrape and a couple deep gashes, but the bleeding has stopped."

Ryan nodded and grabbed his rifle. "Okay, then let's go home."

# CHAPTER 23

R yan headed up the ramp to his office. He'd spent the last thirty minutes stitching up Dog. The morphine still had him doped enough that he didn't fight when Ryan patched him up. The good news was it didn't look like the knife had hit any major arteries or veins. Yeah, there was a fuckton of blood, but that was probably because Dog was moving so much. Ryan sewed him up and gave him a little more morphine to try to keep him still. Of course, he had to carry the animal up to Ethan's room, because the boy was not going to leave his dog.

Bethanie was in there with them now. His bet was they'd all be asleep before the lights on the motion detectors timed out. Muscle memory pushed his hand toward the eighth shelf, seventh book from the left. He tapped the spine of the book and closed his eyes. He knew what he needed to do. He had no choice. Instead of pulling the book forward to unlock the shelf from its position, Ryan spun and shut the office door.

He pulled up his alarm system and checked everything, twice. While he was looking at the status of his alarms, he hit the new button beside the satellite antenna switch. Ethan asked why they couldn't defrost the antenna like a car defrosts the windshield. Brilliant fucking idea. Ryan had let the boy help him install a small heating device. He glanced at the clock and hoped the device had enough time to melt off the snow that had fallen tonight before he reached over and flipped the switch to lift and unfolded his satellite antenna. He picked up the handheld phone and waited for the light on the satellite to turn green.

He threw the encryption key and waited for a steady dial tone. The numbers were pressed with a sense of deja vu that he'd rather not recall. He'd wanted out. He'd wanted a chance at a family, but the bastards had come to his mountain and tried to hurt those he loved. Game fucking on. Lycos blinked. *Those he loved.* He glanced down at the vein of mica in the desk and ran his finger along it. His family. *His.* His to protect. His to care for. His to love.

"Operator Two Seven Four."

"Sunset clearance, third operative."

"Third operative? We show you as archived."

Lycos blinked rapidly at the comment. So, maybe the operator wasn't an AI program. "Circumstances dictated my retrieval. Send me to Bengal. Now."

"Standby."

Ryan dropped his head into his hand and winced. He pulled away and looked at the tender flesh of his palms. The rage he held barely contained boiled closer to the surface. Ethan could have died. Those bastards could have killed him, or he could have missed that ledge and fallen... He squeezed his eyes shut and channeled his venom. He reached for the pouch where he'd dropped Midwest's keys and cell phone.

"Status?" Bengal's demand cracked like a whip across the connection.

"Secure Hotel."

"I pass you Pole."

"Glitter. They found us."

"What the fuck are you talking about?"

Lycos leaned forward and detailed the events since he'd arrived at the mountain. Fuck, was it only four hours ago?

"So, the threat is neutralized? I'll send a team to clean up the debris."

"I'll clean up my own mess, and the threat isn't neutralized. There are nine other teams circling this area."

"We'll remove you."

"No fucking way."

"They'll find you."

"Not if I find them first."

"Nine teams? You said there were three men on the team that showed today?"

"Yes."

"So, your plan is to hunt down and kill over twenty men, by yourself, on United States soil, and you think we're going to be okay with that?"

Ryan leaned back in his chair and stared at the cell phone in front of him. "I have a way to do it. If I don't go after them, they will continue to hunt us, and Bethanie and Ethan will never be safe. I'm going to send their handlers a message. One that will get, and hold, their attention."

"I'll need to get authorization and man... I'm not sure they're going to give it."

"I'm not asking for permission. I'm informing you of my decision."

"How long do I have to work this?"

"I'm calling in my markers. When protection for Bethanie and Ethan gets here, I'm gone."

"Fuck me, Lycos, you're putting my nuts in a vice here."

"No, I'm really not. You can walk away from this. I'm archived, right?"

"Technically. I see where you're going with this, but I don't like it. It leaves you out there without assets or help."

"I'm never without assets, besides we all know accidents happen. Even on US soil."

"We can't protect you if the local LEOs nab your ass."

Lycos laughed. "Local law enforcement? As if, man. As if."

"I'm still sending this up the chain."

"Do it. Your woman told me Ethan was family. Remind them of that when you brief them."

"I won't have to, man. Off the books, do you need anything from me?"

"Keep our side away from here. If they are in the way, they'll wake up dead."

"Roger, I copy all. Take care of yourself, my friend, and this is from me, not the company. You do whatever it fucking takes."

Lycos sneered as Bengal's evil growl reached him. "As long as it takes. As long as it fucking takes."

He disconnected the call and dialed a phone number he'd memorized long ago. He waited for the voice message to drop, and when the beep sounded, he simply stated. "I'm calling in all my markers. Mountain safe house. Yesterday."

Lycos cracked open the back of Midwest's cell phone. He examined the inner components carefully before he powered it up. He needed to manipulate the lock screen to open it, which took less than four minutes. As soon as he had access, he disabled the carrier's signal and set the phone on the counter.

Once the phone was opened, he accessed the last numbers called. A smile spread across his face. *Gotcha motherfuckers.*

He spun in his chair, moved his bookshelf out of the way, and entered his vault, although it took two attempts to get the scanner to read his swollen hand. He headed to the back and opened his faraday case where he extracted a thin laptop computer. He grabbed several cords and brought the machine back to his desk. He hooked the laptop to his satellite feed, plugged it in, and then hooked the phone into the computer. He bypassed the startup screen and opened the program he wanted from the c: prompt. The screen flickered and went dark. Lycos watched as his program manipulated the global navigation satellite system and built a 3D model of the mountain. His system used predictive calculations to fill in the blanks that regular satellite systems couldn't.

His fingers flew over the keys, and the system pinged the telephone numbers of Midwest's recent calls. He watched as his target locations populated. None were moving, which made sense as it was currently blizzarding outside and almost midnight. He waited for the program to finish populating the numbers before he unhooked the cell phone and scanned the text messages and emails that were downloaded on the device.

Lycos powered down the phone and unhooked it from his system. He rolled his shoulders. He was beyond exhausted, and he needed to check on Bethanie and Ethan. He closed the laptop, putting it to sleep before he unplugged it from the satellite antenna and brought that down. Stifling a huge yawn, he flipped through the alarm system. It was quiet. For now.

He opened the door and froze in his tracks. Bethanie was asleep outside his office. She'd wrapped in a blanket and propped herself against the cave wall. He took two steps forward and squatted down. "Hey, you."

She blinked and smiled up at him. "Hey."

"How long have you been out here?"

"I dunno." She yawned so hard her whole body shook. "I didn't want to interrupt. I could hear you talking to someone, but I couldn't hear what you were saying."

Yeah, he knew that. Soundproofing was difficult in a stone cave, but he'd muted his office with every technique he could design. "I guess we need to talk." He didn't want to have this conversation, but it was probably better they got it out of the way as soon as possible.

"Yeah." She nodded and dropped her head back against the wall. He winced as she sucked air and reached up to rub the back of her head. "Damn, that hurt."

He sat down in front of her and leaned back against the wall of his office. "Bet it did."

"Why did you kill the men tonight?"

Ryan drew a breath and let it escape slowly. He extended his legs and crossed his feet before he spoke, "I killed them because if I did not, they would alert others to where we were. I had no option. In order to protect you and Ethan, and yes, myself, they needed to be eliminated."

He watched as she examined her thumbnail. "Are we safe now?"

"No."

Her eyes flew to him. "Why not?"

"Because there are still twenty to thirty men out there who are searching for you and Ethan."

"What are we going to do? Do we need to leave?"

"That is exactly what you aren't going to do. I'm going after them."

He watched emotions flit over her face. She frowned deeply and shook her head. "You can't go. What will happen to us?"

"An associate is coming to stay with you. Someone I trust implicitly."

She gathered the blanket and leaned forward, crawling across the hall. He lifted his arm, wincing as his muscles protested the movement. She leaned up against him. He dropped his arm and she settled, tucking along his side. He looked up at the ceiling and said a quick thank you. At least she wasn't terrified of him.

"Harvey killed someone, in front of me. I was holding Ethan. She wasn't much older than me. He told me he'd kill me and leave Ethan to starve to death if I didn't do exactly what he wanted."

"Harvey was a monster."

She nodded her head. "But you're not." Her voice was small and hesitant but firmed. "You, Ryan Wolf, are a protector.

"I've never lied to you. You know I've killed people while doing my job." *And earlier.*

"For Guardian?"

"Yes."

"The weapons in there, do you know how to use them all?"

He chuckled. "I do."

"Will you teach me how to use them?"

He cocked his head so he could see her. "Why?"

She sat up and stared at him. "I'm so damn tired of being a victim. I'm tired of needing someone to take care of us. I can't live like *this* anymore. I need to be able to defend myself. I need to have that. I need to know..." she clenched her fist and held it against her heart, "...here, that if something ever happened to you, I'd be able to take care of Ethan and myself. Teach me how to use those weapons. Teach me how to not be afraid. *Please*."

"I can do that. I'll show you both how to use a handgun tomorrow." After he dropped Midwest's body down the chute Ethan had fallen into. The other bodies were going into the ravine in their car. Damn shame the car was going to erupt in flames. Of course, that would be done on his way down the mountain, after he made sure Bethanie and Ethan were tucked in and had protection. Local law enforcement would investigate if the fire was called in. Of course, they wouldn't find a damn thing other than an unfortunate accident due to inclement weather and poor road conditions.

"Does it make me a horrible person that I'm not upset about you killing them? I mean, inside I really wish you didn't have to do it. It was our fault you were forced into that position, but I'm so relieved that you did and that they're gone and I—"

Ryan put his finger under her chin and lifted, stopping her emotion-driven words. "You are not a horrible person. Period. You are a mother who is relieved a threat to her son has been eliminated. You're going to have huge emotional swings. This isn't going to be easy for you to process. It is also natural to see me in a different light." He dropped his finger and hated he no longer had the right to pull her into his arms. He figured he'd lost that when he'd admitted he'd killed those men.

She sat up straighter and examined him. Her brow furrowed for a moment before she jerked her head to the side and then back to look at him. "Why would I look at you differently? You saved us."

"I killed two men and left the third to die."

She nodded; her brow still tightly furrowed. "Yes, to protect us."

Ryan stared at her for a moment. "You're not repulsed by the fact that I've killed?"

She shook her head. "I've seen monsters. I know what they do and why they kill. They kill to intimidate. To show power, to punish, to imprison. You killed to free us. Does it make it right? No, but it doesn't convict you of some atrocity in my eyes."

"What about Ethan?"

"He can never know about this. As his parents..." Bethanie's mouth snapped shut. "Sorry, I didn't mean to..."

Ryan reached out and took her hand in his. "When you two first arrived on this mountain, I couldn't fathom having either of you in my space. Then you went and got lost." Ryan laughed and shook his head. "Woman, you have no idea what a royal pain in the ass I thought you were."

"And stupid."

Bethanie lifted an eyebrow at him, which caused him to laugh again. "Well you did almost make a popsicle of yourself, but yeah... The entire time I was searching for you I was telling myself that getting you both off the mountain as soon as humanly possible was the best thing for everyone. I didn't want anyone here. I liked being alone. It was all I knew." With the exception of his time with Moriah, and there was no comparison to be drawn between the two women. None.

"But you asked us to stay."

Ryan nodded, but studied her small hand in his rather than look at her. "I did."

"Why?"

He met her gaze and smiled. "You and Ethan brought me to life. I was dormant, suspended in a vast cushion of nothingness I worked damn hard to believe I wanted. I built this home, all the while telling myself I'd be content, complete, and happy to live out my days alone when, in reality, I built this home for a family." *Moriah knew that when he didn't.*

"A family?" Her whisper echoed his words.

He nodded and watched Bethanie's eyes fill with

tears, but he didn't look away. Ryan held onto that connection, to emotions that were foreign, and messy, and loud. He embraced the feelings that drove him crazy because he didn't know how to deal with the disaster internalizing them left in their wake. He clung to the desperation he felt when he'd seen Ethan on that ledge and the mind-numbing dread that had encased him when he'd seen the blood on the trail this afternoon. Emotions he'd shielded himself against as a preemptive strike against the entire world now coursed through his veins, and he *did not* know what to do with them or how to explain them.

He shook his head and swallowed hard. *Time to sac up.* "I asked you to stay because I think I am in love with you. I don't know for sure because I've never experienced it, you know? I just... I can't lose you. Either of you."

"I don't think I love you."

*Karma, you fucking bitch.* Ryan pulled away, but the grasp of her small hand on his arm stilled him.

"I don't *think* I love you because I *know* I love you. I know it because Ethan taught me what it means to love. One day you'll wake up, and you'll realize loving someone isn't as terrifying as it seems. Loving someone gives you a center and a purpose. Love isn't something to be feared. I love you. I know Ethan loves you, too. My past and yours are horrid. Ethan was born out of a madman's lust for an heir. Yet the three battered strands of our lives combined together can make us all stronger. Love does that,

Ryan. Love makes us stronger than we think we are. It allows us to do things we never dreamed we could."

He lifted his trembling hand to her face and cupped her cheek. Tears crested from those beautiful blue eyes, dropped down, and skittered along the pad of his thumb. He shook his head. "I don't understand how you can love me."

A sad smile spread across her face. "I know. One day you will. I promise." She turned her head and kissed the tender flesh of his palm. "We need sleep."

"We do." Ryan stood and offered her his hand. She carefully took the offered assistance, but gripped him by his wrist rather than his shredded flesh. She followed him as he opened Ethan's door. The boy had moved from his bed and was lying rolled in a blanket beside Dog, his hand buried in the animal's scruff. The dog lifted his head when the door opened. He chuffed quietly and lay back down. Ryan tiptoed in and checked the bandages. There was a small amount of fluids, but no new bleeding. He reached down and stroked the soft fur on Dog's muzzle. "You did good today."

Dog lifted his tail and gave a few thwacks against the flooring. Ryan covered Ethan's hand. "You did a hell of a job, too, young man." The kid did what it took to survive. Granted, if he had anything to say about it, the boy wouldn't be leaving the house until he was old enough to vote, but still... Ethan was a survivor, and smart, and so much like his mom.

Ryan stood and walked to Bethanie, who was leaning against the doorjamb. "Let's go to bed."

Bethanie woke up and stretched against the vast expanse of warm skin spooned up against her back. She could feel Ryan's morning erection against her bottom. She stilled and listened to his steady breathing. She pushed back into him and wiggled her hips a bit.

Ryan hummed and tightened his arms, pulling her closer to him. A lazy roll of his hips against her released a waiting a hum of desire from her, too. He did it again, and she met the movement. His hand traveled down to the bottom of her sleep shirt and lifted it.

He groaned and rotated his hips when his fingers failed to find any panties. She smiled and ground back into him and raised her top leg up toward her chest. He rolled his hips, and his cock pushed up, sliding against her as his hand cupped her breast.

She reached down and positioned his shaft at her core. He lifted his leg, paralleling her position and pushed into her. She arched her back; the bite of his thick cock was delicious and too much, all at the same time. His hand slid from her breast to her hip, and he held her still as he rocked back and forth, working himself into her. Her body opened for him, and they both groaned when he seated fully inside her. Their union in this moment was a validation of life, of their need for each other.

"I don't deserve you." Ryan's words fell like a prayer in her ear.

"You do. We deserve this. Make love to me."

He withdrew from her and moved them, so she was under him. Bethanie wrapped her arms around his neck and pulled him down to her. "My love."

He draped over her. Their bodies touched and melded into one as he entered her again. Her hands snuck down his muscled back, moving along with his hips. Her hands slid lower and grabbed his ass, asking without words for a stronger, harder connection.

He covered her mouth with his, stealing her breath and depositing it next to the heart he already owned. When he lifted away, she was desperate for air and for this man. She pushed his hair away from his face. He was hers.

He lifted his leg and changed the angle of his thrust. The slight change stirred the brewing storm inside her and shuttered all attempts to relish anything but the sensations his body was creating inside her. His neck muscles strained above her and sweat trickled from his brow. She felt her insides peak and tighten before that blessed snap of delight lit her body up. Her fingernails dug into his back, and he bucked against her, thrusting deep and hard. She gasped and climaxed again as he came inside her.

She panted underneath his weight; her body

ravaged by shudders of residual delight. "I like waking up that way."

Her breathy words drew a low chuckle from him, and he slid out of her, rolling to the side. "I could do that for the next thirty or forty years." He cupped her neck and pulled her in for a kiss. His lips swept hers, once, twice, and again, before he pulled away.

"I love you," she whispered across the few inches that separated them.

"I have to leave you. I have to protect you and Ethan." His thumb stroked her cheek.

"I know." She understood the need to protect, to shield, to make sure the ones she loved were safe. Ethan had taught her that lesson.

"I'll be back."

"We'll be here."

"Mom, Dog needs to go outside." They both jumped at Ethan's voice right outside the closed door. Bethanie squeaked and shot under the covers.

"I'll be right there, Bud," Ryan called over his shoulder and laughed when she folded the sheet down and peeked out.

"I think we need to have a talk about closed doors." Bethanie held the sheet against her.

Ryan chuckled and rolled out of bed, standing up gloriously naked. "I thought I had, but Dog is a priority."

"That he is." Ethan loved that animal.

"I'll take care of them; you grab a shower. After breakfast, we'll figure out a way to work on handgun familiarization. My associate should be here by nightfall or latest, tomorrow morning." Ryan slid into his blue jeans. Commando.

Bethanie blushed and swatted away her thoughts about how to capitalize on his nakedness. "He works for Guardian, too?"

"He does."

"What's his name?"

Ryan frowned and glanced back at her. "The name I know him by is… classified. I'll have him introduce himself when he shows up."

"Classified?"

He made a noise that sounded like an agreement when he pulled his sweater over his head.

"Is your name classified?"

He chuckled. "Not the one you know me by."

She sat up, pulling the sheet up with her. "You have a code name or something?"

"Or something." He smiled and winked at her.

He'd given her a glimpse of what he'd done for Guardian. She could draw her own conclusions, but every equation equaled the same summation. She loved the man he was and what he did for Guardian was a part of that man. "I'll never say a word. You're safe with me."

He walked over, leaned down, and kissed her. "I'm beginning to realize that."

# CHAPTER 24

Thanatos stood outside the safe house and leaned against the debarked tree that held up the left side of the porch. The heavy, wet, snow that his four-wheel drive had sloshed through this afternoon was in the process of a slow melt, leaving a muddy mess.

Mother Nature's defrost was an efficient way to remove the signs of what had happened here, but Thanatos's trained eyes missed nothing. Lycos had sanitized the cabin. The smell of chemicals told him it had been recently. He'd inspected the inside of the abode. There was a mattress missing from a bed frame, and the sun-bleached flooring showed where a rug had been removed. The small outbuilding behind the safe house had a similar chemical smell. Of course, the most telling indication was the two dead bodies currently occupying the cargo space of the SUV parked outside the house.

He couldn't decide if the shallow wounds on dead body number one had been inflicted to cause fear or if someone other than Lycos had killed the guy. Maybe someone weaker? But the fact that the man's nose was smeared across his face suggested Lycos was being purposeful in the slow death rather than putting the man down. Interesting. Wasn't his usual dispassionate style.

The second guy, well, he'd been mauled. Probably that damn wolf of Lycos'. Thanatos rolled his shoulders, pulled out a cigarette, lipped, and lit it. He inhaled a lungful of the toxic fumes and relaxed. Lycos would know he was here. His eyes flew to the tree line when a bunch of sparrows, or whatever the fuck the little birds were, took off into the air. He leaned forward and smiled as Lycos appeared out of the trees. The motherfucker walked like a damn wolf, prowled like the predator he was. Thanatos glanced around furtively, looking for the damn beast that always lurked somewhere near.

"Where is the poodle?" Thanatos offered his hand when Lycos' stride brought him close enough.

Lycos tipped his head toward the four-wheeled coffin. "Son of a bitch stabbed him. Twice."

Thanatos did a double take. What the actual fuck? The beast wouldn't attack without provocation. As much as he didn't care for the lion-sized dog, he was well trained. "Did they get the drop on you?"

"No, the bastard grabbed my kid."

Thanatos felt his jaw unhinge and drop. Shit, the echo of his chin hitting the wooden porch could be heard in Alaska. "You're going to have to explain that, mate."

"Figured. I need you to watch him and his mom. I need to take care of business. Personal business."

"Personal? Since when do you deviate from protocol?" Thanatos lifted his cigarette and pulled a long toke.

"Since I left Guardian."

He released the deliberate exhale of smoke. "So, I think I'm going to need a strong shot of Irish Whiskey."

"Come with me." Lycos turned and headed back into the tree line.

"Going to leave the stiffs?"

"I'll take care of them tonight when I go down the mountain."

"And you're going after…?"

"Stratus. They're after my family."

Thanatos hopped off the porch and grimaced at the ankle-deep mud, but he was too invested in what-the-ever-loving-fuck was going on with the lone wolf of the group. Seriously, of all people, Lycos was the last person he'd ever peg as having a family. How the fuck had he hidden this?

"I think you should start talking." Thanatos fell into step behind Lycos and naturally mimicked his footfall. The man was a ghost in the forest, and

Thanatos wasn't. He'd be able to survive, but his forte was the urban jungle, not granite mountaintops.

"Three months ago, this woman shows up at the safe house…"

Thanatos had tripped twice and muttered, "You're fucking with me, aren't you?" at least five times by the time they made it around the face of the mountain. Thanatos took in everything, the words, the mountaintop trail–minus the two outcroppings that he'd stumbled over—and the stoic presentation of the events of the last three months that came in staccato bursts from the man leading him.

"So, you are going after Stratus." They paused at what appeared to be a narrow passageway of weather honed rock. He leaned against the massive boulder that seemed to have been placed in front of the passageway.

"I'm going after those who are coming after me."

"Could take a hot minute. You sure you want to be away from them that long?" He shoved his hands in his jacket. "Fuck, man, you realize it is springtime in the rest of the world?"

"Spring here, too." Lycos shrugged. "I have to neutralize the threat."

"Why are they after them?"

"Long story. She can tell you, but basically the boy's father was deep in the organization."

"They are wiping the slate clean."

"Exactly. I'm going to ensure they understand the cost of assuming they are expendable."

"And you don't have any Guardian back up." It was a statement, not a question.

"You can tap out man. I'd understand. This isn't standard operating procedure."

"I'm here, aren't I? But you will buy me new boots. Do you know how much these things cost?"

Lycos glanced down at his feet and laughed. "Get some Timberlands. Designer clothes don't do well up here. You know that."

"True, but when I get a call for help from the last person who would ever call because his contrary, solitary, lonely ass has walked through life solo for over forty years, I came running. You think I was going to stop for a wardrobe change?" Thanatos glanced down at his hand made, Italian leather, ankle-high boots. Fifteen hundred dollars of artesian beauty, ruined.

"Damn good thing we are about the same size. You can gear up with my shit."

"Oh, goodie." Thanatos drawled, earning him a laugh from his colleague.

"Come on, I'll introduce you to Bethanie and Ethan." He circled around Thanatos and headed down a narrow path.

"Dude, I am not living in a fucking cave while you run amuck down the mountain." He would, for Lycos, he would do what it took, but fuck him, camping in Thanatos' opinion was staying at a three-star hotel without a Starbucks in the lobby and no room service.

Lycos lifted a hand and flipped him a middle finger. When they stopped, he leaned over so he could see what Lycos was doing. "Holy fuck. You built a house in the fucking mountain. How very Grizzly Adams of you."

"Fuck you, asshole." He keyed in a code to the panel, and the door slid open.

"Holy fuck, Batman." The vast expanse of a majestic cavern had been turned into a warm, inviting home. "Solar?"

"Yep. Thermal heat from the hot springs. Completely off the grid. Satellite antenna retracts and deploys for contact with the outside. We've been building a hydroponic garden in the antechamber through there." Lycos pointed as he toed off his boots.

Thanatos kicked off his sodden leather and followed him into the cavern. A heavenly smell of meat and herbs... and freshly baked bread assailed him. He swung his attention to the portion of the cavern that had been allocated as the kitchen.

Lycos pointed up the ramp. "Bedrooms, office, and vault are up there. I'll give you access to the weapons."

"I brought my own arsenal. They're locked in my vehicle down the mountain a bit."

Lycos nodded. "We'll get it, and I'll show you where you can park. The back trail is more user-friendly."

From the other side of the room, a low, vicious growl captured Thanatos' attention. The wolf was lying on the couch, his head lifted up. Just beyond the massive fur body, Thanatos could see small, sock-covered feet. They bounced up and down in time to some unheard beat.

"Knock it off," Lycos growled back at the animal. It huffed and dropped its head again.

"He's hyperprotective of Ethan."

"No shit."

"Hi."

Thanatos returned his attention to the kitchen area. A petite blonde with a shock of short curly hair and huge blue eyes stood with a dish towel in her hands. The woman smiled at Lycos. She was absolutely stunning. Beautiful in a way that was natural and buoyant. He swallowed hard. Fuck him, the woman was breathtaking.

Lycos crossed the space and wrapped the woman in his arms. Thanatos averted his eyes, suddenly finding the dropped lighting intriguing. He'd never tread on Lycos' bond with the woman or the child.

Seeing Lycos like this reminded him of Asp with Lyric, and Anubis with Sky, hell even Bengal and Jewell. He glanced at the wolf who had lifted his head to watch the public display of affection. Moriah was also involved with someone, and if the rumor was correct, it was a long-term thing. Thanatos hadn't been back to the ranch in a while although he'd routinely sent little Kadey gifts. Anubis' kid was cool, and she deserved good things.

"Bethanie, may I introduce..." Lycos lifted an eyebrow.

Thanatos stepped forward, appreciating the assassin's discretion which allowed him to present the cover with which he was most comfortable.

"Dolan, Dolan McDaid." Thanatos let a bit of his natural Irish brogue roll through the words.

"It is nice to meet you. Thank you for coming, for allowing Ryan to do what he needs to do."

Thanatos cocked his head and lifted an eyebrow at Lycos. Ryan? That was a new cover.

The man shrugged. "She knows they won't be safe unless we address the situation." He glanced over at the couch.

Ah, well, Thanatos tucked that information into his back pocket. "If that food tastes half as good as it smells, the pleasure will be all mine."

"Come on, I'll give you the lay of the land, then we'll eat before we get your gear."

Thanatos waited for Lycos to separate himself from his woman and followed him up the incline. He felt like an interloper in a cartoon filled with hearts and flowers. Who in the hell would have guessed that Lycos of all people would find this kind of happiness?

Well, not him, but he'd do whatever it took to ensure the man could grab hold of it and keep it. If that meant babysitting his woman, kid, and killer mutant wolf, he'd put on his Uncle Dolan persona and play nice. He could do it.

CHAPTER 25

One drew a deep breath and released it. Her irritation at the unexpected communication waned as Three continued.

"Of the twenty-one assets we had in the area, we can confirm two died in a car accident coming down a mountain during a blizzard. One was caught in a crossfire between sheriff's deputies and a robbery suspect. The suspect evaded apprehension. Two died when a bridge they were traversing collapsed. Local police have determined the bridge, which was older than dirt to begin with, had finally succumbed to age and imploded when our men drove over it. Then we have four men missing. They were going into the area on foot. There is another that has not been found. He was the third member of the team that plummeted over the cliff during the snowstorm."

One clicked her fingernails against the smoked

glass of her desk. "Accidents. Unfortunate accidents and the ones on foot could be running silent."

Three nodded. "That was my opinion, too; however, we had a report this morning. Two more of our people have died. Carbon monoxide poisoning. The heater in their hotel rooms malfunctioned."

"It is a rural location. Unfortunate, but understandable."

"Until you realize that only those two rooms had malfunctioning heaters. That is twelve of our best operatives, dead or unaccounted for."

"Is there any intelligence on agency operatives in the area?"

"None. The man in the truck we ID'd via traffic cameras has not hit on any of our databases. I'm concerned that the woman has a protector—one we shouldn't discount."

One sighed and leaned back in her chair. "We still have nine assets in the area."

"Yes."

"Double the incentive for her termination. I want this over." One leaned forward to terminate the communication.

"I have already done that. Our enforcement arm is still unconvinced."

One's eyes snapped to Three. "Then convince them. If they are worried they will perish should they move forward, they need to know they will cease to exist if they do not."

"Sometimes force doesn't work." Three shook her

head before dropping it to her hand and rubbing her brow. "Perhaps we should consider another candidate."

"Death always works. Finding another candidate will not be considered until all options are exhausted. Reminding you of this is troublesome. I thought you stronger."

Three lifted her head. The ice in her eyes contradicted the tiredness that lined her face. "Are you questioning my ability?"

One cocked her head. Her hand hovered over the mouse which would terminate the call. She blinked once and then nodded. "I must admit, I find that I am." She hit the mouse and cut the communication.

Lycos hooked his latest victim's phone to his laptop. The phone records downloaded, and his map lit up with four other locations. He memorized three of them and powered down the machine. The fourth was one he already knew. The head of the serpent as it were. The number was shielded. That number would be his last effort. He put his computer into the backpack he carried and headed out of the dive hotel he'd spent the night in. His eyes traveled to the west, to the mountain he couldn't see and to his family.

Hunting was ninety percent setting up in strategic places to sit and wait for his prey to come to him; however, he was through waiting. He had five numbers left, three of which he'd been able to ping today. He was done being subtle. The leather jacket he wore crinkled as he slipped his black nylon back-pack on and straddled the motorcycle he'd been using since he'd come down the mountain. He put on his gloves and then pulled on his helmet. His shoulder holsters were well hidden in the bulk of his coat as he pulled out onto the road.

The removal of the men so far had been rudimen-tary. If anyone could connect the men to Stratus, they'd see what was happening was a systematic purge of those who were looking for Bethanie and Ethan. Obviously, his shots over the bow, so to speak, weren't as effective as he would have liked. Time to up the stakes.

Ryan stopped and reached into the inside pocket of his jacket. He pulled his phone out and glanced at the flashing dots. He watched as two moved away from him on this road. Given his current location and the direction the third was traveling, he'd have to hurry. He secured the phone to the mount on the handlebars of his motorcycle. He dropped the face shield on his helmet. Time to go to work.

The first car, a rust bucket with an old woman driving and an even older man in the passenger seat, wasn't his target. He passed them carefully, giving the elderly couple no reason to notice him. Once he rounded the bend, he accelerated. He leaned into the curves of the old back-country road, his knee inches from the asphalt, as he accelerated and glided through hairpin curves and treacherous switchbacks. When he saw a car in front of him, he leaned over the engine of his Harley for a better look at the license plates. The SUV had New York plates. A sneer lifted the corner of his mouth. He slowed long enough to confirm the vehicle he trailed was his target. The yellow dot on the phone was now red. *Bingo.*

He held the throttle steady with his right hand as he reached into his jacket with his left. He scanned the road in front and behind him for other traffic then withdrew the Desert Eagle from its holster. He held it low as he rolled the accelerator and sped up.

He put on his blinker as he pulled out from behind the SUV. The use of a blinker indicated a law-abiding citizen. That simple act would mislead the driver. Ryan leaned out of the lane to clear the road ahead, as any motorcycle rider would do, and then accelerated. Two men. The driver wasn't looking at him; he was glancing at the passenger, who held a cell phone to his ear. Ryan positioned himself at the driver's side passenger door and lifted the forty-five. The first kick of the weapon exploded window glass and brain matter as the passenger's brain misted against the windshield in front of him.

Ryan accelerated and swerved as the driver's reflexes jerked the SUV toward him. He aimed and pulled the trigger twice. The driver slumped at the wheel. He decelerated and used the right rear brake on the right-hand pedal and the right handlebar brake to bring his bike to skidding stop. The SUV sliced in front of him and plunged down into the ditch beside the road. It hit a deep rut and flipped nose over tail once before Ryan toed his bike into gear and hit the accelerator.

He powered forward as he double checked the phone between his handlebars. The other target car had turned and was coming back toward him. The motherfuckers had been talking to each other. All right. He could deal. Jousting had always been an interest.

He rounded the curve and saw the SUV barreling toward him. The passenger pushed through the passenger side window and leveled a rifle at him. Ryan laughed. Unless the motherfucker was Wild Bill Hickok, the son of a bitch had a ten percent chance of making the shot. He'd take those odds, all day every day.

Pressing his chest low to the bike, he hit the accelerator. The approach to the SUV played out in his mind like a movie. The rifle bucked repeatedly. The vehicle crossed the broken white line on the old road. He drew a long, even breath and judged the distance between them. The driver wanted to run him down. Well, he'd go down all right, but on his terms.

He hit the brakes and decelerated as he laid his bike down, kicking out from under it as it hit the pavement. The bike, being heavier than he was and having momentum, careened under the SUV. As his ass skidded on the asphalt, he tucked and rolled, a controlled burn, which was more than he could say for the SUV. Even at fifty miles an hour, running over a pile of metal caused catastrophic damage.

Ryan pulled one Eagle out of its holster and stood. With his right hand, he placed the weapon in his left and then awkwardly extracted the other and limped forward. The weapon in his left hand hung lifeless. He'd dislocated his shoulder or separated it, but he needed the weapon out and available. The leathers he wore had saved his skin, but he fucking felt like he'd been through an asphalt blender. His vision was fucked up. Ryan blinked and realized his visor was pitted, scratched and cracked. He tried to flip the visor up, but it wouldn't budge. He glanced toward the SUV. Dammit. He dropped to his knee and worked the chinstrap to remove his helmet. He flipped it off onto the road and staggered up again.

Lycos had just gained his stance when the passenger door opened and a man fell out, holding himself against the armrest of the door. The rifle swung up at the same time as Ryan lifted his handgun. He fired twice and felt the bite of shards of pavement as they hit at his face.

The man fell, still suspended from the vehicle. The strap of his seatbelt kept him from hitting the ground in a gruesome replica of a rearview ornament.

He advanced on the driver's side door and opened it. Blood seeped down the man's face, but he was still breathing. A cursory search provided the man's cell phone before he took aim. The echo of the shot rang in his ears. Methodically, Lycos moved to the other man, grabbed his phone and made his way to the field past the road. He pushed farther into the interior of the sparsely populated area.

He used the first sturdy tree he found to force his shoulder back into joint. He fell to his knees and immediately vomited, the pain crushing his consciousness. "Fuck me." He rolled to his ass and moved his arm carefully—and worked on breathing at a normal rate—nearly impossible when he had to get his backpack off. Moving that shoulder was not a fun thing, but he did it.

Lycos winced when he saw the back of the pack. His leather had protected his skin, but the nylon of the pack had obviously left fabric all the fuck over the road. He pulled his computer out... in pieces. Fuck him. He wasn't going to stop until he could go home and know that there was no longer a threat.

He pulled his pay-by-the-minute phone out and laughed. He actually had three bars out here in the middle of nowhere. He punched in the numbers and leaned back against what was left of his pack. He was secluded, to an extent. At least he was out of view. That would have to do for now.

"Operator Two Seven Four."

"Sunset clearance, third operative."

"How would you like your call routed, Third Operative."

Yeah, definitely not an AI. "Send me to Bengal."

He waited and listened to a series of clicks and

whirs as the system encrypted the call, at least from the other end.

"The line is not secure." Bengal's voice came across the connection.

"Yeah, I know that."

"Are you secure?"

"I'm… hell, I'm kinda tore up, but I'll live. I need to access your wife's systems." There was a long pause. "For what purpose?"

"I have a telephone number I can't track. The same number is on all of the minion's phones. I need to end this."

"Others still remain? We've been monitoring the local LEO's down there. You've been busy."

"You'll hear some serious shit soon. I took it public."

"As in how public?"

"As in bullets-through-brains-type public." Lycos sighed and winced. "I need a location on that number. I'll handle it, but I need that fucking address. I'm sending a message."

"What signature will the message have?"

"None. Just a guarantee. One they can't afford to disregard."

"And if this telephone number is information Guardian needs?"

"I wouldn't need your assistance if my computer hadn't died." Hell, if he could get to an internet connection and a computer of any sort, he could jump his hard drive and access his program, but getting to a computer wasn't an option right now.

"But it did die, and you want me to pull my wife into this mess."

"I do. Give me twenty-four hours, and then you can take any action you want. I'm calling it in, brother. Every time I was there for you, for them. I'm calling it in. Get me the address and give me twenty-four hours. You'll never hear from me again."

"Give me the number and call back in an hour."

The line died, and Lycos turned off his phone. An hour. Okay. He'd just close his eyes for a few moments. The sun felt damn good, and he was shielded from the cool winds. He let his body relax for a few moments before he systematically tightened and contracted the muscles in his legs, arms, chest, shoulders, and back. He was bent, not broken, even though his arm wasn't going to be a hondo for a couple weeks. He'd deal.

He'd make his way to this address, send a deadly message, and get out. First, he needed to figure out exactly where he was. Ryan opened his eyes and scanned the horizon. The mountains were located to his right. Okay. A vehicle was the next requirement. Considering he was ass planted not a mile from the roadway, hitching a ride to the next small hamlet wouldn't be too hard. Unfortunately, that would make him memorable, so he'd wait until night, go back to the road and walk into town. Not optimal, but he'd jack a truck from a farm or from the hamlet and drop it on the way to the address.

He glanced at his watch and gave an abbreviated laugh. Abbreviated because it fucking hurt. The crystal of his watch was shattered and missing. There were no minute or hour hands, but the second dial swept around the circumference of the face as if nothing had altered its course. Hell, if that wasn't an example of how things kept chugging on no matter the disasters in life, nothing was.

The hours and minutes of life weren't guaranteed. But in the background behind the insanity of normal people's lives time still moved on. Seconds ticked forward, regardless of who was there to mark the time of events like life and death.

He palmed his phone and dialed the number, one last time.

"Operator Two Seven Four."

"Sunset clearance, third operative."

"Third operative, stand by."

"Are you prepared to copy?" Bengal asked.

"Send it."

He rattled off the address.

"Thank you. Twenty-four hours, and if I can, I'll ensure the target doesn't crawl away. But I need to send a message, and that means the fucker has to be breathing."

"Understood. You do whatever it takes, my friend. As long as it takes."

"Wrong. Twenty-three hours and fifty-seven

minutes. And lose this number. All markers have been pulled."

"Understood. It was good to know you. Take care of yourself."

"Live a good life, my friend. I have a feeling we'll be seeing each other at family functions."

"Someday." He hoped like hell it would happen.

"I'm clear."

Lycos powered down his phone, took out the battery and gave it a toss. He glanced at the sun and closed his eyes. He had hours before dark. The only thing to do was wait. He closed his eyes.

Lycos parked the second car he'd stolen in the last six hours three blocks away. He walked the distance, looking for alarm systems, cameras and guards. The three cameras he saw where wide-angle lenses. He pulled the University of Miami hat he'd taken from the first stolen vehicle over his face and kept his head turned away and down.

The door was deadbolted, which, let's face it, kept honest people honest. He wasn't that version of humanity. The door took forty-five seconds to circumvent. He hit the stairs. His body complained with every push forward. His left side was nothing but a massive bruise including his ass, which flamed with red and black splotches from the back of his thigh to the small of his back. Fuck him for looking at the damage in a gas station bathroom.

He stopped outside the door of the address he was given. S. J. Canalis, Private Investigator. A pale light broadcast through the frosted window from somewhere further back in the space. Lycos looked up and down the hall. *Fuck. This.* He extracted his forty-five from its shoulder holster.

His size thirteen boot landed beside the handle of the door and the flimsy door shattered around the lock. Lycos stepped through the opening. He leveled his weapon on the woman who sat behind the desk. He saw everything. Her eyes flicked to the gun on her desk. He made a show of pulling the hammer back on the weapon in his hand. The metallic click was louder than any explosion.

She lifted her hands and leaned back in her chair, crossing her legs, as if he was going to be distracted by her legs. Give him some credit. He wasn't a hormonal teenager. He moved forward and glanced down at her desk blotter. Thirteen names with lines running through them. There were four more. He nodded at the names.

"Decided to save you four... for seed."

"As if I want to have more like them. May I ask why you're taking my men out?"

Lycos leaned forward and pressed the weapon to the woman's forehead. Her eyes grew huge as he advanced. "We are going to do this the easy way... to begin with."

"So, you're going to kill me?"

Lycos laughed and lifted the gun away a split second before he dropped the butt of it against the woman's head in a resounding crack. She slumped in her chair. "No, bitch, you're only going to wish you were dead."

He made quick work of gagging and tying her up. He glanced at the clock on her computer. He had hours before the city would stir, longer before anyone would come to the nondescript office building, and even more before someone would notice the door to the office at the end of the hall was broken.

He searched the area and found a flat rate mailer in her top drawer. He chuckled as he turned off her cell phone and dropped it into the cardboard postal pouch. He did a hard shut down of the computer on her desk and quickly disassembled the tower collecting dust beside the desk. He pulled the hard drive and dropped it into the same box. Pulling a stickie off the top of the stack, he dropped a quick note on the paper and sealed the flat rate *if it fits it ships* container. If Bengal's wife could find anything useful on the electronics maybe he'd earn a marker or two he could use in the future. He pulled his laptop out of his pack and removed the 2.5-inch hard drive. He had to rig the connection to the 3.5-inch hard drive sled he'd removed from the woman's tower, but he managed it. He started his program and watched the monitor as the computer connection acquired the internet and downloaded a GPS map of the world. Perfect.

The woman groaned and winced as her head jerked up. He'd tied her hands to the arms of her chair and her feet to the prongs of the roller wheels.

"Well good morning, sweetheart."

Lycos laughed at the fuck you noise she made.

He grabbed her hand and showed her the lock pick he held in his hand. "We are going to have a conversation."

She narrowed her eyes at him, and this time enunciated around the gag, "Might as well kill me."

"Oh, I plan on it, but I want some answers first." He lifted her index finger and positioned the lock pick. "Why are you after the woman and the boy."

"Fuck you." The muffled, barely discernible words spewed around the gag.

Lycos felt nothing as the woman contorted in agony. Her screams, although muted, were horrendous and he should have been moved, but he felt nothing. This woman had sent men after his family. She'd coordinated the efforts. She was the one who knew the next step in the chain.

He waited until she regained consciousness. As her tear-streaked face lifted, he held up the lock shiv again. She screamed and shook her head back and forth. "Ready to answer questions?" She nodded and cried. "Why are you looking for the woman and the child?"

"Woman only." The words were hard to distinguish through the gag, but he managed.

His eyes narrowed. That didn't compute. Period. If they wanted to clear Harvey's slate, they'd need to… Unless it had nothing to do with Harvey.

He cocked his head and smiled at her. "What does she know?"

"I don't know!" The woman screamed the disclaimer over and over.

"Shhhh… okay, then you don't know." He waited for the woman to settle down. "What is the telephone number you call to report in?"

Her eyes went crazy wide, and she fell into hysteria as she cried, shaking her head.

"See, this is what we are going to do. You're going to give me that number. No one will ever know. I'll leave, and in a couple hours someone will find you. You can tell everyone it was a robbery. Your handlers won't even have to know."

She shook her head, still crying.

"Or we could do this the hard way." He reached for her middle finger and positioned the shiv under the nail. She screamed again and begged.

Lycos leaned in, "What was that? You'll give me the number?"

The woman really was a mess. Snot hung from her nose as she cried and nodded. He tapped her finger, making her jump. "I'm not a patient man."

Getting the digits between the pleading cries was tedious, but in the end, he had the number. He took out his pay-as-you-go phone and dialed. She cried and shook her head back and forth, trying to push her chair away from him.

"You might want to be quiet, or they're going to guess you gave me the number." He listened to the phone ring.

A system of clicks and whirs commenced before a manipulated voice answered. "Who is this?"

"You'll never know, but I know you. I know how to find you. I'm a black door asset which no longer belongs to your world, but I will come back, and I will find you."

"What do you want?"

"The woman, forget she exists."

"It isn't that simple."

"It is." Lycos countered.

"I have people I answer to."

"Then convince them. You won't be my first kill, and just for your information the fact you are a woman doesn't matter in the slightest to me. Evil exists in both male and female form."

There was an audible pause, but the implication was that he'd guessed correctly. Stratus had long been rumored to be run by a female council known as the Fates. Moriah had told him that Guardian had captured one. "There are only two of you. Convince the other. Let this go."

"What motivation do I have to do so? We can find you."

"Thirteen men have tried. I can kill the other four

in the field, now if you'd like, or you can remove them. I have already visited their pretty coordinator."

"As is indicated by the GPS lock we have on you."

"So, you know I am capable."

"Why is the woman important to you?"

"Personal reasons."

"When things get personal, life becomes messy."

Lycos laughed. "I like messy. Comply or die."

"What incentive do I have to comply?"

Lycos stood and turned to face the computer monitor. He cupped his hand to the phone and whispered, "Because if you don't, I'll come to 6900 Royal Palms Drive and I'll kill you. You cannot hide from me. Leave her alone. Your word, Fate, or your death. Your call."

"She is released. We will never go after her as long as you both stay in the dark."

"Keep your word, Fate, or I'll hunt you through the bowels of hell."

"I don't make commitments I can't keep."

"See that it stays that way."

Lycos terminated the call and dropped the phone into his pocket. He yanked the smaller drive from the computer and tucked it into his inside coat pocket. Glancing at his broken watch, he decided to make one more call.

"Operator Two Seven Four."

"Sunset clearance, third operative, tell Bengal to haul ass to my location. I have a present for him and disconnect this number from the switchboard. It may be compromised before he reaches this location."

The woman chuckled. "You might want to hurry; I believe he is poised to strike. Goodbye, Third Operative, it has been a pleasure."

Lycos hung up and gave the office one final sweep to ensure he'd left nothing. He looked at the woman. "Both the good guys and the bad guys are converging on this location will all speed. I wonder which one will win? If I were you and the good guys get here first? I'd roll hard on Stratus and the Fates and beg for protective custody. If your boss' assets arrive first? You'll be dead."

He put his stolen ball cap back on and pulled it down over his face. The jarring of the stairs as he traveled down them didn't hurt as bad as it had going up. Perhaps because the accord he just struck with the devil had taken some weight off the load he was carrying. He turned right out of the building and walked as quickly as a casual pace would take him. He needed a car and a way back to the mountains. At forty-three, he was finally ready to start his life.

CHAPTER 26

Lycos pulled into the covered and camouflaged parking area on his mountain and smiled. A fine sheen of dust and dirt covered Thanatos' vehicle. His friend hadn't had to leave. Lycos had abandoned his old truck, which was the only way Stratus could have tracked them to the mountain, in Charlotte before he purchased a new vehicle, in cash, under another name. He'd loaded it full of groceries, presents for both Bethanie and Ethan, and yes, a full case of gallon jars of peanut butter. He was home. He'd purchased a new laptop and checked to make sure the four men who were in the area searching for them had been called off. They were scattered across the continental US, but he'd be damn sure to keep track of those signals. He'd also bought twenty new wildlife cameras with motion detection activation devices with the intention to blanket the mountain. He'd know if anything came close.

He grabbed a few bags out of the cab and headed up to the back entrance of the cave. The trail had been used recently. He could see tracks for three sizes of humans and one dog. He keyed in his code and set the bags down as the door slid shut. Within seconds, Dog was at the edge of the cabinets, teeth bared in a fearsome snarl.

"You better knock that shit off," Lycos growled back. He laughed as the dog twisted and jumped in the same action. The animal barked, which was rare, before it launched at him. One hundred and twenty pounds of wolf hair hit him, knocking him into the wall.

"Ryan! Mom! Ryan's home!"

He absorbed the additional body that flung against him. Between the boy and the dog, he was covered from shoulder to floor. He glanced up as she flew to him. Her eyes glitter and her smile stretched from ear to ear. Her legs wrapped around his waist as he lifted her up. "You're home!"

Fuck, yes. He was home. Finally.

He heard Thanatos entice Ethan out of the house. His friend got it. Lycos couldn't explain how they made it to the bedroom, the walk up with her in his arms was a blur. But the world slowed down when he dropped her to the mattress. It slowed enough to register two individual heartbeats.

He wished he could have taken his time when he

claimed her again, but his need to possess her, fill her, drove him to mount her like a wild man. She was with him, though. Her words pushed him harder and faster. She broke apart in his arms, and he shattered along with her.

She refused to let him move away and rolled on top of him. Her chin cupped on her hands as she laid on his chest. "Are we safe?"

"We are." At least as safe as he could make them.

"And you won't have to leave us again?"

"Not for any reason I can think of." He reached up and ran his hands through her curls. Her hair was getting longer.

He listened as Ethan's chatter and Thanatos' laughter filled the bottom cavern. "I suppose we should go down and help unload the truck."

Bethanie shook her head. "Let them do it. I need you inside me again. I need to know you're home. For good."

*Oh! Shit!* He sat up, and she scrambled to keep her balance. "There they are." He moved her to the side and dashed out of bed, grabbing his jeans. He snatched them and jumped back in bed, launching her small body in a bounce as he hit the mattress. He pulled her back to him and slipped his hand in the front pocket of his jeans. "I got something for you."

"You did? What?" She lifted up, the sheet pooling at her hips. God, she was beautiful. He withdrew his hand and opened his closed fist, exposing a black velvet box.

"What… is this a…"

He lifted the lid and watched her eyes flood with tears. "Yes. Yes. Yes. Yes."

"I haven't asked you yet." He laughed and rolled her over onto her back. "Bethanie Clark, would you marry me?"

Ryan really liked the way she chose to answer him.

# CHAPTER 27

Thanatos waited until the family retired for the evening. He'd watched over Lycos' woman and child, and he got it. He understood how Ryan could step away from his life for this woman and the boy. Hell, if he'd been lucky enough to be the person at the safe house when they arrived... he closed his eyes and rolled his shoulders. This wasn't his destiny. Happiness on a mountaintop wasn't his destiny. Although Bethanie was the type of woman he could see making sacrifices for. He'd even consider staying out here in the godforsaken wilderness for a woman like her, and the idea of an insta-family didn't send him running away to the nearest bar, which said a lot about where his mind was planted.

He glanced at the kid's jacket hanging on the peg next to the one he'd claimed from Lycos' vast array of outdoor clothing. The boy was smart and funny, and he was a good kid. Yeah, he could see why Lycos walked away from Guardian. He had one hell of a bundle of incentive.

Thanatos slipped his feet into an old pair of Lycos' hiking boots. The guy would have to deal with them going missing. He grabbed the coat he'd commandeered and turned to leave the cavern for the last time.

"Leaving without saying goodbye?" Lycos leaned against the cabinets. His massive watchdog ambled over and sniffed at Thanatos' feet. He'd never really gotten comfortable with the dog, but he trusted that the damn thing wouldn't eat him. Maybe.

"No sense in making a scene."

"Thank you for watching over them." Lycos walked forward and extended his hand. "By the way, you're the only human besides the three of us that knows this place exists."

"Damn good thing I have a shit memory." Thanatos took his brethren's hand and clasped it. "You take care of those two. If you don't, I'll have to come back and kick your ass."

"You could try." Lycos smiled at him.

And that was something that he hadn't seen before either. Thanatos dropped Lycos' hand and nodded. "Have a great life, man." He turned and headed out the back entrance.

"Thanatos?"

He turned at Lycos' soft call.

"Dude, if you ever need a place to exist, off the grid, you come to me. To us."

"I appreciate that, but I would never bring heat down on you or them."

"By the time the next snow falls, this mountain will be rigged. No one will be able to get within miles of us. If you need me, I am here for you. I will always be here for you. Markers or no."

Thanatos smiled and gave Lycos a two-finger salute before he keyed the code and left the warmth of the home Lycos had built. He ghosted down the dark trail to his vehicle. The road off the mountain was a slow drive, and Thanatos used the time to push all those pesky feelings back into the compartments he kept them in. He was the last of his group of Shadows. Well, except for Tempest, and no one really knew if he was alive.

He waited until he passed Charlotte before he turned on his phone. Notifications pinged for his dead drop email. He opened it and read the reporting instructions the code spelled out for him. He pulled a U-turn using the emergency cut-throughs and headed back to Charlotte and the airport.

Guardian needed him. That privilege would have to be enough. His dreams of having what others had were just that, dreams. Thoughts like that were easily weeded from the graveyard plot where his previous life had been buried. What he did, and who he did it for, was his purpose in life. He existed to eliminate those who prayed on the weak, defend those who had no voice, and defeat those who would bring disaster to humanity. He was a Shadow, a warrior, and for a man such as he, that identity would suffice.


## THE END

Continue on for a sneak peek of SEAL Forever by Kris Michaels!

FOR A SNEAK PEEK OF

SEAL Forever

TURN THE PAGE!

**SEAL Forever**
Written by Kris Michaels
Copyright 2019.
**Chapter One**

Creed Lachlan pushed the throttle up on the four, 1,480-hp, diesel V-drive, inboards until the power under him lifted the nose of the one hundred-sixty-five-foot luxury yacht out of the glassy, late-afternoon, Atlantic. He held the controls at half power, listening to the throaty rumble with a skilled ear. He'd modified this baby's quad engines, and she was pushing enough horsepower to beat any tropical storm back to the safe harbor of Key West's Cow Key Channel. The gauges showed exactly what he needed to see. *Angelo's Princess* was once again purring, hitting all cylinders. The gauges held true as Creed inched the throttle forward. He flicked the throttle up a quarter inch. The plane of the bow surged further upright, and he braced against the pull as he balanced behind the wheel. He gripped the steering controls and tightened his muscles as he steadily increased the power to the motor. At the throttle's top end, he was almost flying the yacht over the water. The exhilaration from the deep growl of the motors and speed of the boat fed an addiction he'd been trying to forget. Like most of the men in his career field, he'd grown accustomed to jolts of adrenaline. *Check that... prior career field.*

When he'd been forced to retire, he'd commanded SEAL Team One. Six platoons. Ninety-six SEALs and a headquarters element—all before he fucked up his knee. Blew it out six ways from Sunday and needed a complete knee replacement. Oh, the Navy had offered him a job *'commensurate to his physical limitations.'* He'd take a pity job the day his rosy, red ass sprouted blossoms. Instead, he'd shown a middle finger to the paper pushers and had left on his own terms. At the advanced age of forty-three, he'd retired. *Fuck.*

Since then, he'd buried himself in the family business. His parents had built Lachlan Maritime Industries from the ground up and were still strong pillars within the Key West community, even though they'd handed the reins over to their three sons.

The coastline of his home reappeared as he brought the *Princess* out of her breakneck pace. Like a trained thoroughbred, she relaxed under his expert hand, and the deep vee of white froth behind her lessened to almost nothing. The heavy roar of the diesel engines died to a bass murmur. Creed took a moment to soak in one of the most beautiful sights in the world. Sunset in Key West. The setting sun glistened off the flat waters west of Cow Key Channel and painted the sky in epic orange and purple. Creed turned on the *Princess'* running lights and pulled back on the throttle to coast through the no-wake zone. He rounded the northeast side of the island and headed the yacht back to the massive commercial pier his father had built. As he approached, two figures trotted down the dock. They scrambled to tie off the *Princess* as Creed nudged the one-hundred-and-sixty-five-footer into its berth.

"I was getting worried about you, old man."

Creed glanced up but ignored his brother's smart-ass comment as it floated through the cabin's open window.

"What happened? Finally lose your hearing?"

Creed shifted his eyes again to glare at his brother. The little shit. He was about four inches shorter than Creed's six-feet, six-inches and easily eighty to ninety pounds lighter. Where he hit the gym regularly and had the bulked-up muscle to prove it, Thane had a swimmer's body. Hell, Thane's sun-bleached hair was more blond than brown. The only thing Thane had in common with either of his brothers was the color of his eyes. All three had deep blue irises, ringed in dark black circles and laced with flecks of gold. It seemed to be the only genetic gift from his mother's side of the family. Thankfully. His mother, all four-foot-eleven inches of her, had a fire-laced temper with a hair trigger that brought all three of her boys to heel. Nobody messed with Caroline Lachlan. Nobody.

Creed didn't give his brother the courtesy of a response before his attention returned to the engine logbooks.

"Yo, dude, we're going to Sam's tonight. You in?" Thane braced himself on the doorjamb and leaned into the bridge of the yacht.

Creed kept writing but asked, "Cruise ships all gone?"

"Yeah, the last one pulled out about an hour ago." Thane glanced at his watch. "Missy should be there by now. She's going to hold a table for us."

Creed nodded. He could do with a cold beer. "I'm in."

"Seriously?"

He lifted his head at the sound of his brother's shocked voice. "Yeah, why?"

"Because you've never come with us before?" The 'duh' was implied.

"And still you ask every time." Creed returned to his work.

"Yeah, you know miracles do happen, and old, cranky shits like you are allowed to have fun."

"I'm only ten years older than you."

"And you *act* like you're ten thousand years old.

Dude, you wake up, work out, come here and then go home. Wash, rinse, repeat. Day after day, week after week, month—

Creed snapped his book shut. "I get it."

"Do you? Do you really?" Thane crossed his arms and blinked like an owl before he shook his head. "I don't think you do. We live in a paradise, complete with sunshine, good food, great rum, teeny-tiny bikinis and hard, hot little bodies inside those almost nonexistent pieces of string. And still"—Thane paused for dramatic effect—"you live like a fucking monk."

Not quite. His brother made some big assumptions. "Partying until three in the morning has never been something I enjoyed." That was the God's honest truth. He'd never been interested in parties or the type of people who lived for the thrill of that atmosphere. His mom said he had an 'old soul.' These days his soul felt older than dirt.

Thane shifted on his feet. "What exactly do you enjoy, Creed? I mean it's been almost a year since you've been back. You don't date, at least not that I've seen. What exactly is it that gives you pleasure? Dude just tell me, and I'll find it for you. I know there has to be something out there for you." His voice softened, "Man, whatever it is that will bring back the man I used to know, I'll find it. I hate that you are so damn empty. I see it and it kills me."

Creed stood, automatically testing the cobalt-chrome device they'd replaced his knee with. His mind still believed the thing would fail. The doctors said that was normal. Normal. As if. He drew a deep breath and turned his entire focus on his brother and forced a smile. "You can't find what doesn't exist, but thanks for the thought."

Thane quipped, "You need a woman in your life."

"Not interested." Not any longer. He'd fucking searched for that elusive woman. Hell, he had the list. Truth be told, he wasn't asking for a supermodel crossed with a physicist. Looks faded; he knew that. He hadn't been looking for some image of perfection. He wanted a real woman, someone genuine who could hold his interest. As said woman's competition was his job, well, his former job, it had been a tall order. Over the last twenty years he'd dedicated too much time carrying on strained conversations with women whose names he promptly forgot to hold out any hope there was someone for a man like him. Obviously, he wanted a fucking unicorn, because the woman he'd been searching for didn't exist. There was never that 'click,' and no he wasn't channeling a romance novel or a *Lifetime* movie. He tucked his books under his arm, pocketed the keys to the million-dollar vessel and slapped his brother on the back as he exited the bridge.

Thane fell into step beside him. After a moment, he cleared his throat. "Danica is going to be there tonight. She's been asking about you. I'm supposed to hint that she's a good catch."

He stopped short, and his brother crashed into his

back, bouncing off of him as he turned around. "Say what?"

"Well, Mom and Missy are worried, too."

He extended a finger and pointed it at Thane. His brother stiffened and backed up another step. "You're telling me that *your* wife and *our* mother are trying to set *me* up?" Incredulous didn't begin to cover the shock of that thought. He was forty-four-years old. If he wanted to get laid, he did. He just didn't make a spectacle of it. Fuck him for being discreet.

"Ah... yeah." Thane blushed and rubbed the back of his neck. "I promise I'll run interference tonight. Everyone will be there, and if you aren't interested in Danica... well then man, you're dead."

Creed chuffed. "Fuck you."

"She's *hawt*." Thane licked his finger and touched something imaginary making a sizzling sound.

He'd seen her hanging around with Missy. The girl *was* attractive. Okay, *hot*, but dammit, he was forty-four, and he had no desire to become a sugar daddy. He wanted the company of a woman that could actually hold a conversation and didn't post three hundred selfies to social media throughout the night. He kept walking and tried to picture what a date with Danica would be like. It was useless. He shook his head to clear his thoughts and muttered under his breath about the yacht he'd just run. He made a note on the invoice that they needed to send in the clean-up crew to wash and detail the ship before the owner took possession of her. Just for good measure he glanced over his shoulder at his brother and grumped, "She's barely legal."

Thane presented his fingers and made an act of counting before he piped, "Twenty-two."

Creed snorted. "That qualifies as barely legal, and she's literally half my age. I was in college at Annapolis when she was born. Think about that."

"She's the trifecta! Young, legal, nubile and H.A.W.T." Thane hustled along behind him.

"Idiot, that's four things, not three. Does Missy know you have hidden desires for this girl?"

"What's four then... a quadfecta? Who says they're hidden? Missy and I have had some awesome sex after talking about our fantasies." Thane made a growling sound behind him.

Creed stopped short, and his brother bounced off of him—again. He turned and held up a hand. "Never, and I mean never, tell me about your sex life. I don't want to know. Some things you can't unhear or"—he pointed toward his head—"mentally unsee."

A shit-eating grin crossed his brother's face. "But you did picture it, didn't you?"

"I'm having second thoughts about going to Sam's with you."

He could just as easily have a drink at his house. His cottage was small, but it was his, free and clear. The little home had been wiped out during the last hurricane. Having money saved, plus the insurance policy on the house and no real home in the military, he'd rebuilt his cottage with fourteen-inch-thick cinder block walls and even elevated it higher than the building code required. It was his forever home where he had planned to retire with a wife. He hadn't realized his retirement would come so soon.

"Right?" Thane's question made him realize his brother had been droning on.

He entered the massive storage warehouse where they dry-docked over four hundred boats. He glanced at his brother. "Right, what?"

Thane pulled up and scowled at him. "Dude, weren't you listening?"

He shrugged. "I rarely listen to you."

"Wow, I think I might be hurt." Thane put his hand over his heart.

He opened a spiral notebook for his notes that he carried along with the log books of the *Princess*. He ripped out a blank page and handed it to Thane.

The man's eyes bounced from the paper to Creed. "What's this for?"

"To file a hurt feelings report. You tell me all about those bruised emotions. Submit it, and in twenty or thirty days I'll send you a response guaranteeing I one hundred percent don't give a shit. You know, just to make it official." He spun on his heel and headed to his office on the far side of the warehouse.

"You know if you weren't my brother, I'd think you were a dick."

He turned and walked backward as he spoke, "You *are* my brother, and I still think you're a dick."

"Only because I am!" A smile split Thane's face as he threw the words across the building.

He shouted back, "Glad to know you have a skill!"

"We're leaving in a half hour!"

Creed lifted his hand in acknowledgment and chuckled. It had been a while since he'd been out with his brother. A drink or two while avoiding the trap Missy and his mother had set for him should be doable. He was a fucking SEAL after all. How hard could it be to avoid a tiny, five-foot-nothing blonde?

Evidently, pretty fucking hard.

# ABOUT THE AUTHOR

USA Today and Amazon Bestselling Author, Kris Michaels is the alter ego of a happily married wife and mother. She writes romance, usually with characters from military and law enforcement backgrounds.

Made in United States
Troutdale, OR
11/12/2023

14528064R00209